# IN LIGHT OF FIRES

# AND

# FOGGY MORNINGS

# IN LIGHT OF FIRES

# AND

# FOGGY MORNINGS

### Stories from a Small Town

### in the 1950s

### That Are Absolutely, Positively True.

### Sort of.

**Sonora, Ohio**

Fred Whissel

*All drawings and photographs either taken or acquired by the author.*
*Cover: Brother Jim looks at Dad and his fishing friend at Ellis Dam.*

Copyright ©2007
By Fred Whissel

**DEDICATED TO THE PEOPLE WHO LIVED IN AND AROUND SONORA, OHIO, DURING THE 1950s. WITHOUT THEIR UNWITTING PARTICIPATION, THIS BOOK WOULD NOT HAVE BEEN NECESSARY.**

For purchase or other printing or publication information, please contact Lulu, 3131 RDU Center, Suite 210, Morrisville, NC 27560 USA, on the web at http://www.lulu.com

ISBN: 978-0-6151-5177-9

*Lulu first edition 2007*

Printed in the United States of America

# TABLE OF CONTENTS

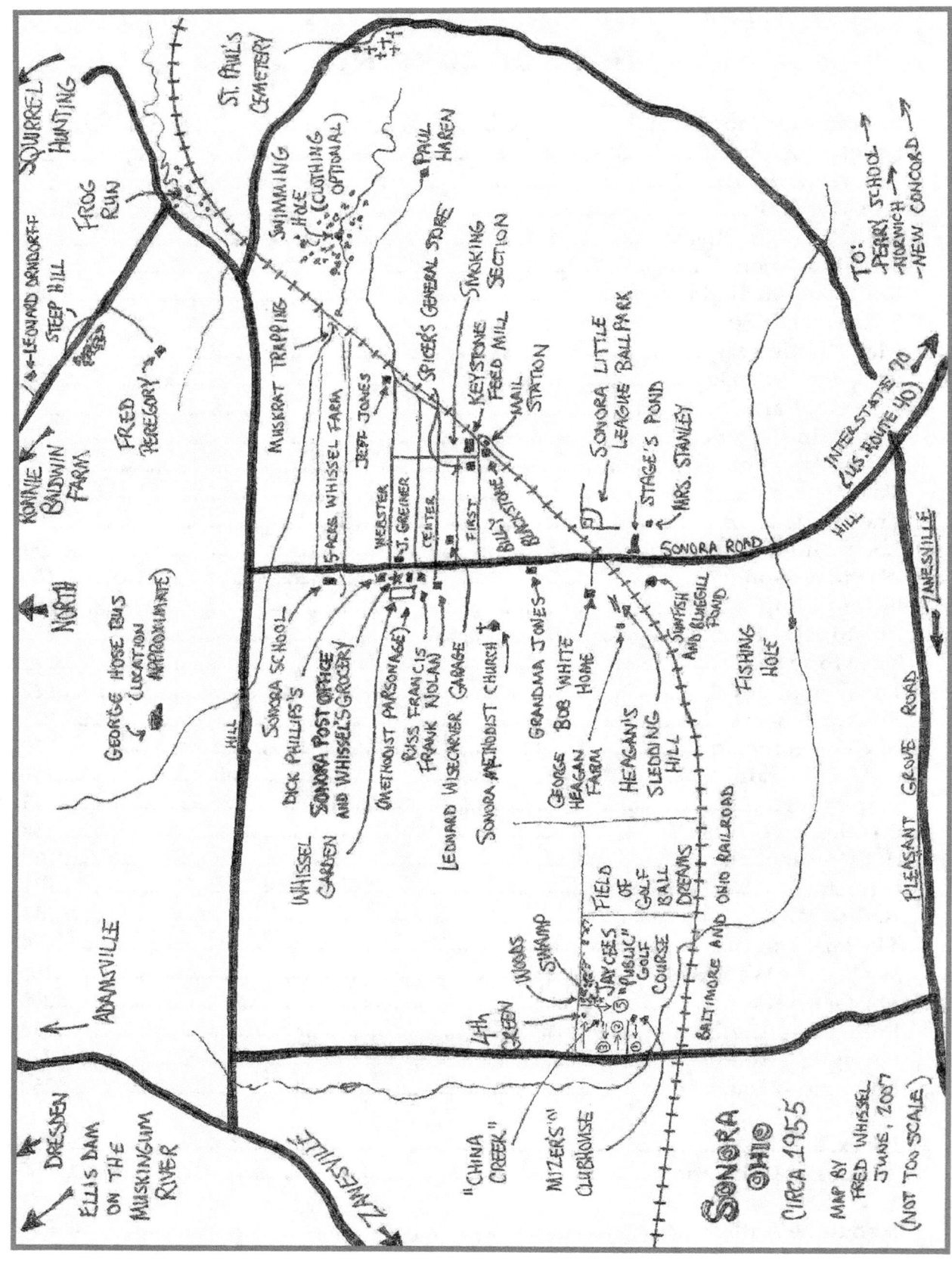

# CHAPTER ONE

# Scouting Around

In the 1950s, there was a lot of stuff that the average kid in Sonora had to learn. A girl had to learn how to cook, how to sew, how to knit, how to wash clothes, how to iron, and a few other essentials that would some day make her a good American housewife. (This was before females became liberated.) A boy had to learn how to hunt, how to trap, how to fish, how to take a car apart and put it back together using most of the parts and pieces, how to play various games, how to celebrate assorted holidays and sports victories, and a few other essentials that would some day make him a good American husband. (This was before females became liberated.)

Most of the things a girl needed to learn she could get from her mother. Most of the things a boy needed to learn he could pick up on the street. Or he could ask his father. But if he really got desperate, he could turn to the Boy Scouts of America. In the Boy Scouts of America you could learn almost anything about almost everything that you almost never needed to know.

I joined the Boy Scouts in November of 1957, in one of those acts of desperation. At the ripe old age of eleven I was getting on in years. I suddenly realized that I still had a few things left to learn. But Sonora didn't have very many streets, and Dad had already taught me pretty much everything he knew that was worth knowing (or so I thought). So I made a few discrete inquiries, and soon discovered that most of the answers to life's toughest questions could be found in Scouting: how to build a forest fire by using only two rocks; when to do a good turn; whether or not to help old ladies cross the street. Important stuff like that. I decided to sign up.

## - OF FIRES AND FOGGY MORNINGS -

Sonora itself didn't have a Boy Scout troop, but there was an outfit that met every Thursday night at 7 p.m. in Perry Elementary School, about four miles east of Sonora on U. S. Route 40. After scanning my Little League baseball practice and game schedule, I figured I could just manage to fit this weekly troop meeting in, if I didn't stop to take a shower after a game or a practice. So one night I had Mom drive me down to Perry School to check it all out.

Troop 171 of the B.S.A. met in Perry School's gymnasium, which was twice as large as Sonora's whole three-room, sheet-metal school building put together. The Scoutmaster for this troop was named Jerry Ramsey. He was a thin, bony, red-haired guy of above-average height with freckles and buck teeth, and was in his late twenties or early thirties. He reminded me of Mickey Rooney as Andy Hardy, only much taller and older. His assistant scoutmasters were Joe Orndorff and Jack Kelly. Joe was a rough-cut country boy who lived north of Sonora who was then in his teens. Jack was almost the same age as Jerry Ramsey and was nearly as thin. The last time I heard the name Jack Kelly he was the guy who played Bret Maverick's brother in the 1960s television western series, which was one of my favorite shows. But I don't think it was the same Jack Kelly. Jack Kelly the assistant scoutmaster never wore a black hat and a white shirt with frilly wrist cuffs and collar—at least not when he was our assistant scoutmaster.

The first thing I learned from Scoutmaster Ramsey was that any of us who had uniforms were expected to wear them—to meetings, to camp-outs, on day hikes, to church, to school on special occasions, and at all other times duly designated by Scoutmaster Ramsey. That mandate was followed immediately by Scoutmaster Ramsey's further imperative that any of us who did not yet have said uniform were expected to get one, no later than yesterday. After attending a couple of meetings, and feeling conspicuously out of uniform in my knee-less blue jeans and plain white cotton tee-shirt, I asked Mom to take me in to Bintz's Department Store in Zanesville to obtain my official uniform.

Bintz's, a business that took up the entire corner of Third and Main Streets, had a whole back room on the first floor devoted to official Scouting stuff—Cub, Boy, Eagle, and probably Girl. They not only had complete Scout uniforms, from collapsible cotton caps to shiny leather shoes, but they also carried a wide selection of official camping equipment, official hiking items like compasses and maps, and a lot of other official things that would probably come in very handy some day if your parents could afford them. Like the complete, official campfire cooking kit, with metal pot, pan, plate, and collapsible cup—all held together by a clever, swing-around, screw-clamped handle that was secured by a wing-nut. This neat kit came in a green canvas fabric cover that was stamped with the Scout emblem. It had an adjustable carrying strap that let you sling it over your shoulder, like a woman's purse. Along with an official canteen, the official campfire cooking kit allowed you to be ready for any food preparation emergencies that might pop up. There were multi-tooled knives that you could do everything in the world with— even cut. And there was a tricky little cross-hatched aluminum tube, about as big around as one nickel and about as long as a paper tube of them, with a screw-on cap that pivoted on two arms out to an angle. Inside this tube you could carry enough matches to camp out for a whole week and keep them perfectly dry, even if you fell in a creek on the very first day. If nothing else, I had to have one of those. And an official Scout hatchet. I could never be a real Boy Scout without an official maple-handled

**My Official Scout Handbook—with my Mohawk Patrol inscription. Page 553 tells you how to avoid Ohio's vicious alligators.**

hatchet, with a real leather holster stamped "Made in Japan" that had a snap-down button flap for easy access. You never knew when some dead tree was going to jump up and grab at you while you were trooping through a cemetery at twelve o'clock on a dark Halloween night and you would have to whip out your official Boy Scout hatchet and chop off a couple of its limbs and branches just to teach it a lesson.

Other than the uniform, which came in both a sissified short-pants version and the macho long-pants one as well, every Scout was expected to purchase an official Scout Field Book, which at the time was a 552-page encyclopedia of indoors and outdoors skills that cost only $1.25, plus tax, where applicable. With this bulky but authoritative book in hand you could tie a knot, read a map, track a duck, build a fire with only one match (or a well-concealed cigarette lighter), bake bread in the raw ashes of a forest fire

My brother's 1943 handbook.

that wasn't your fault and you didn't mean to set, identify a deer, avoid one of Ohio's vicious alligators, mount colorful bugs and butterflies by pinning them to a sheet of cardboard while they were still kicking, save someone from overheating by giving them artificial perspiration, and properly fold the American Flag into a tight triangle with some of the 48 stars showing. It also had the words to various songs. Since I never saw a single vicious alligator in Ohio's dangerous woods, this must have been a pretty good book. If you had to do something that wasn't covered in the official Scout Field Book, you probably didn't need to do it.

Our typical Thursday night troop meeting would begin by reciting the Scout Oath, Scout Law, Scout Motto, and Scout Slogan, giving the Scout Salute, shaking hands with the Secret, split-fingered Scout Shake and swearing on a stack of olive-green Bibles that we would take a Scout Shower (in water that had been purified by Boiling for three minutes) before we came to the Scout Meeting next week. We would then break up into smaller groups of two or three to work on our "merit" badges. Merit badges were small, iconic uniform patches that symbolized the doing of a lot of hard work and the achievement of at least some degree of proficiency in such essential skills as lifesaving, marksmanship, swimming, first-aid, and forestry. The more-ambitious among us could concentrate on things like public speaking, aerodynamics, hog and pork production, snow skiing, and deepwater seamanship. Being located in southeastern Ohio, Sonora didn't have a lot of ski resorts or salt-water seaports, so anybody who wanted to work on the snow skiing or deepwater seamanship merit badges had to use a lot of imagination. I don't remember ever working on anything except tying rope knots, and I got most of those wrong.

In good weather (which to Jerry Ramsey was anything short of a tornado or a blizzard) our whole troop of ten would trek into the deep, second-growth woods behind Perry School and look at the trees. I never saw a tree I didn't like. There were oaks and ashes, pines and poplars, elms and maples—until Scoutmaster Ramsey pointed them out, I had never been able to see all of those trees for the forest. But once we learned to identify them I stopped at more trees in the woods than the average dog, to look at their leaves, examine their bark, and compare their real-life, living-color shapes with the blurry black-and-white silhouette drawings in my official Scout Field Book that never seemed to match up. Scoutmaster Ramsey told us it was important to learn the names of trees, and I could see why. If one of those suckers was ever struck by lightning, and happened to fall on me while I was walking through the woods, I would be able to call it by name (among other things) before I died.

I became a member of the Mohawk Patrol, which with only four members was the poor relation of Troop 171. John Vestre was our patrol leader, mainly because somebody had to do it and he was the oldest, although I thought he took way too much pride in exercising the rights and privileges of an appointed position that he had gotten basically by being born at the right time. The other members of the Mohawk Patrol, alphabetically and in reverse order of age, were David Francis and Bobby Shirer. We got grouped together mainly because we were all from Sonora, while the six members of the Pioneer Patrol were all from anywhere else. (This was before the term "discrimination" came into common use. Back then, the same practice was referred to as "just keep away from us.") The official motto of our Mohawk Patrol, which we adopted after considerable deliberation and much official soul-searching, was "Let the Pioneer Patrol Do It." As good Scouts, we were prepared to do that daily, or more often if at all possible.

I don't believe I ever earned a merit badge, although I should have been awarded two: one for search-and-rescue operations and one for winter camping. I should have gotten my first merit badge for spending several days, one night, combing the hills and dales around Leonard Orndorff's farm, armed only with a half-bright official plastic Boy Scout flashlight for protection against Ohio's vicious alligators. We were out there searching for our assistant scoutmaster, Joe, who was Leonard's son. I can't recall whether Joe actually got lost on his own farm or just wanted to get away from it all for awhile but his lengthy and unsupervised absence of a couple of hours precipitated an all-out search-and-rescue effort, involving dozens of Scouts, many ordinary citizens, representatives of Muskingum County's

**Arriving at Camp Somethingorother or Whatchamacallit**

law enforcement community, members of the township's volunteer fire department, and several otherwise intelligent hunting dogs. I can't remember whether or not we ever actually found Joe, but I suppose we did. At least we all stopped looking for him.

My toughest challenge as a Boy Scout occurred during that first winter, when our whole troop packed up in pickups and went off to Camp Somethingorother or Whatchamacallit, located somewhere in Ohio, I think, maybe up around Newcomerstown. It was an official Boy Scout camp, for official Girl Scouts, too, although we really had enough to do without looking out for them, so we just skipped that part.

We arrived at Camp Somethingorother or Whatchamacallit late in the afternoon on a dry but frigid day, and checked in at the main and only lodge, a fairly large log structure with a big open-ceilinged room, two one-room log wings and a huge fireplace in the middle of the main room that was made out of field rock. Scattered throughout the lodge were shaky wooden bunk beds with worn-out springs under paper-thin mattresses that had been folded neatly in half by the previous campers. I don't know

12

exactly why, but there must have been some unwritten Scout rule or law that said that after you had slept in a bed you had to fold the mattress in half. Apparently, that was to alert the next camper that you weren't still sleeping on the mattress, in case he couldn't tell by looking at the big lump. The most noticeable feature of the fireplace was that it had no fire, nor was there any stacked wood nearby to make one, and that perhaps explained why the temperature inside the lodge when we arrived was about 40 degrees below zero and three thin mice were skating in circles to the mouse music from *The Nutcracker Suite* on the solid ice surface that used to be an official bucket of wash water.

While most of us straightened up our beds, unfolded our mattresses, and unrolled our sleeping bags, a few others went out to find some firewood. Unfortunately, since our little band of others must have been hard upon the heels of at least one earlier Scout troop in similar straits, there was no easy firewood to be found anywhere in the immediate vicinity, especially in the dark. That discouraging discovery resulted in some fast flashlit axe work on the local tree population, by some of us who apparently had not yet learned that some trees are dead and burn well, while other trees are living, and wouldn't burn if their lives depended on it.

Shaking, shivering, and sheltered in all of the clothes that we had brought, any other clothing that we could borrow, and all of the mattresses that we could fold up around us, we shouted encouraging words and other less-polite epithets at the experts who were trying hard but unsuccessfully to build a fire. After burning up all of the loose paper that had been lying around in the lodge and still not able to keep the green wet wood ablaze, our firelighters appeared to be taking a new interest in their official Scout Field Books when someone brought in some small, dry branches. Rubbing these sticks together rapidly, in close proximity with a few flaming kitchen matches, they finally got a fire going. Throughout the night we all had to take turns rolling out of our sleeping bags and peeling off our mattresses to feed the fire more green wood every half-hour or so. Even then the interior of the building never warmed up above 30 below zero that night and the three mice became very good at doing figure eights. (A few years later one of those same mice skaters took the bronze medal at a Winter Olympics. The last I heard, they were still searching for it.)

The next morning, going outside in the bitterly cold air in a futile attempt to get warm, we built three or four huge campfires near the lodge, in pits that had been specially constructed for the purpose. We thawed ourselves out with an official Scout breakfast of bacon and eggs, cream of

13

wheat, Lipton's tea, hot cocoa, and coffee. We then set out to do what we had come to do, official Scout stuff like identifying trees, tying knots, and classifying rocks.

By the end of the day, having Scouted the campground as thoroughly as we could, we were really looking forward to spending another night in the ice-skating arena, freezing our official Scout butts off. That's when Jerry, our trusted Scoutmaster, who would never intentionally mismaster us, who always knew approximately what he was doing, who was a born leader of men (or at least of a troop of ten Boy Scouts), decided that we would probably, maybe, possibly be a lot warmer if we just scattered our sleeping bags all around the two blazing campfires and slept outside, in the open air, not even indoors, on the cold, dry, crackling frozen leaves that covered the hard, cruel, un-folded-mattressed ground.

The next morning we all awoke with an official blanket of six inches of cold, wet snow upon us.


My Boy Scout career came to an abrupt halt one night in the following summer when I was a bit tardy for a regular troop meeting at the Perry School gym. I was coming in late again from a Little League baseball practice. Inviting me to step outside (for what I feared was going to be an unfair official fistfight), Scoutmaster Ramsey said I was going to have to make up my mind, once and for all, whether I was going to be an official Boy Scout or play (ugh) Little League baseball, because I just couldn't do both at the same time. It was an either/or, take-it-or-leave-it, damned-if-you-do-and-damned-if-you-don't type of proposition, with no room for negotiation in-between, and he demanded an immediate, best-and-final, show-me-the-money answer.

I don't think I ever saw Jerry Ramsey again.


My olive-green long-pants uniform is long gone, along with the complete cooking kit and the snap-covered hatchet and the neat little tube with the pivoting top that kept your matches dry even if you fell in the water. I have forgotten most of the names of trees, and can't tie rope knots any better now than I did back then. But I still have my official Scout Field Book. I keep it right next to my Little League baseball glove that was autographed by a machine that went around impersonating Al Kaline. You never know when a good how-to book like this might come in very handy when you need to do something official, like helping little old ladies cross the street to avoid Ohio's vicious alligators.

Helping little old ladies cross the street to avoid Ohio's vicious alligators was one of the prime duties of a Boy Scout in the 1950s. Behind the huge catalpa trees is Dick Phillips's house. Dick's backyard sidewalk leads to his garage, on to which he built a shop to sell TVs and do electronics repairs. He hired me to paint a sign. I thought a big U.S. flag would attract a lot of attention, but I somehow mounted it upside down. Dick said that was okay, because it caught your eye. However, he thought the sign needed some words. So I added "Dick Repairs and TVs" on three lines. Dick liked that, because it told the story pretty quick without causing a lot of confusion. Unfortunately, a lot of people started to get upset with Dick, accused him of being unpatriotic and a pornographer, and mentioned something about riding him out of town on a (B&O?) rail. Dick tried to tell them it was all a misunderstanding, but then my brother accidentally set fire to one of Dick's front porch posts. (*See Chapter 18: "Radio Daze."*) Dick quickly decided to close his shop before things got even worse. Owning your own business can be tough.

# CHAPTER TWO

# The Whizzer

The year was 1959. For my thirteenth birthday my dad bought me a motorbike. It was not exactly legal back then (or now) for a thirteen-year-old to operate a motorized bicycle on Ohio's public highways. But most highway law enforcement officers tacitly gave young riders the benefit of a doubt if, when seen from a distance, they *appeared* to be of legal age. They apparently had agreed that if the lawmakers in Ohio's General Assembly had been *truly* concerned about underaged motorbikers, they would have made violators pay a stiffer price when apprehended, charged, and convicted, like the death penalty or something.

So I didn't feel real guilty about riding my new Whizzer motorbike whenever and wherever I wanted to. Besides, I looked both young and dumb for my age. If ever I got stopped by the state highway patrol or a county mountie, I rationalized, I could probably claim ignorance of every traffic law in the state and get away with it. And if that didn't work, there was always the thing with amnesia.

I could see it coming. After a hot, 30 m.p.h. highway pursuit, lasting most of a minute, one of Ohio's finest would flash his lights, bark sharply at me through his electronic roof megaphone, and order me to pull over to the side of the road. He then would flow out of his big black volcanic cruiser like hot lava, through a fissured front door that had Ohio's official gold-lettered seal of approval on it. Rising to his full eight-foot height, he would poke a bad-looking billy club into a steel loop on his leather belt and rest his right hand on the notched ivory handle of a .38-caliber pistol, which always rode ready for instant access in an unsnapped hip holster. With a menacing look on his face, he would amble up behind me, hoping to intimidate me with his practiced authoritarian bearing. However, having watched his ominous approach in my Whizzer's rear-view mirror, which did not make objects look any smaller than they actually were, I would not be intimidated. Instead, I would merely be shaking in my shoes.

"May I see your driver's license or temporary learner's permit, young man?"

This guy didn't waste any time, asking the toughest question right off the bat. He obviously was a no-nonsense type, committed to some narrow-minded pursuit of Truth, Justice, and the American Way. Well, I could try lying, but he probably had been at the head of his State Patrol Academy class in Lie Detection 101. Nothing I could do now but play the old amnesia card.

"Where am I? Florida? What is this thing I'm riding? Who are you? Who am I?"

This story, to my complete surprise, he would fail to buy. He would give me a verbal warning, order me to push my bike home and park it for a couple of years, and say the next time he caught me riding without a valid permit on one of Ohio's precious highways he would throw his book at me. Since I had already checked out the size of his little book, I knew it couldn't hurt all that much. I would thank him anyway for being so officious and forgiving, wait alongside the highway until he drove out of sight, and then continue riding on my merry way—until I got pulled over again, probably by the same officer.

I can vaguely remember going in to Zanesville with Dad on a hot day in the middle of July in his short-bed red Chevy pickup truck with the outside-in fenders that always seemed wrong-side out to pick up my new Whizzer. Actually, it was not really a new Whizzer, but a used Whizzer in good condition that was new to me. We drove to a small smelly shop on West Main Street that sold both motorcycles and motorbikes, along with bike and biker accessories and repair parts. The shop's main showroom garden was planted nearly wall-to-wall with fully grown motorcycles, ready to harvest and ride. The whole shop smelled of oil, alcohol, grease, gasoline, cleaning solvents, and apparently every other liquid and solid that anyone could ever need for two-wheeled motoring. The alcohol, I suspected, was stocked mainly for use by the several salesmen and mechanics, to be mixed with 7-Up, Squirt, or some other ten-cent bottled beverage from a dusty red Coke machine in the back of the showroom.

## - OF FIRES AND FOGGY MORNINGS -

One small section of the glass-fronted shop had been set aside to display new and used motorbikes and related paraphernalia, such as windshields, helmets, chains, belts, and other cycling essentials. There were chrome clutch-belt covers, half-moon headlight visors, and several styles of exhaust mufflers. Apparently, it just wasn't enough for a high-octaned biker to blow black high-carbon exhaust straight out his rear end. You could buy any style of muffler, from a simple reticulated tube that flexed to fit your own personal positioning preference, to a big chrome tubular tank affair that terminated in a tall thin tail fin that would have put any of the late-Fifties Plymouths, Chryslers, and Dodges to shame. There were even long plastic streamers in popular patriotic colors, including yellow, to dangle from the ends of your ribbed plastic handgrips to prove to the whole civilized world, once and for all, that you really were as uncivilized as everyone had long suspected.

Being from a very small town, with a population of about 200, if you counted all of the dogs, cats, and free-ranging roosters and chickens, I had been brought up on and around bicycles. My first bike was a 20-inch trainer with two small side wheels that were designed to prevent tip-overs but were really useful for only about the first ten seconds or 25 feet of training, whichever came first. Once I got the hang of using the bike's momentum to keep it erect, the training wheels came off. After a year or so of learning the ins and

My first bike, a 20-inch trainer. I am the one with the holster. My best friend David Francis holds the rifle. The parsonage is at right, Jack Greiner home at rear.

outs and bumps and bruises of bike riding, I traded in the trainer for a red 24-inch Roadmaster with white pencil trim, battery-powered headlight,

18

and taillight, molded white rubber mud flaps, behind-the-seat genuine artificial black leather tool bag, and a chrome, spring-loaded luggage rack that straddled the rear fender. At first glance this bike seemed to have everything on it that a young bicyclist could hope to have. But it wasn't long until I bested the basic package by adding a generator-powered miniature stop light to the rear fender. It had green, yellow, and red lenses and was supposed to work just like a real stop light when you slowed down or hit the brakes, but it never did. However, I never really expected any of the drivers who came up behind me to pay much attention to this little light anyway. It was really there more for show than for go, slow down, or stop, and was probably almost invisible at a distance of only 20 feet. By the time a rear-approaching driver could have seen it and reacted, I would already be fated for the two-wheeler's heaven.

My red 24-inch Roadmaster became my first official vehicle for long-distance bicycling and was also my first attempt at "motor" cycling. This notable advancement was achieved by putting a half-inflated long balloon in the closed side kick stand, so that it was rubbed by the rear-wheel spokes to simulate the throbbing sound of a motor...until it popped from heat and friction after anywhere from five to fifteen seconds of furious pedaling. I went through more of these "motors" than any of the lead-footed stock-car drivers did real ones at the two dirt tracks near Zanesville.

At our back porch screen door with my new 24-inch Roadmaster. Note the head and tail lights, mirror, mud flaps, rear carrier, and baseball glove. Not the season to add a squirrel tail to each grip.

My final rung on the bicycle ladder was reached with a 26-inch beauty that was soon perfected by certain other innovative but absolutely essential modifications. Strictly in the interest of science I put a 24-inch wheel on the front with a 26-incher on the rear, tried a 26-inch wheel on the front with a 24-inch one on the rear, used a 24-inch wheel on the front with a

20-inch one on the back and, of course, mounted the handlebars straight up or straight down and turned them completely over. Such scientific experimentation eventually led to new ways to ride the bicycle, along with frequent trips to the nearest hospital emergency room. Having grown bored with building short board ramps to approach with blazing speed and jump off to "new record" distances to demonstrate our daring like early Evel Knievels, and having gotten soaked-to-the-bone too many times to count in rain-filled mud puddles, my friends and I eventually decided to test our balance (and sanity) by sitting backwards on the handlebars of our bikes and peddling around the pot-holed streets of Sonora, paying more attention to where we had been than to where we were going. That was a big mistake.

Of necessity (see above) I soon became an accomplished bicycle repairman. To begin with, my constant alterations constantly were in need of adjustments, or my bike was frequently breaking down. Then there were the normal maintenance items such as loose nuts, broken bolts, and a hard leather seat that needed at least daily reconfiguration. Before long I could take a Bendix-braked back chromed axle apart and reassemble it in less than an hour without losing more than two or three bearings. Over the years, by my as-needed borrowing of the Sears Craftsman-branded wrenches that Dad said were off-limits under penalty of death

The Perfect Companion to Your Motorhome

120 mpg, 25 mph, One year factory warranty

For a dealer near you, call (714) 563-9982

Or see us at www.whizzermotorbike.com

Whizzer Motorbike Company
2051 E. Cerritos Avenue, Suite C, Anaheim California 92806

**A recent magazine ad for the perfect motorhome companion, which now costs between $1,800 and $2,000. My used Whizzer cost Dad maybe $150. Check out the miles-per-gallon.**

or something even worse, and by unintentionally forgetting to return any of them, I had gradually accumulated one of the better tool kits in town among other thieves my age. So it was only to be expected that, on one memorable day in July of 1959, Dad finally gave up on retaining his few remaining Craftsman wrenches, and determined that I was at long last ready to ride the rough paved road of life, on a bicycle that was powered by a real motor.

That is exactly what the Whizzer company's seldom seen motorbike was. Within a heavy-duty 26-inch bicycle frame they mounted a 2½ or a 3½ horsepower four-cycle gasoline engine that could tool you along on heavy-duty wheels and tires at near-highway speeds. The power of the single-cylinder engine was sent to the rear wheel by two fabric-reinforced rubber V-belts, one large, one small, that shared a spring-tensioned cast-iron pulley that was mounted just under the bike's oversized seat. When you squeezed a chromed clutch handle with your left hand the under-seat pulley was pulled downward and loosened both belts, particularly the smaller one in front (the clutch belt) that was spun by the motor's exposed, vertically mounted flywheel. This clutching action allowed you to slow or halt the bike's forward movement without killing the engine, by using the standard bicycle pedal brake. For added braking power, and to increase your overall thrill of riding, there were front wheel disc brakes that tightened when you squeezed a second handle with your right hand. If you accidentally squeezed this hand brake, and somehow survived, you soon learned that it was not a real good idea to use the front-wheel caliper brakes alone to stop the bike—unless you wanted to discover how Peter Pan felt to fly. Releasing the clutch handle allowed the under-seat spring to pull the pulley upward and tighten both belts, thereby causing the engine to send its awesome power to the much-larger pulley that was bolted to the chromed spokes on the left side of the rear wheel.

As with larger motorcycles, twisting the Whizzer's right plastic handgrip controlled the speed of the engine, and thus the speed or acceleration of the bike. The Whizzer had no gears to cause a rider any concern or confusion about shifting. By twisting the right hand grip one way or the other, more or less gas and air mixture was fed through the carburetor into the air-cooled cylinder, the single reciprocating piston increased or lost revolutions per minute, and the bike moved faster or slower.

In a similar manner, the left handgrip was twisted one way or the other to open or close a valve in the single cylinder that caused full or reduced compression of the fuel-air mixture as the piston cycled up and down. At the same time, this grip motion permitted or cut off the electricity-generating magneto's "spark" that ignited the compressed fuel-air mixture. When the valve was open, the reduced compression allowed the engine to be turned over fairly easily; when the valve was closed, the compression was much higher, and turning over the engine then was like trying to push a car uphill in first gear against a headwind in a hurricane with the brakes locked and a brick wall before it.

Due to the use of a magneto, the Whizzer did not need a battery, either to power a starter motor, as with some other motorbikes and motorcycles of then and now, or to provide electricity for the mandatory headlight and tail light. As magnets set into the flywheel spun past an internal coil of wire, electricity was sent to the single spark plug to ignite the air-fuel mixture. The magneto also powered any

A slightly earlier model of my Whizzer, showing the large main drive belt, the flywheel/clutch belt (under cover), and the rear U-shaped stand for starting that I very seldom used.

accessories. This endless source of electricity was instantly available—whenever the engine was running. But when you were out riding a Whizzer at night and the engine suddenly stopped, you quickly learned the meaning of the simile "as dark as the inside of Satan's heart," and also gave some thought to the metaphor "hell on wheels."

To start the Whizzer's engine, you backed the bike up onto its squared-U kick stand that could be pivoted up and down from the rear axle, and pumped the pedals until the engine turned over on its own. You could also choose to pedal the motorbike down the road like any motor-less bicycle until the engine agreed to run. Well, there was actually a third way to fire up the engine—if you had iron lungs, the Tin Man's missing brain, and Superman's testicles made of steel. You could simply run down the road alongside the Whizzer, until the engine turned over, and then make a flying leap onto the bike and hope to land somewhere on the padded seat instead of on the much-harder two-gallon metal gas tank in front of it.

On the first July morning that I took my new used Whizzer out for a spin, I went for the run-alongside-it method. This clearly did not prove to be the best available choice. I ran all the way from Sonora Road down Webster to First Street, all the way from Webster down First to Main, all the way from First up Main to Sonora Road, and finally hopped on the bike, squeezed the clutch handle to loosen the belts, and coasted slowly down the moderate Sonora Road slope in front of my Grandma Jones's house. During that entire Sonora speedway circuit, I never heard even the first cough or pop from the engine. I didn't quite wear out the rubber soles of my high-top Converse tennis shoes on that joyless jog, but they could have heated at least one large igloo in Alaska for an entire winter just by sitting them on a blubberless stove. You could have turned my raw lungs inside out and used them for sandpaper. You could have launched my leaden legs into outer space, and they would have generated their own field of gravity.

Barely able to walk, let alone run any more alongside the Whizzer, I parked the recalcitrant bike just off the street, stumbled up

COLLAPSING ON GRANDMA'S FRONT PORCH JW 2007

the Great Pyramid of Grandma's front steps, climbed her Long March stretch of sidewalk, crawled halfway across the hundred-yard football field that once was her small, vine-framed porch and had just enough strength left in one finger to overcome the ridiculous spring resistance of her doorbell button. Grandma, as she was known on rare occasion to do, came to the door.

"Water," I gasped, collapsing into Grandma's thin, elderly arms. "Water."

Having been born and raised in an earlier era where a woman's place was in the home, and more specifically in the kitchen, Grandma wasn't what you would call real mechanically minded. About all she knew

of planes, trains, and automobiles was that if you got into them they sometimes took you somewhere. But Grandma knew enough about internal medicine to recognize some of the more obvious signs of an overheated grandson's imminent demise. She helped me in to her living room, sat me down on her big soft sofa, got me a tall tumbler glass of the pure-gold ice water that she always kept stashed in a green cut-glass pitcher in her ancient refrigerator, and asked me what on earth had happened.

"What on earth has happened?" Grandma asked me.

Grandma Minnie Jones, in one of her favorite poses at her home.

After two more tumblers of ice water, I was able to answer. Grandma apparently had not yet noticed my new used birthday present, which was leaning comfortably at the foot of her street-side sidewalk on its lowered side kick stand. It was probably still basking in the glory of its recent victory of having run me more than half to death. I had no doubt that it was silently planning its next no-go move. I pointed in the general direction of the bike, wheezed a couple of times for effect, and described the bike for Grandma in somewhat glowing if undeserved terms. For some reason, Grandma seemed to think I was nuts.

"I think you're nuts," Grandma said, seeming to think. "Why do you want a bicycle that you have to push everywhere, instead of ride?" Grandma was apparently confused by my unanticipated praise of the bi-wheeled beast that had nearly done me in.

"It's not a bicycle, Grandma," I panted, still quaffing big gulps of her ice water. "It's a motorbike. It has a motor, so you don't have to pedal it."

"So why do you have to push it all over town?" she asked.

Grandma was, perhaps, more mechanically minded than I at first gave her credit for being. I had not yet dared to ask myself that same mechanical question.

"Well, normally I would just have to push it a little ways," I wheezed, "to get the engine started. Then I could jump on it, and ride it without any more pushing or pedaling. But I haven't been able to get the engine going."

"I've never heard of such a thing," Grandma declared. "A bicycle with a motor that you have to push to ride." She paused to reflect on that a moment—and to determine just who was to blame for this latest crisis to come knocking at her door. And then it erupted, the volcanic question that I had known all along that she would ask, ever since I collapsed into her arms: "Did your dad get you this thing?"

Even after thirty years, Grandma was still suspicious of the man who had married her youngest daughter. She still doubted his marital motives, as though no man in his right

My first bike was *actually* a trike. With my sandbucket swinging from the handlebars and outfitted in coveralls and cap, I'm all ready for work. Maybe I should start by fixing those rickety steps to our backyard shed.

mind would have married her daughter—my mother—without having some ulterior motive or nefarious plan up his sleeve, some hidden scheme. ("Oh, it's a nice wedding ring and all—but what does this man expect to get from you in return?"). In Grandma's mind, to her way of thinking, she had cleverly arrived at the real crux of the motorized bicycle question.

## - OF FIRES AND FOGGY MORNINGS -

"It was a birthday present," I admitted, with reluctance, seeing no way out of this one but to tell the truth, which was always my last, most-desperate option. As usual, my frank admission left Dad all on his own, out on a limb without a paddle.

"Hah! Some birthday present," Grandma concluded, her immediate suspicions now confirmed. "A bicycle that you have to push to ride. I should have guessed it. My goodness gracious!" Grandma always said "My goodness gracious!" whenever she wanted to use an exclamation point to emphasize her jury-like convictions.

The show was over. The fat lady had sung. The curtain had fallen. It was time to run the roads and streets again.

Having almost completely recovered from my non-motoring ordeal, having nearly drained Grandma of an entire week's supply of ice water, having all but failed to convince her that my new used motorbike really was a significant step forward in the progress of all mankind, and having dug an even deeper hole for Dad with Grandma than he had been in before, I thanked her for all of the water and for the legs and lungs rest, and said I had better be going. She walked me to the door and watched me walk back to my bike. As I squeezed the clutch handle to reduce the engine compression and make the heavy bike much easier to push, and began walking it back up the gentle Sonora Road grade to Main Street, Grandma stood on her vine-shrouded front porch with her arms crossed, and monitored me all the way, occasionally shaking her gray-haired head from side to side in sheer amazement. Or maybe it was something closer to sympathy for her Don Quixote grandson, who was tilting at his new used Whizzer windmill, and losing.

As I went by George Smith's pleasantly aromatic, recently mowed front yard and his freshly roto-tilled garden, on the left, and by my spinster Aunt Faye's hideous, unpainted-clapboard house/briar patch, on the right, I ran alongside the bike again, still trying to get the engine to turn over. Not any nearer to success, I decided to roll down the first cindered alley on my right, and wheel the Whizzer into Leonard Wisecarver's cement block and corrugated aluminum garage. If old Leonard couldn't get my new used bike running, it just wasn't going to run.

# CHAPTER THREE

# Ace Mechanic

Leonard Wisecarver was the Sonora area's ace mechanic. People from miles around brought a mishmash of machinery to his shop for repair or restoration. He was always taking something apart or putting it back together, re-tooling worn components, or installing new ones, making whatever machinery that he worked on purr like a fine Swiss watch. As though to testify as to his mechanical wizardry, there was not a single old rusting, wheel-less auto sitting anywhere near Leonard's shop on wooden blocks that had knocked him to his mechanical knees. His clients all believed that Leonard was personally related to every gasoline engine that had ever been made, and he certainly always smelled like it.

Leonard had no useful teeth, or at least he had long been missing an awful lot of the normal number, due probably to the chaw of Workman's tobacco that he kept constantly in motion in his mouth, occasionally spitting the acrid juice towards the nearest open space on his floor. He never wore anything but a pair of greasy coveralls, greasy black laced work shoes, greasy checkered cotton or wool shirt with the sleeves rolled up past his greasy elbows, and a greasy battered railroad engineer's hat that, over the years, had conformed itself perfectly to the shape of his head. Leonard was a thin, wiry, greasy man, of just under average height, with a constant, eighth-inch stubble of dense, salt-and-pepper beard, who seemed to be the same age throughout the whole 1950s decade as he did when he died, which was many years later. (Did I mention that he was always greasy?)

## - OF FIRES AND FOGGY MORNINGS -

Leonard had a severe stutter, that pushed the tumbling thoughts of his quick mind into your deciphering ears with a rapid tongue and lip movement, producing a sort of smacking sound that appeared to be somewhere between a dip and a dup. These shotgunned stutters he injected liberally into every conversation, regardless of the subject, its complexity, or the time of day.

Leonard loved motorcycles. He seemingly always had a big Harley Davidson hog sitting off to one side in his dimly lit garage on the grease-hardened dirt floor. He kept this monstrous motorcycle covered by a canvas tarpaulin, and it was always freshly polished and ready to ride. He took his Harley out for a throaty spin only once or twice a week, except during the winter, probably just to keep a charge on the battery.

Taking my Whizzer to Leonard Wisecarver for help to get it started. His big Harley sits under the tarp cover at left. Although I drew the garage with board siding, I think it actually was constructed of cement blocks. His home is at right rear.

Afterwards, he polished the hog's paint and chrome to perfection, before putting it back under wraps, where it would once more be protected from all of the airborne pollutants that Leonard himself generated. The chrome-encrusted Harley must have weighed ten times as much as Leonard did, and I often wondered how he would ever get it off him if it tipped over on some back road some day and pinned him under it. Anyone coming to

28

Leonard's rescue may have heard him cursing and stuttering way down under the Harley, but might have thought he was simply fine-tuning the engine.

If Leonard couldn't fix my wheezing Whizzer, nobody could. Over the years I had taken all of my toughest bicycle business to him, and he had never failed to diagnose and defeat the problem. Best of all, he had never charged me a dime. I was able to get fresh air for my leaking tires whenever I needed it—all I had to do was wait for Leonard's old homemade air compressor to pressurize its tank. I could borrow any of his wrenches and screwdrivers that I somehow hadn't yet stolen from Dad—as long as I used them *inside* his alley-entered garage. Like my uncle, Jeff Jones, down by the railroad tracks or like Albert Galloway, up by the church, Leonard was always willing to weld or braze any of my broken metal parts with his acetylene/oxygen torch. Although Leonard never charged me anything for his services, unlike my penurious uncle Jeff or the always-prudent and slow-walking Scot, Albert Galloway, he probably added in some extra charge whenever Dad brought in one of his own repairs. Welding fuel and brazing rods certainly were not free, even in the Fifties, when a single dollar bill would buy you four gallons of gas and you would get back change.

Throughout all of my elementary school years, I had been friends with Leonard's two older sons, Donald and Coley, and with his younger stepson, David Huffman. Both Donald and Coley, who were a year or so ahead of me in school, had at some point acquired their own used Whizzers before I got mine. We were the only Whizzer riders in Sonora, and we spent many long days cycling through the surrounding countryside, in search of sexual excitement and other outlaw-like intrigue, like young Marlon Brandos. Although we always created a lot of the latter (in our own minds), we never found any of the former. Maybe Marlon had more luck.

I pedaled my Whizzer down the slight slope of the cindered alley, and coasted it silently into Leonard's garage. (As they usually were, the two big, bi-fold corrugated steel doors were open.) From the back of his well-greased shop, standing at a well-greased wooden workbench, Leonard watched me enter. He interrupted whatever he was doing, and sauntered over, the thick black used motor oil from his current project still dripping from his greasy hands. He wiped up carefully, with an old cotton rag that may once have been clean, and took his first official note of my new toy.

"Dup...dup...dup...dup...dup...dup... I see...dup...dup...dup... I see you have a new toy," Leonard sputtered, his scraggly bearded lower jaw working overtime to keep up with his thoughts. "Why...dup...dup...dup...dup... ain't it running?" Leonard never was one for beating around the bush, when there was a mechanical problem to be solved.

"Beats me, Leonard," I replied, shaking my head back and forth in mandatory deference to his mechanical genius. "Dad just got me this thing for my birthday" (as he probably already knew, Dad most likely having consulted him long before the actual purchase). "It was running okay yesterday when we picked it up in town, but I haven't been able to get it to fire a lick this morning. I've pushed and pedaled this stupid thing from one end of Sonora to the other, and it just won't start."

"Dup...dup...dup...dup... maybe...dup...dup...dup...dup... maybe it's flooded."

"Could be. I've certainly choked it enough—and if it had a neck I'd be real happy to choke it some more. I've tried starting this thing with the spark on, spark off, throttle open, throttle closed, choke on, choke off. I don't know what the heck's the matter. Wanna try it?"

"Dup...dup...dup... sure."

Leonard hopped on the bike with the agility of a man years younger than he actually was—an age which, apparently, was never known to anyone who ever knew him—and began pedaling it down the alley. Nothing. I was about to ask him if he wanted to go down to Grandma's for a glass or two of her ice water before he got too parched out when, after pedaling about fifty feet farther, he stopped, reached down under the gas tank, and made some slight adjustment to the carburetor with the flathead screwdriver that he always carried in a greasy back pocket. He resumed pedaling, but did not go another ten feet before the sick engine coughed asthmatically and pushed a puff of greasy white smoke out its finned exhaust pipe. Leonard stopped again, did some more fine-tuning, and continued pedaling. Almost immediately, the engine began running, moving the bike forward on its own. As it sputtered along, Leonard reached down to the carburetor again, and made a further adjustment. The engine was sounding smoother all the time.

When he reached the end of the alley, at its intersection with First Street, Leonard turned left and continued riding the motorbike northward.

I could hear the engine purring as he went past Center Street, over to Webster, turned west towards our home, and then hung a right onto Sonora Road. It was a good 10 minutes before I heard Leonard coming back down the alley. He coasted the now-warm Whizzer into the garage, intentionally killed the engine, and pedal-braked the bike to a satisfied stop—much like Marlon Brando himself might have done.

"Nice...dup...dup...dup...dup...dup... bike," Leonard stuttered. He got off the Whizzer, and backed it up onto its rear-mounted starting stand.

"What was the problem?" I asked, showing a heartfelt respect and appreciation for his well-known diagnostic skills.

"Oh...dup...dup..dup...dup... it just needed the carburetor...dup... dup...dup... adjusted. It should...dup...dup...dup... be okay now." To prove his theory, Leonard hopped back on the bike, flipped the carburetor choke handle, pumped the pedals a rotation or two, and twisted the left-hand grip to increase the compression and engage the spark. The engine turned over on its own, and smoothed out when he reached down and flipped off the choke. Using the right-hand grip, he revved the motor several times, listened for it to backfire, and seemed satisfied that the engine was running properly. Twisting the compression/spark grip once again, he killed the engine, emitted a deep sigh of satisfaction, and dismounted.

"Okay...dup...dup...dup...dup...dup... okay now," he assured me.

"Sure sounds like it," I boasted, again expressing my admiration for his work. "How much do I owe ya?"

"Oh...dup...dup...dup...dup...dup...dup... there's no charge," he replied, motioning me out with a wave of his greasy hand. I thanked him as I rolled the bike off its starting stand, hopped on, and began pedaling down the alley. With a twist of my left wrist, the engine boomed to life, and sounded much better than any of the thousand balloons that I had mounted for a motor on earlier-owned bicycles.

As I sped away, I could just imagine old Leonard watching me, standing there rubbing his greasy hands again on his greasy overalls, still diagnosing the health of the four-cycle engine through the deep-throated sound from the muffler, grinning from one hairy ear to the other. Once Leonard got my Whizzer running it ran for years. In all four seasons, including some days during Sonora's on-again off-again winter, I rode the motorbike either alone or accompanied by Coley and Donald for hours each day, week in and week out. We circled Sonora's square, up the streets and down the alleys, until our bikes almost made the turns automatically. We rode day and night, rain or shine, hot or cold. We went for miles up into "the country" on loose gravel roads that could have sent us skidding out of control in a split second, making complicated trips on the unmarked back roads that stretched to what would amount to several city blocks, if plotted on a map. We took Route 93 all the way to Adamsville, some ten miles north, and ran Adamsville Road to Zanesville, some seven miles west. Never having a license, or even a learner's permit, we snuck in broad daylight through Zanesville's darkest alleys, almost never using the main streets, hoping that we would not be seen and stopped by a curious cop (and we apparently never were). We came back from Zanesville on the old East Pike—the Federal Government's U. S. Route 40—or on the county's graveled Pleasant Grove Road, and often whizzed the paved mile over to Zanesville's Municipal Airport, more just to look around than to watch for any planes that were coming in or going out. We went east to Bridgeville and farther east to Norwich, and a couple of times even ventured to ride "Old 40" all the way to New Concord, where –unknown to us—the future astronaut John Glenn had some years previously progressed through the same high school that we would soon attend. We had a whole circuit that we often made and timed, starting at our grocery store in Sonora, going south to the top of George Hill, west on Pleasant Grove Road, north on County Road 198 by the Jaycees Golf Course, east on C. R. 64, down Jack King's Hill to the Sonora Road intersection, and back into town—a distance of some four-and-a-half miles on perilously pocked secondary and gravel roads that we covered in less than fifteen minutes, unless a mean-spirited dog or two came chasing after us along the way, hoping to tear off a leg or pantleg, or we had to dodge overstroked golf balls at holes one and three as we whizzed past the public golf course that, privately, was off-limits to us Sonora trash, thanks to Gary Mizer, the course "pro."

We wore out dozens of clutch belts, and burned entire tanker loads of regular gas. When our wire-reinforced half-inch clutch belts got so stretched that they would not grip a pulley any longer, we coated them with gobs of sticky belt-renew stuff, or wrapped them in rolls of friction tape—which we bought by the dozen—and immediately lost all engine clutching, until the sticky new coating wore off or the friction tape wore down, which was a major inconvenience at all stop signs, traffic light intersections, and any other time we wanted to stop without killing ourselves or the engine. We ran our tubed tires until we had no tread at all to steady us on icy or rain-slicked roadways, then replaced them and did it again. We were often miles in any direction from our homes, hours removed from any sight of us by anyone we knew, with nothing more than a pilfered Craftsman Crescent wrench, a pilfered pair of Craftsman pliers, and a couple of pilfered Craftsman screwdrivers to repair whatever mechanical ills befell us, without a penny in our pockets, and who knew how much gas left in our tanks, as good as ghosts to friends, family, neighbors, pets, distant relatives, casual acquaintances, and most of all moms.

We had some real fine times, on our Whizzers.

# CHAPTER FOUR

# Little Wooden Pliers

The small town of Sonora had a fair number of skilled craftsmen in the 1950s, but none stands out in my memory like old George Hose.

George was who you found listed in the dictionary when you looked up the definition of recluse. He lived about as alone as a person could be, in an old, caution-sign-colored school bus that didn't have any wheels on it but wasn't going anywhere anyway. You had to hunt hard to find his bus-house. There was a lane in the second-growth woods north of Sonora that started at the foot of Jack King's hill (by the creek where we turned

SUMMER (AND WINTER) HOME OF GEORGE HOSE

over rocks under the bridge in the summer to find crawdads), and if you followed this lane long enough for it to disappear you not only got yourself lost but eventually came out somewhere in the vicinity of George Hose's non-transportable school bus.

George came into Sonora maybe once a week or so to pick up a few assorted grocery items at our store, and to check his mail. He never brought a tote bag or a wheelbarrow with him, because he never packed home a whole lot of either groceries or mail. Most of what George lived on he somehow must have grown in the woods, within a clearing of weeds, although I don't recall him ever having much of a garden. He must have lived on grass or leaves.

When George came to town, it was easy to miss him as he ambled along the side of Sonora Road, his gimpy gait supported by a sturdy carved wooden cane. He was non-descript. He was—or had been at one time—a big man, big-boned, rough-hewn, and rustic. But in the 1950s, George was all but worn out. He dressed in drab, loose-fitting clothes that looked like they had been cast off as unwanted by the Goodwill store. His ragged-edged suspenders held up faded floppy cotton pants that had been form-fitted by long and constant wear. The thin gray-white strands of hair on his head, always extra long, were only partly corralled by one of those bumpy, broad-brimmed campaign hats like Teddy Roosevelt used to wear (although Teddy never would have recognized it on George). And George always had a sharp, two-bladed pen-knife in one of his pockets, with short sticks of wood in another.

LITTLE WOODEN PLIERS A lA GEORGE HOSE

George could do things with a well-honed pen-knife that most people couldn't even imagine. He could carve the standard whittled objects out of a piece of old wood with both eyes closed and one hand tied behind his back. With his eyes open, both hands free, and a good piece of hardwood to work with, he could make you a new car that carried six passengers and got pretty fair mileage. Given a sharp knife, a few pine boards, and a workweek to do it, George probably could have whittled you a whole two-story house, with an attached garage and a separate backyard gazebo. But what George really specialized in making was little wooden pliers.

There was something magical about George Hose's little wooden pliers.  He would take a single piece of moderately hard wood that was fairly dry, and while you watched in amazement he would quickly turn it into a pair of two-inch, fully functional pliers that had bowed handles, strong jaws, and a finely whittled scissors joint for smooth movement. If you wanted, you could probably apply enough pressure on a pair of George's little wooden pliers to pinch your finger without snapping them in two. But you didn't dare put them to any such test so much as marvel at the fact that these little boogers actually worked, and had been whittled in two joined pieces from a single piece of wood. They not only worked, but were as symmetrically made any pair that could have been machined from metal. George's pliers should have resided in America's national museum of things that people actually make but really shouldn't be able to.

George was locally famous for his little wooden pliers, which he always gave away—never sold—to the first kid watching in wide-mouthed amazement who asked for them. His whittling reputation may even have extended far beyond the Sonora area, but I doubt it. I never saw George's picture in the paper, and never saw a feature story about his works of art in any magazine. He was an unknown artist. He probably never got the fifteen minutes of fame that Andy Warhol would later claim that he deserved.

One day George Hose died.

When George Hose died, Sonora lost by far the community's finest whittler, along with its sole source of those little wooden pliers that really worked. They just don't make them like that any more. But, then, they probably don't make any of those little wooden pliers either.

# CHAPTER FIVE

# Billy Blackstone

Billy Blackstone was blind in one eye, but he could see just fine out of the other. I don't know how, but Billy seemed to be able to get around with his one eye almost as well as the two-eyed rest of us. He did not appear to have any special difficulties in discerning either depth or perspective.

As long as any of us could remember, Billy had been plagued by a prominent white spot on the cornea of his right eye. It closely resembled a nearly full moon, but it was obvious that none of the insensitive kids in our sensitive neighborhood had ever recognized the resemblance, for Billy immediately would have been nicknamed "Moony." That's the way small-town kids were in the 1950s, before the whole world, Bob Dylan's times and all of the rules in society changed, forcing everyone to be more politically correct. It was a cruel life back then, but only the victims were able to fully appreciate it.

I never knew how Billy had come to have the white spot on his eye, but I never thought to ask him. Apparently, no one else did either, for I never heard it mentioned. Billy's blindness was simply one of those things that you accepted. You had two arms, two legs, two ears, one nose. Billy Blackstone had a white spot on his right eye.

Billy was the only boy in Sonora with such a physical handicap, and that somehow made him a lesser person. He was almost always the last one in line when it came to playing games, getting served, signing up, sitting down—nearly any activity involving an order of selection. He was also usually in the final few when sides were chosen for games such as baseball or basketball, although he did make our eighth-grade basketball team—as a backup, not as a starter). He was even second-rated when it came to non-athletic competition, such as stand-up spelling bees, or simply queuing up to get on a school bus.

I can't believe that Billy was not acutely aware of how he was publicly ostracized constantly. He must have noticed the denigrating looks

The ace b-ballers of Sonora (I think we almost won a game once). Front, at bottom left, is Billy Blackstone, my cousin Bobby Jones, and Tommy Russell. Middle left, the author, Harold West, and Bobby Shirer. Back left, Paul Jones (no relation) and Harry Filkill. My uncle, Dunkin' Dave Steinman, managed the team.

and heard the snotty little barbs that were subtly intended to put and keep him in his proper place. But Billy never seemed to let it bother him. He was, seemingly, always happy, always eager to join in group activities, always hoping that he would be accepted as just another one of the guys. But he never was, really. He was always an outcast.

Billy was dark-complected, the apparent result of close inter-racial communication somewhere along the line. He had straight black, shiny hair that was always long, always loosely lapping in the wind. He wore mainly blue jeans and plain, short- or long-sleeved cotton shirts. In itself, Billy's off-color countenance was also a handicap, because there were few other kids in town who affected such a look, and they likewise were socially down caste. It wasn't so much an intentional racial thing as it was a matter of simple skin tone, about the same as being the one kid in town who had red hair. (His name was Gregory Fisher, and he always seemed to have the latest and most popular electronic toys.)

Billy had the additional handicap of living on the side of Sonora—near the old Keystone feed mill—that was generally regarded as wrong, particularly by those of us who lived on the side of town that was generally regarded as right. It was like being on the other side of the tracks without actually having any tracks to cross. There was even a clear difference between Billy's house and the ones around it. His was not well-kept. His had no weekly mowed lawn, nor any yard whatsoever that was not always overgrown with weeds. What paint there had been on the dusty clapboard siding of the Blackstone house had peeled off long ago, or now hung on to its outer walls by the thinnest curled edge. Accidental holes in the glass windows were routinely repaired with rags, wadded and stuffed. And the old, parts-shorn cars and trucks that sat rusting in the property's front and side yards would never run again.

It is unfortunate that Billy never seemed to get a fair shake. His were not the highest grades in any class or on any test, but you could always tell that he was trying hard to learn. He generally understood the concepts being taught by the teachers in our three-room, eight-graded school at least as well as some of the others who always took home better report cards. It was like Billy was destined to receive mediocre marks, in both school and life, no matter what he actually deserved or tried to earn. Unless a test had to be graded strictly by the numbers, with all of the answers being either black or white, right or wrong, Billy automatically scored lower than he should have, while others less-deserving automatically scored higher. Billy's answers to life's questions left no room for any gray interpretations.

Billy was a study in character. Time and again I would see him treated unfairly, and time and again he would return for more. He was beat up or put down on a regular basis. He was nicknamed "Blackie" more as a skin-color epithet than a shortened form of his last name. He was always left out by the "in" crowd. He was never regarded as normal. He was not even respected as "special" (unlike the physically or mentally challenged of today. Billy was just odd. Yet, in spite of everything, as though all of the mistreatment that he suffered never made any difference to him, I never heard him call anyone else a name, never saw him treat anyone else like he himself was treated, never noticed him take out the tremendous frustration that he must have experienced on another person, or kick a dog, or show even the slightest sign that he wanted to get back at the world for putting him in his unfortunate position. Billy simply accepted his lot in life, and went on his way.

He did not attend church, that I recall, but Billy was one of the most Christian persons that I ever knew. I regret now that I never got around to telling him so, and I never will. About ten years ago, Billy Blackstone put a loaded pistol to his head, and pulled the trigger.

# CHAPTER SIX

# Religious Affiliations

Our next door neighbor was always a Methodist minister. No, that's not right. The person who lived next door to us had not always been a Methodist minister, but whoever lived next door to us was always a Methodist minister. Although the face changed occasionally, the title stayed the same.

Sonora had only one church, so if you wanted to go there you either became a Methodist, or you went somewhere else. I became a Methodist because my mother said so. One day I was enjoying my Constitutionally protected freedom of religion; the next Sunday I was sleeping through an uninspired sermon on a hot summer day like everyone else. I never knew exactly when and how I went wrong.

Sonora had several practitioners of the Catholic faith, but they were easy to keep track of, because they were all in the same family, the Harens up on the hill. Since there were no Catholic churches in or near Sonora, the Harens went to church seven miles away in Zanesville, where the largest and most conspicuous Catholic church stood at the head of Main Street. Not only was this huge church firmly footed on Zanesville's highest hill, with a good view of most of the worst bars in downtown Zanesville, but it was also crowned with a dome, atop which was some winged golden statue that, because of the size and the location of the church, was already halfway to heaven. There may have been a few Presbyterians in Sonora, a handful of Lutherans, and probably several Baptists, but no Jews. Like the Methodists and the Catholics, all of those religious people sought out their own respective houses of worship. Sonora may even have had among its few hundred residents an atheist or two, who were always going straight to hell, not just on Saturdays or Sundays but every day of the week, if you asked any of the other true believers.

The reason we always had a Methodist minister living next to us probably had something to do with that house being the official Methodist parsonage. Every time one minister and his family—if he had one—moved out, another one moved in. Over the years I paid many visits to the next-door parsonage, and came to know each of the resident ministers and his family members fairly well. I gradually came to think of them as almost normal people. I often mowed the ministerial lawn, to pocket a few precious points toward my eventual after-life destination, practiced trumpet solos for church performances to the piano accompaniment of one minister's wife, played chess and Scrabble with them, even drove in to Zanesville with one young pastor in his Chevrolet convertible to get a

Perched in our backyard apple tree, where I got most of my useful education, reading a comic book (no doubt one of the Classics). The Methodist parsonage is at left rear, its garage at right. Two fuel-oil drums for our dining room stove are hidden in the small shed under the tree. At rear are the homes of Russell Francis and Glen Reed. Nothing woulda been fina than to be in Carolina in the morning. Maybe.

frosty A&W root beer and play miniature golf. I now believe that my periodic presence in the parsonage may even have inspired a few Sunday sermons, for some of them seemed aimed squarely in my direction.

Because of my sign-lettering talents, which admittedly left a lot to be desired (although Dick Phillips seemed satisfied well enough with my "TV and Radio Repairs" lettering on the side of his shop), I was sometimes coerced into painting one or more posters announcing the annual summer vacation Bible school. These signs were staked out in the maple-shaded front yard of the parsonage, where they would catch the attention of almost nobody passing by, or were tacked to a telephone pole at the corner of Sonora Road and Main Street, where they would be seen by almost everyone who walked or drove by. My colorful signs, over the years, must have stimulated many thoughts about the Methodist Church and its parishioners, although I'm not certain that they did anything to increase the annual enrollment in vacation Bible school. For some reason, the church leg of Main Street intersecting with Sonora Road was known as Old Country Lane. It had about as much resemblance to an old country lane as the rest of Main Street did to Atlantic City's Boardwalk, but if that name nonsense made the other Christians in town feel any better about sweating out Sundays in church, it was okay with me.

Every summer, the most religious kids in town would spend several of their precious vacation days in Bible school, memorizing Bible verses ("Jesus wept" was always the first one memorized), coloring and cutting out significant scenes from Biblical events, and otherwise crafting clever reminders of the Christian thing to do. Most of the vacation Bible school classes were held in the multi-partitioned basement of the church— although some were held on the lawn outside—mainly, I believe, to give any of us who were thinking about sinning some idea of just how hot it would be where we were going if we did. That was the only explanation I ever came up with for them running the church's furnace full-blast in the middle of July.

I could never figure out why vacation Bible school even existed. I think it must have been one of those last-shot brainstorms conceived by a den of mothers somewhere who needed concrete evidence that their sons and daughters were making progress towards Christianity after all. But if you were aged ten or under, church was where you had to go anyway, because your mom was going to make you. And if you were slightly older, you already knew that what you did with certain magazines in the privacy of your own bedroom was probably going to stunt your growth or cause you to go blind, so you didn't need to go to any church school to learn the whys and wherefores. Especially in the middle of the hot summer, with the furnace running full blast.

Attending Sunday School I could justify better. Your whole Sunday morning was already shot to heck by having to dress up in clean clothes and go to church and sit through a long sermon by a man on the pulpit who had only a short railing to protect him if the crowd didn't like what he was saying. Since you were already there, it didn't much matter if you had to spend another half-hour hearing still more about floods, feasts, and famines, saints, souls, and sinners, or heaven, hell, and high water, because you weren't going home anyway until the fat lady sang or the minister finally found the point for which he was searching.

This photo could have been even worse—it could have been in color. My new Easter suit was pastel blue, with matching brown shoes. Our backyard fence, at rear, was white. The grass was green. The sky was blue. "Hello, again. This is Den-ny Tay-lor, singing so-ongs to you...." (I guess you had to be there. Remember radio?)

For most of the Methodist community in Sonora, as probably elsewhere, Easter was a much bigger deal than Christmas. The main thing in Sonora's church at Christmas was the Christmas Eve celebration, when our poor excuse for a church band tortured half the town with songs like *Joy to the World* (congregationally subtitled, *The Band's Stopped Playing*), *Hark! The Herald Angels Sing*, and *Oh, Little Town of Bethlehem*, which we played with the most longing that we could muster, never having even visited the place, let alone seen it stilling lie. After the music, much to the relief of the Sonora souls who had flocked together to suffer through our performance, our band would disband for another full year, and a Santa whose suit never seemed to suit him would ho-ho-ho up the center aisle, and scare the bejesus out of all of the youngest members of the congregation. Those staunch celebrants who had stayed for the duration were then rewarded with a one-way gift exchange, apparently the church's way of symbolizing the significance of Christ's coming or apologizing for all of the minister's senseless sermons over the past year. As an extra added bonus, each family was presented with a two-pound straw basket of indigestible rock-hard chocolates, a bruised green apple, and a bag of bruised and battered tangerines— apparently the very best our church shepherds could find to substitute for gold, frankincense and myrrh.

There was a lot less circumstance, but far more pomp at Easter, when the point seemed to be that, in order to be a good Christian, you had to be dressed in pastel pinks, blues, yellows, and purples. On this special Sunday, many people in Sonora actually walked to church, even if they had a car, just to smell the fresh spring flowers like daffodils, tulips, and lilies along the roadside. I suspected that many of these churchgoers also wanted to show off their new Sunday-go-to-meeting suits and dresses that would have to do them another twelve months before they got new ones. Those who did come by car, or perhaps by truck from the surrounding "country," had to be especially careful not to get any oil or grease on their new duds while they stood around outside the church and waited for the bell to call them in, and checked out what everyone else was wearing so they would have something to talk about when they got home. Once inside the church, there was no way for anyone to escape the stifling heat, even with all of the stained-glass windows open,

Christmas photo with Mom, sitting on her piano bench. The Teddy Bear (Roosevelt – *See: "The General Store"*) must have been for somebody else. We always had the best-looking worst-looking tree in the house. Bar none.

the four overhead fans spinning at full-speed, and the paper hand-fans flipping back and forth faster than the minister's arms, as he tried to add new interest and emphasis to the same Biblical passages that he quoted the last time many people were here, on Easter Sunday a year ago.

Contributing to the torture of the stifling heat, which always took its greatest toll on your neck, that was choked by the too-tight buttoned-down collar of your new white shirt and a noose-knotted black tie, were the agonized efforts of the church organist, who had prepared for this special occasion by practicing almost the whole preceding week. Every so often, the minister would ask the organist to reveal her most recent musical revelation, while he collected his thoughts or recovered the notes that he had just dropped on the floor. More often than not, he would also call upon the assembled flock (a.k.a. the congregation) to raise their voices loudly unto heaven, apparently in a very commendable but completely futile attempt to drown out the organ.

The desire to be a Methodist church organist is an affliction that sometimes struck even the most unprepared and unrepentant among us in the 1950s. My mother, for instance, had always been somewhat susceptible to the lure of musical participation in various gatherings, and had long volunteered her voice to praise the Lord on Sundays in the twenty-member church choir. But it wasn't until one of the ministerial wives, Marian Carl, assured her that she had some untapped instrumental talent, that Mom's mysterious church organist ambitions finally surfaced. One day, Mrs. Carl began giving Mom in-parsonage piano lessons, and after a few hours of perfecting her own peculiar version of *Chopsticks,* Mom was forever hooked on pianos and organs. She acquired one of each, and at some point a small harpsichord that came up with its own chords. After a few (long) years of practice, Mom stepped forward from the general congregation, to serve the Lord as substitute pianist at the church. Eventually, she became The Organist, and took her blessed cherry bench almost every Sunday thereafter, for years, and then decades. When she wasn't playing in church or practicing at home, Mom seemed to be either hosting or attending one of the King's Daughters Class parties, where they also did a lot of singing and piano playing, or participating in other church functions. Mom practiced her religion religiously.

My attitude toward Methodism and our endless parade of minister neighbors took a whole new twist with the arrival one day of Tim McArthy, one of the few young ministers that Sonora received straight from the seminary. Tim was one of the most philosophically liberal ministers who ever entered the ranks of preaching-what-they-practiced Methodists, and he approached his new assignment with way more applied psychological fervor than any of the others that Sonora ever had. Tim was very studious. He spent a lot of hours each week researching the facts and figures for his Sunday sermons. Many times at night, you could hear him talking to God (or somebody else) in his upstairs writing room, spouting off scriptures like he was some sort of Moby Dick or Jonah in the whale, over and over again. By Sunday morning, Tim would be so well-versed in the story of his sermon that at least half of everything he said passed straight over the sweating brows of his confused congregation without even slowing down; the rest of it they simply ignored or disagreed with.

Tim was ushered out of Sonora's one and only pulpit as soon as heavenly possible by the church fathers and church mothers when his first term was up. They made no effort at all to renew his contract for another season, or even trade him for a couple of preachers in the minor leagues, which I personally considered to be a huge mistake. Tim and I had shared many good times and intelligent conversation, at least on my part. He had also told me some really rotten jokes that he seemed to think were funny, such as the one where the city slicker went in a country store and saw several old fellows sitting around a warming stove, apparently telling jokes. Every few minutes, one of them would shout out a number, and the others would laugh. At first confused, when the city slicker asked the store owner about the curious practice, he was told that the men had been telling the same jokes to themselves for so long that they finally had decided to number them and just shout out the numbers, to save both time and effort. After watching them for a while longer, the city fellow decided to try one of his own. "Eighty-four!" he shoured. No laughter,

The Rev. Thomas McArthy

nothing but stern looks. He tried again: "Sixty-seven!" No reaction. When he asked one of the old men what he had done wrong, the man explained: "Well, sonny, some of us got it, and some of us ain't."

In addition to being a struggling comedian, Tim was also a fair Scrabble player, although his frequent use of religion-based Greek and Latin words against me appeared to border on cheating. Tim also read *Playboy* magazine religiously, and occasionally invited me over to the parsonage to discuss Hugh Hefner's *Playboy* philosophy in great detail. But we never actually looked at the pictures. As soon as Tim was exiled from Sonora I got my own subscription to *Playboy,* so I could look at the pictures any time I wanted to.

Sonora Methodist Church visitors in the 1950s would have recognized this half-completed version of the huge painting that hung behind the pulpit. The author must have been around fourteen years old at the time the color oil painting was begun. I have no idea why I never finished it.

# CHAPTER SEVEN

# THE SEVENTH SON

Reputedly the seventh son of a seventh son, Frank Nolan was thought to possess mystical powers that were simply beyond anyone's understanding or full appreciation. Certainly none of the kids in Sonora had a clue. And while we had our doubts about the actual existence of his powers, we wisely decided to leave Mr. Nolan pretty much to himself, and play no pranks on him for which we could be held personally accountable. We also kept in mind that, if ever we were bitten by a venomous snake, poisonous spider, or one of Ohio's vicious alligators, Frank should be the first person we called. You never could tell when Frank's mythical powers—if they really existed—might be used to bring you back from the dead, and there was no sense taking a chance of writing your own obituary by getting on his wrong side. Besides, the word was, Frank had been Sonora's justice of the peace, back in the frontier days when Sonora still had justice, peace, and a justice of the peace. So Frank, apparently, was one of those guys who would just as soon shoot you as save you. Given a choice between getting shot or being saved, the best option was obvious. We may have been dumb back then, but we weren't exactly stupid.

Frank was a sort of FDR-looking fellow, with some of the stronger facial features of Bella Lugosi. He always wore drab, baggy clothes, and a lumpy old felt fedora, and lived alone at the end of an alley that was really the non-paved end of Center Street west of Sonora Road, in a boxy, gray, two-story frame house that apparently never saw a second coat of paint. The closest I ever got to being inside Frank's house was when it caught fire one afternoon, filled the whole town with a lot of smoke, and had to be saved by the Perry Township Volunteer Fire Department. Since occasional house fires were the most spectacular and best-attended public events in

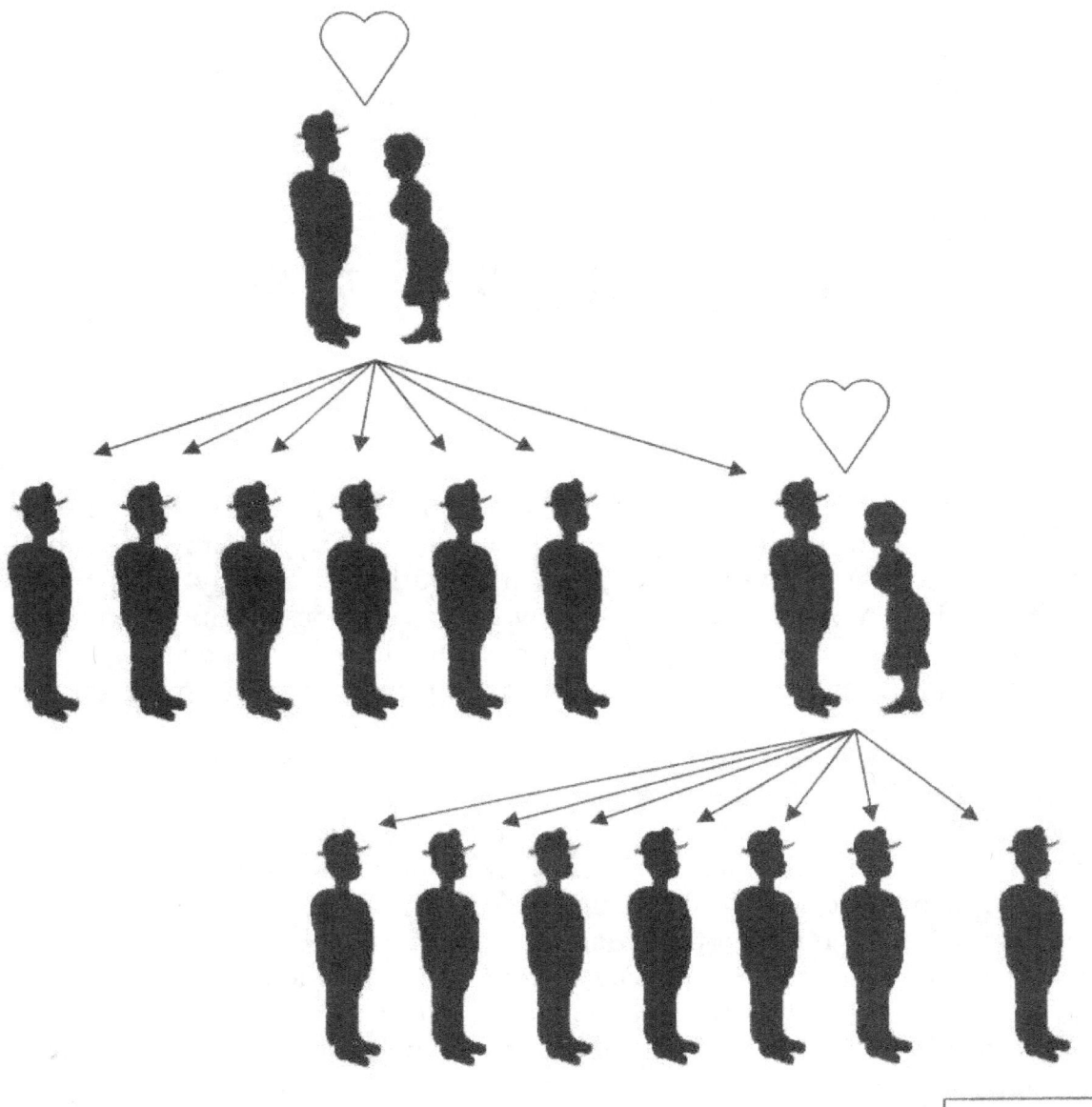

FRANK

Sonora, I usually tried to go to them, as a curious but disinterested observer, along with everyone else in town. People rushed to middle-of-the-night fires in their robes and pajamas, since there was a good chance that a fire would be extinguished before you got there if you stopped to dress. Daytime fires were far less popular, and most people attended those fully clothed. A nighttime fire offered the additional excitement of seeing hot, luminescent sparks shooting high into the black sky, and watching the bright orange flames paint constantly changing silhouettes on the surrounding homes, barns, sheds, trees, yards, dogs, and people. A daytime fire just couldn't compete with that for sheer spectacle, unless there was some sort of gas explosion or something, which couldn't always be arranged. When Frank's house caught fire in broad daylight, we had to suck what excitement we could get from it, knowing full well that there wasn't much chance of it exploding, or doing anything extraordinary. They got Frank's fire out before most people could even show up. So it wasn't one of the worst fires we had ever seen, but it would have been a lot more impressive if it could have been started at night.

I never knew anyone who had to test Frank's alleged seventh-son powers by getting bitten by a venomous snake, a poisonous spider, or one of Ohio's vicious alligators. I had never even heard of anyone being shot by him. Frank probably couldn't have saved anyone anyhow. You had to doubt the mystical healing powers of a seventh son of a seventh son who couldn't even put out his own house fire in broad daylight.

REMAINS OF RUSS FRANCIS HOME AFTER FIRE (AT LEFT IS HOME OF FRANK NOLAN - ALSO ONE OF SEVERAL FIRE SITES IN SONORA.)

# CHAPTER EIGHT

# Major Little Leaguers

Bob White, it seems, was one of my distant uncles. It was not that Bob lived very far away, which he didn't, but that he had acquired his relative distinction through some complicated family arrangement. Bob's two daughters, Beverly and Dixie, were about my age (except Beverly was older) and were cousins of mine, twice or three times removed. The way I figured it, in the 1950s, that must have made Bob my uncle—at the same relative distance, twice or three times removed.

I never knew exactly what that meant. Did it mean that Bob used to live somewhere else and had picked up and moved his family two or three times, finally settling down in Sonora? Did it mean that he used to be a brother of one of my real uncles, who was a real brother of one of my real parents? Had Bob been kicked out of our immediate family for committing some unspeakable sin? When and how had he gone wrong? Why was Bob so unpopular that he had to be removed from relativity? Did Albert Einstein know about my Uncle Bob? It seemed to me that there were an awful lot of unanswered questions surrounding this man. I eventually came to think that Uncle Bob's real relation relevance was that Minnie Huffman Jones, my mother's mother, and thus my maternal grandmother, was Bob White's aunt. That

**Uncle Bob**

obviously made Bob White my Grandma Jones's nephew. When you were somebody's nephew, back then, apparently you were also somebody else's uncle. Since Bob was Grandma's nephew, he was forced to be my uncle. Ironically, and to add to this lineal confusion, Grandma's brother, Shiner, was Uncle Bob's nearest neighbor. (Shiner's real name was Kelly, and he was married to Lizzie. Minnie and Kelly's sister was Ida, who became a White when she married Ben, and their son Bob's sisters were Vera and Helen. Helen married Elton Wheeler, and they lived directly across the railroad tracks, near the station house, next to Jesse Bagent, who lived next to Ida White, Bob's mother.) I have no idea what that made Shiner and Bob—nearly far-removed close-second neighbors? Fourth cousins joined at the sister? In a small town like Sonora in the 1950s, it seemed like most of your neighbors, and half of your friends, were either close or distant relatives, often at the very same time. That caused an incredible amount of confusion among the younger members of a family, and you didn't dare attend an annual reunion without a Bible in your hand, wherein you had stuffed a kind of *Cliff's Notes* cheat sheet on all of your relatives that made the Book of Genesis look like a common telephone directory. Life was not easy for a small-town kid in the 1950s.

Whatever his relationship, Bob and his all-female family lived in one of Sonora's oldest, largest, and nicest houses, a ninety-year-old, two-story

structure that was perched on a massive stone foundation in a grove of some 20 or 30 tall old oak, maple, and other trees down by the B&O railroad tracks, where they ripped right through Sonora Road. A cindered, two-tracked lane snaked through the ancient timber, from Sonora Road to the far setback house, which was easily the largest in Sonora. It had been built by a man named J. W. Stiers, who was an apparent relative of Isaac Stiers (maybe his near-distant nephew or close-second cousin), who had platted the town of Sonora in 1852. Bob also had the largest front yard in Sonora, about two acres square, and mowed it several times during the summer with a sickle bar that was attached to the side of an old Ford or Ferguson tractor.

The biggest social occasions in Sonora occurred whenever the Whites held a summer family reunion under those tall trees. These family gatherings included not only the Whites, but the Heagans, the Haneses, the Huffmans, the Joneses, the Whissels, the Smiths, and anybody else who didn't have any idea who their relatives were, but could use a good meal. The reunions always featured table after table of covered-dishes, and literally hundreds of people of all ages mingled a whole afternoon in the shade of Uncle Bob's big trees, gobbling up baked beans, hot dogs, apple pie, and other delicious home-made items on the pot-luck menu.

One of the top Sonora home-run hitters shows his distinctive wide stance. I also played a mean third base. At right is Seymour West. At left, in the open dug-out, is our team. Somewhere in the bleachers, I suppose, is Mom. She always was.

My Uncle Bob's biggest claim to fame, however, was his knuckle ball. I don't know whether he had ever played baseball for a semi-professional team, but he obviously knew a good bit about it. Under Seymour West, our team manager, Bob was an assistant coach of Sonora's always-outstanding Little League baseball team (along with Joe Bishop and, later, Joe Curry). The fact that Bob had foddered no sons himself for the team didn't seem to matter to him. He spent a lot of time, over several summers, helping all of the boys he could to learn the intricacies of America's favorite pastime, and if they had any time left over he would also teach them a few things about baseball. Sonora's Little

League team was always good, not only because of a natural talent for the game that was seemingly inbred in all of us, but also because we were constantly playing the game in back yards and open fields, and were coached by men who had been there and done that and had, somehow, survived. Several times a week, we would play or practice on our own official field, with our own official backstop, official benches, official bleachers, official food stand, and an official American flag on a pole in

**Truly, one of the best Little League teams that ever took the field. Front row, from left, Gregory Fisher, Jimmy Wheeler, Timmy Nolan, unknown, David Francis, Richard Harding, unknown. Second row, Harry Filkill, Bobby Shirer, Joey Haren, Tommy Russell, cousin Bobby Jones, Harold West, Jack Haren. Back row, Uncle Bob White, the author, Paul Jones, Seymour West. We practiced several times a week, took the game seriously, and won a lot more games than we lost.**

center field that we took our caps off to while we listened to a version of the National Anthem that was record-scratched through a single horny loudspeaker before every game.

Our team, known somewhat imaginatively as "Sonora," was always in the running for the league championship. We could beat the pants off

55

most other area teams any day of the week and twice on Sunday, when the doubleheaders were usually scheduled. Our biggest rivals were teams from Zanesville (which had a lot more kids to choose from, and even had "Zanesville 1" and "Zanesville 2" teams), Dresden (which always seemed to have some kid pitching with an unhittable fast ball), and Adamsville (which was our chief rival, simply because they were nearby, and thought they had a better ballpark—which they did, but they were not going to hear it from us). We even had uncomfortable heavy cotton uniforms that were provided by sponsoring area individuals and local businesses, like Bowers Monuments and Whissel's Grocery. (The latter was worn by a strong-armed, stocky built kid who played a mean third base and had a home-run swing that often led the team, thank you very much.) We were so good that even non-parents sometimes came to watch us play; some of them even stayed.

Both Seymour and Bob took turns showing our outfielders how to shag balls, showing our infielders how to keep their gloves ready and heads down, and showing all batters how to time their swing to a pitch precisely and meet the ball with the bat just as it crossed the plate. You could also hit the ball to a particular field or lay it down in the infield if you swung early, swung late, or accidentally made contact. Seymour, a huge, soundly constructed man whose catcher stepson Harold West was just as stocky, specialized in showing our pitchers how to throw hard and fast balls that a lot of times came pretty close to crossing the plate. Seymour had a major control problem with his fast ball that made him even more intimidating than he tried to be. When he stood on the pitching mound, Seymour's throwing arm seemed to rise to a height of about 25 feet, and his fast balls occasionally caught fire from the friction as they approached the plate. When Seymour talked, you listened, or you sat on the bench while your ears cooled down. He had a booming voice of authority, and he seemed to take great pleasure in booming at us often.

Our ace pitcher was Harry Filkill, who also happened to be the biggest kid that any of us had ever even seen, let alone played with or against. Harry had a fast ball that rivaled Seymour's. You sometimes caught your first glance of Harry's fast ball on your way home after a game or a practice, as it burned up while leaving the atmosphere. You didn't try to hit Harry's fast ball so much as avoid it, because Harry's fast ball would leave a red spot with seams on your head if it hit you—and that was if you were wearing a helmet. Going up against Harry without a helmet was like jumping into a turtle-filled swimming hole on a hot day with no clothes on. It sure felt good at the time, but you would probably live to regret it.

Your only chance of connecting with Harry's fast ball came by starting your swing while he was still at his home south of Sonora on George Hill, prior to a practice. If your bat happened to be in just the right spot at just the right time you would hear a crack that was as much a shock to you as to anyone else, and by the time you realized that you had actually hit the ball it was already too late to start running for first, so you just stood there in shock until the plate umpire told you to go back to the dugout and sit down. Harry's slow ball "change-up" sailed by at 150 miles per hour; no one ever measured his fast ball, because nobody ever saw it except Chuck Yeager, and he only saw it once as it went soaring by, leaving his supersonic jet plane looking like it was a hot-air balloon.

Unlike Seymour, Uncle Bob was interested in teaching our pitchers how to throw stuff that you could actually see. Bob's pitching philosophy, therefore, was just the opposite of Seymour's: on the mound it was not might that made right, but sleight of hand.

Uncle Bob had one of the slowest pitches that I have ever seen. You would think that with an old geezer like Bob (who must have been over thirty) standing on the mound some forty-five feet away, taking his good old time about winding up to make the pitch and releasing his knuckle ball, making no attempt at all to conceal his just truly unbelievable one-hand prestidigitation, you would have plenty of time to get your bat ready to strike his pitched ball. But three or

four minutes usually passed between the time Bob's knuckle ball left his contorted fingers and you heard it snap in the center of the catcher's mitt. During this long interval, you lost all track of where you were and what you were doing. While you stood there with your teeth in your mouth, Bob's knuckler took a leisurely trip around the bases, stopped by the food stand for a complimentary hot dog, and went in to Zanesville for a light trim at Landaker's Barber Shop, before it inched by you, waving hello, how are you, now isn't this just a heck of a lot of fun?

Bob's knuckle ball seemed to have about six times the up-and-down and sideways speed as forward movement. The only way to actually hit it was by pure accident. I never saw anybody who even came close. You could take three swings, and strike out on a single pitch. It was one of those showcase pitches that he pulled out only on special occasions such as holidays, or to celebrate the return of Halley's Comet, and then only for demonstration purposes. Like one of the white-hatted guys in an old western at the Liberty Theatre in Zanesville, Uncle Bob never used his remarkable knuckle ball to take advantage of others, never for mere personal gain, but only to uphold law and order in the community, and then only after a lot of hand wringing and personal conferencing with his wife, Dude. If you really wanted to be thrown one of Uncle Bob's remarkable knuckle balls, you had to submit a written request three days in advance, and sign a special form that released him from all responsibility if you ended up in the hospital. Some of us did, and some of us didn't. Some of us didn't, and some of us did.

Sonora baseballer, 1957. Red cap, gray cotton uniform with red-and-white leggings, spikes with real steel cleats. Make sure the glove you get at Clossman's Hardware in Zanesville is big enough, and don't forget the glove oil to break in the pocket. Oh yeah, bring your own 32-inch bat, and make sure you custom wrap the handle with friction tape. That oughta just about do it. Play ball!

# CHAPTER NINE

# Mrs. Stanley's Dogs

We had no witches in Sonora (that I knew of then or know of now), but the woman who was nearest to my mental image of one was named Mrs. Stanley. If I ever knew Mrs. Stanley's first name, it has escaped me. My friends, our family, and I always called her Mrs. Stanley.

Mrs. Stanley lived alone, a few stone's throw south of Sonora, beyond the two parallel sets of Baltimore & Ohio railroad tracks (main and siding), in a decrepit two-story frame house that was surrounded by oaks, ashes, maples, bushy pine trees, and a yard full of weeds that had never met a lawnmower. To reach Mrs. Stanley's house, which apparently few other Sonora residents ever did, you had to wind your way from Sonora Road through the weeds and trees on a rutted, narrow dirt lane. About halfway there, you passed by a large, square, two-story red-brick house on the right that belonged to Mr. and Mrs. Clifford Stage. I think there may have been some family relationship between Mrs. Stage and Mrs. Stanley, but I never knew what it was. I think Mrs. Stage may have been Mrs. Stanley's daughter. Clifford always reminded me of Humphrey Bogart.

Mrs. Stanley was always old, at least 100. She was always white-haired, always supported by a cane and apparently always confined within the far walls of her house. I never saw her outside her kitchen, which was the first (and only) room we entered when I occasionally accompanied one of my parents on the delivery of a groceries order or, later, made a delivery run myself on my bike. We would sack up Mrs. Stanley's phoned-in items, take them to her home, often slip unnoticed into her kitchen, and simply leave them on her table. The bill would be paid later.

## - OF FIRES AND FOGGY MORNINGS -

Mrs. Stanley's mystery, in addition to her near-match to my mental image of a witch—thin, wiry, wily, with small, beady eyes under hanks of unkempt white hair, and squarish little teeth—was her intimate relationship with dogs. Mrs. Stanley did not have just one dog as a pet. When you entered her kitchen, to deliver mainly cans and bags of dog food, you were accosted by the acrid odors of a dozen or more dogs that had been confined to quarters but free to roam up and down the two floors of her house, and do all of the things that you might expect from animals that had no outdoor outlets for their bodily waste-disposal needs. Mrs. Stanley's house was a mess. It smelled to high heaven. You could barely stand to be in her kitchen long enough to leave it.

Mrs. Stanley never seemed to notice that the dogs had made deposits to their waste products bank accounts right under her feet, everywhere on her worn-thin and faded carpets, all over her once-fine furniture, and anywhere else where they had felt the urge. Nor did she ever seem to be affected by the offensive odors. She must have been holding her breath for years, or she simply had grown accustomed to the stench. Whatever the explanation, the smells that soon would have nauseated anyone else apparently became normal and not particularly bad to her. Perhaps the pleasant scent of the surrounding pine trees, wafting through her broken and unrepaired second-floor windows, was always enough to her to offset the eye-burning doggie-do odors. Perhaps she had an unceasing, severe case of nasal congestion. Perhaps she just didn't care.

The houseful of dogs obviously offered almost the only companionship that Mrs. Stanley ever seemed to have, but there were still other dogs tied to several boxes in her yard, scattered among the trees. Those dogs, apparently, were the ones that were not housebroken.

I never saw Mrs. Stanley anywhere in Sonora—and never, during any of our grocery deliveries, did I ever see anyone else inside her house. Only the dogs. Always the dogs.

Mrs. Stanley must have been a lonely old lady. She obviously had been married, and was either widowed or divorced. She was a real mystery. She was one of the many unsolved riddles of Sonora in the 1950s, when almost everyone in town was the subject of one interesting story or another, and almost every dog that you saw on the street had a smile on its face.

# CHAPTER TEN

# One Hot Car

One fine fall day in 1957 Dad drove his old Chevy to the levee of a new car dealership on Newark Road, and came home with a brand-new, fire-engine-red Pontiac Star Chief two-door convertible with white trim, white top, white sidewall tires, and nearly a ton of chrome on the inside alone.

This was one hot car. Dad must have paid upwards of $5,000 for it.

Dad had long been a fan of the Cleveland Indians, and also of Pontiac products, but not until now had he ever gone over the edge of the warpath. All of his previous cars and trucks had been fairly plain and practical. This time, however, Dad decided to make a statement. To most of the people of Sonora, Dad's purchase of the showy new Pontiac seemed to be a statement that he had finally gone nuts. Not since Dick Phillips came home one night with the first color television set in Sonora had anyone bought anything so ostentatious. The Pontiac achieved instant fame as the most expensive car in town. Everyone feared a new rise in grocery prices or postage rates, since Dad was both a local grocer and the Sonora postmaster.

This year, 1957, was a groundbreaking one for Pontiac. The company came up with some six dozen technological innovations among car companies, not the least of which were genuine simulated leather seats that matched the colors of a car's exterior. (Back then, it didn't take much innovation for a car company to outgun the competition.) Dad's new Star Chief had all of Pontiac's standard features and most of the options as well. It had an automatic transmission with overdrive, snap-on fender skirts that provided cosmetic concealment of the rear wheel wells, and custom-fitted rubber floor mats, both front and rear. It had a radio that picked up not only the standard AM stations but FM ones as well, with a whole row of silver buttons that you could push to have a motorized, illuminated marker move right to the station that you wanted to hear. When you turned this radio on or off, the chrome sectional antenna that was nearly hidden atop the right rear fender automatically telescoped up or down, and made a loud whirring sound. This motorized antenna must alone have been proof enough to anyone that Pontiac was a cutting-edge company, poised for automotive design leadership.

The Star Chief had an electric clock, a slide-rule speedometer, and powered seats that you could move not only back and forth but also up

and down. It had power steering, power brakes, power door locks, power rag top—I think it even had power hubcaps. I know it had to have a powerful lot of air in its big whitewall tires, because the weight of the massive "continental kit" that enclosed the spare tire and provided chrome ports for the dual exhausts caused the whole car to slant towards the rear. Even sitting still, the Star Chief looked like it was going 90 miles an hour.

Under the hood of this Detroit dragster was an engine that just wouldn't quit. Most of the time, it just wouldn't start either. But when you finally got it running, overcoming its predisposition to flood at the first sign of rain, sleet, snow, hail, fog, frost, wind, or clear, sunny weather, you knew you held the reins of a whole herd of horses. When you sat there in park and popped the accelerator pedal, the entire car would rock from side to side, suggesting the tremendous torque that the engine could transfer to the rear axle. You got the impression that you were sitting on the starting line at a quarter-mile drag strip, waiting for the lights to change from red to yellow to green.

Most street car engines in the 1950s had a single carburetor. Some of the eight-cylinder engines had two. Dad's Star Chief had *three* two-barrels, mounted all in a row, and it was almost impossible to keep them in tune. The car was worse than a Fifties-era Jaguar, which nobody ever drove, except to the garage for a tune-up, and back home. The Star Chief's optional 347-cubic-inch, eight-cylinder engine, for which Dad had dropped many extra dollars, was listed as capable of developing 317 horsepower. It probably produced that much power before leaving the driveway.

Dad's drag star demon would *move.* Even pulling the far-too-heavy continental kit, you could go from a dead stop to 60 m.p.h. in about two seconds flat. The car's acceleration was incredible. You could feel your eyeballs punched back against the seat when you put the pedal to the metal. When Dad was driving down the highway at 60 m.p.h. and called upon the engine for an extra kick to

**Look closely, and you will see my Grandma Jones in the front passenger seat. Obviously, she was waiting for Mom to drive her somewhere. She didn't like to ride with Dad, but sometimes she would wave at him as he drove by.**

leave a passing show-off teenager in a horsed up hot-rod eating his dust, the car leaped forward like it was mounted on springs. If NASA could have found a way to run the Star Chief in outer space without oxygen, we would have reached the moon at least twenty years sooner, in about two hours max. Dad once told me about a guy with a similar model (but with no continental kit) who lost an illegal drag race when he floored the accelerator and spun the rear tires right off the rims.

This Pontiac's real forte, however, was not its acceleration, but its top speed. No one still alive could tell you exactly what it was. The speedometer ended at 120 m.p.h. but you reached that point with the accelerator pedal only about halfway to the floor and the car still in the garage. Until they invented interstate highways, to straighten out all of the curves on secondary highways, where it was usually too dangerous to drag, there wasn't a stretch of road in Ohio long enough to unwind Dad's Pontiac all the way. I know for a fact that this street car would snicker at 140 m.p.h. as it passed by (don't ask me how I know that), and it probably could have edged 160, if asked politely.

Of course, Dad's boxy Star Chief got only three-tenths of a mile per gallon, but it had a large tank, so you could go almost all the way from Zanesville to Columbus—a distance of some fifty miles—without having to stop more than once or twice along the way for gas, if you had a stiff wind behind you. However, with hi-test gasoline costing less than thirty cents a gallon back then, and with Dad able to get all of his gas at wholesale as the operator of a service station, he could well afford to keep the Star Chief's tank topped up.

Knowing he was going to bring this car home one day, Dad built a whole new garage just for it alone. It had a poured concrete floor that I carved my initials into when it was wet and a wide white-pine door that slid on an overhead rail, just like we had on our barn. Dad apparently made a slight miscalculation in the interior dimensions of the garage, and you were forced to run the car's front bumper right up to the stud wall if you wanted to close the garage door. And you had to keep the Star Chief almost all the way over to the right as you pulled in, until its chrome side trim strips nearly scraped the wall, if you wanted to open the driver's side door far enough to get out. But if you had watched your weight, and you held your breath, you usually didn't have much of a problem exiting the car once it was inside Dad's new garage.

Including the garage, the Star Chief had come equipped with almost every possible option, except for the most essential item in a 1950s hot car. And it wasn't long before Dad was able to find the perfect one of those. He came home one day with a clear plastic steering wheel knob with a chrome band that clamped around the wheel. It was held on by two screws, and contained the very same photo of Marilyn Monroe that

Hugh Hefner had used as the centerfold in his premier issue of *Playboy*. The full-figured female movie star was posed completely naked, with her knees and ankles squeezed tightly together, long legs angled demurely off to one side, beckoning right arm bent outward from her flawless face, hand fluffing her sea of flowing hair, abundant bosoms thrust forward proudly—just like the big knobs that protruded so prominently from the chrome front bumper of Dad's car. Marilyn shamelessly displayed her assets for all to see, on a red silk cloth that perfectly matched the exterior of Dad's car. Marilyn and the Pontiac people must have worked very closely together for a long time to achieve this color coordination accomplishment.

Mom, of course, hated Dad's little knob, not just because it got in her way when she was driving but because she had a sort of philosophical, puritanical disagreement with him about whether such things should be seen in a car. I think Dad won this one by pointing out that far worse things, physically, had been seen in a car. But I never saw Mom lay the first finger on one of Marilyn's famous knobs—Dad's or anybody else's.

I, on the other hand, knew we had a real winner here, in this barebosomed breaking of the usual rules against the public display of female body parts. There were things in life that you had to pay for, and other things that people would pay *you* for, and this seemed to be a perfect example of the latter. It wasn't long before I pleadingly borrowed Dad's keys to the Pontiac (I think it was on one afternoon while he was sleeping soundly before going to his night shift job at the Hazel-Atlas glass house in Zanesville), and had an extra set of keys made just for me. I had no intention of risking any damage to the car by actually driving it out of the garage. I had other, more mercenary, entrepreneurial plans for it. Whenever Dad was at work at his job in Zanesville, eight miles away, I was at home in business in the garage. As Mom minded our grocery store and post office, she may have noticed a steady stream of young boys from all over town headed back towards our garage, and probably found their constant

Thanks to Marilyn, I ran a pretty successful backyard business. You might say it was all boom and bust. Then again, you might not.

66

curiosity about Dad's new car amazing. She also probably wondered why my pants pockets always seemed to be chock full of nickels and dimes.

These young boys weren't lining up just to see Dad's Star Chief.

For five cents, they could get a glance at everything Marilyn Monroe had to offer.

For a dime, I would start the engine.

One thing Dad's big red Pontiac Star Chief didn't have was a tightly secured steering wheel knob. After I noticed that, I always kept a screwdriver handy, in case Dad ever tried to tighten it. I couldn't have him putting me out of business. When the Star Chief's engine was off, Marilyn was certainly something to see. But when all of those horses were running, and the whole big Pontiac was shaking, and Marilyn's entire luscious naked body was throbbing ... well, it was certainly worth the extra nickel.

My brother Jim, who burned down our outhouse, thought he had a real hot car, too, and it probably had more gadgets than Dad's Star Chief. At top right, over the pop porch, is my bedroom window, from which Jim ran a radio aerial wire over to Dick Phillips's porch post and caused a fire. As anyone can plainly see, I was not even in my bedroom at the time, so I could not have done it.

Another view of Jim's 1948 Ford, with the weird antenna and a big firehorse (?) for a hood ornament. I was still in training at the time, but I was still strong enough to keep Jim's car from tilting any more sideways. Note the pop cases.

# CHAPTER ELEVEN

# The Flying Tigers

We have raised two whole generations of pre-assembled, remote-controlled modelers, who have absolutely no idea what it was like to make and fly a model airplane in the 1950s.

To begin with, it took far more time and effort to "make" a model airplane back then than just slipping Tab A into Slot B. And you didn't fly the plane that you carefully assembled. It flew you.

Today, model airplanes of an amazing assortment of size, shape, engine, and fuselage designs can be purchased ready-to-fly, with a remote control unit that has more buttons, knobs, and levers than our earliest space shuttles had. Just add fuel and fly. If the model doesn't come off the shelf already assembled, you can probably pay the all-knowing acne-faced teenager who clerks the hobby store to put it together for you. On a real slow sales day, you could probably even pay her to fly it while you just stand by and watch.

Not so in the 1950s, when I somehow acquired a fifteen-inch long brown plastic terror, with a helmeted little pilot under the clear plastic cockpit canopy. It was the spitting image of the World War II Pacific workhorse, the single-engined, tri-propped P-40 Flying Tiger. This was a model plane that you not only had to assemble, but also had to learn how to fly, in a trial-and-error process that was a lot of trial but even more error. With its wide one-piece wing loosely rubber-banded to the fuselage, for quick and relatively shock-free detachment upon the inevitable crash, this little speedster could lay you out in at least a dozen ways before you could even say Lucky Lindbergh.

## - THE FLYING TIGERS -

Many of today's model airplanes are powered by electric motors or pelletized fuel. My P-40 Flying Tiger was a genuine internal combustion-engined powerhouse that was faster than a speeding bullet, and more deadly besides. All you had to do was breathe a few whiffs of its pure ethanol liquid fuel and you were flying high, with or without the plane.

The P-40's fuel tank was an integral part of the engine, and was located just in front of the fuselage. You filled the miniature tank by using a piston-like pump that was attached to a pint fuel can. This streamed fuel through a clear, soft-plastic tube that was connected to your choice of two vertical pipe outlets located atop the tank. Although only one of these pipes was needed to get the fuel into the tank, the second pipe allowed the fuel that you were pumping into one pipe to squirt out the other, shoot up into your eyes, and send you home from the field in a half-blinded condition to fly again another day.

Assuming you got the tank filled with fuel while preserving your eyesight, the next challenge was to attach the leads of a six-volt lantern battery to the engine's "glow plug" using a standard alligator clip that was almost useless in this application. The glow plug, which was essentially a spark plug, was the top cap of the engine, and screwed on. It needed to be of a screw-on design because you repeatedly had to remove the plug, using a small special wrench, turn it upside down, squirt a bit of fuel into it, and connect the battery briefly to make sure the plug's tiny wire element had not burned through. You bought these glow plugs by the dozen, because that's just about how many seconds they were each good for once you had the electrified alligator clip attached.

A P-40 Flying Tiger model

With the tank fueled, and the plug aglow, your next magical trick would be to prime the engine's two open side ports with enough fuel to get it going but not enough to flood it out. This required a substantial amount of skill, and accounted for most of the glow plug failures, because too much fuel would not allow the plug to heat up properly and too little fuel would cause it to overheat and quickly fry the thin wire coil. How you determined the right amount of fuel priming was by sacrificing the skin on half of the knuckles on your fingers.

According to the pre-OSHA printed instructions that came with the .049 horsepower engine, the preferred way to spin the propeller, and thus to begin the self-perpetuating internal combustion process, was to hook it to an attached spring, which you crank-wound a half-turn and then released. This, of course, never worked. All it seemed to do was irritate the obstinate engine enough that it would refuse to even pop, primed or unprimed. Eventually, you came to the conclusion that the propeller had

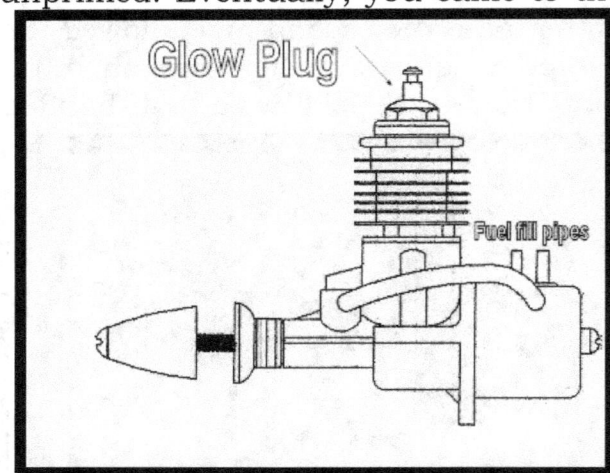

to be spun faster with more torque—whipped into a frenzy, as it were—and the only way to do that was to rotate the recalcitrant prop with the tip of your index finger. (I'm just guessing but I'd bet money that this model airplane was manufactured by the same company that made my Whizzer motorbike.) *(See Chapter Two: "The Whizzer")*. When the glow plug was properly primed, and the propeller was properly spun, there was a reasonable (one in a million) chance that the reciprocating piston in the engine would begin the combustion process and the engine would run. This was almost impossible to achieve in reality, however, because the precise amount of fuel flowing to the glow plug was determined by yet another devious device, called the "fuel adjustment valve." This needle-like valve, which was kept under tension by a spring on its shaft, was supposed to be opened either one-quarter of one revolution, one-and-one-quarter revolutions, or somewhere between all the way closed and all the way open, depending on how you read the instructions, which if I recall correctly were written by a Japanese guy who was apparently still sore about losing the war, and had come up with his own way of striking back at us American dogs.

Not only did the needle valve have to be set absolutely right to begin with before the engine would even fire, let alone continue to run, but the temperature of the engine seemed to have a direct impact on the valve's setting. If you accidentally got the engine started, and if it continued to run for its entire possible two minutes and nineteen seconds, the only way

My brother Jim, who burned down our outhouse, takes a spin at the propeller of my P-40 Flying Tiger, while I prepare for take-off and onlookers maintain a reasonably safe distance. At far left, alongside the alley running beside the B&O railroad tracks, is the home of Jake Jordan. Across Webster Street is the home of Uncle Jeff and Aunt Rita Jones, adjacent to the home of Albert and Lillie Russell. At top right, hidden in the woods, is the dammed pool for individual and group skinny dipping. (I never actually looked at the pictures.)

to go for a second flight, after refueling, was to readjust the fuel valve to compensate for the now-hot engine.

Assuming the needle valve was properly set, and was engine-temperature compensated, there was no guarantee that a manual spin of the propeller would even start the engine, because nine spins out of ten times the engine would backfire, and the propeller would be kicked backward in a vile attempt by the mean-spirited engine to break your index finger. So the trick was to spin the propeller with just the right amount of speed and force, and then withdraw your finger and any other loose appendages that could determine the heredity of your children from the prop path as quickly as possible.

## - OF FIRES AND FOGGY MORNINGS -

Once you had the engine started, the next step was to readjust the needle valve for maximum speed, because you couldn't use the same setting to both start and run the engine. This also was a trial-and-error process, during which you usually turned the valve too far in one direction or too far in the other, and the engine would stutter to a stop, forcing you to refuel, reconnect the battery, re-prime the ports, and resubmit your index finger and other parts unknown to the fickle propeller of fate. Even if you didn't kill the engine at this stage, it still usually took so long to adjust the valve for top running speed that you would have to refuel the tank on the run, as it were, in order to have enough fuel left to actually get the plane off the ground.

With enough practice, a skilled pilot could make two, three, maybe even four flights on a long summer's day, assuming he skipped all meals, remained on the field of battle, and didn't need to go to the bathroom too often.

Flying model airplanes in the 1950s was a two-person task, not just because you needed to have somebody else standing by to take you and your severed index finger to the hospital, but also because there was no way to leave the plane running and get to the end of the control lines by yourself. My older brother, Jim, was a favorite co-pilot of mine, because he could usually be relied upon to go through the prop-spinning process without too much complaining, and didn't expect too many flying minutes of his own in return. Plus, his fingers were a lot bigger and tougher than mine.

Unlike today's pansy products, model airplanes in the 1950s were flown with control lines. Today's radio-controlled planes have buttons and levers on the hand-held remote control panel to adjust ailerons, elevator, stabilizer, flaps and engine speed, turn ten watts of lights off and on, raise and lower the landing gear, wave a tail-mounted American Flag, drop live bombs on the home of the neighborhood bully, and serve all in-flight meals. We, on the other hand, had two thin strings, each about 30 feet long, that ran from a thin plastic bar on one end to the left wing of the plane on the other, and once in a while actually operated the plane's horizontal elevator (the moving part of the small rear "wing" to you non-pilots). When you finally got the engine started, assuming there was still enough daylight to see the plane from a distance of thirty feet, you had to rely upon a friend—or an older brother—to hold it from moving forward until you could run to the circle-center end of the control lines, get them untangled, check the tower for clearance, review your last will and testament, kiss your butt good-bye, and call for the plane's release.

Once the plane began its combined taxi and take-off run, you would notice all curious onlookers within a five-mile radius quickly ducking for cover. But that often proved to be entirely unnecessary, because the spinning propeller had a tendency to get caught up in the high grass (anything taller than the infield dust of the local baseball diamond) and the plane would flip its way forward into model airplane oblivion. You would then have many more pieces of the plane at the end of the run than you had at the beginning, not to mention an unusable tangle of control line. Few takeoff efforts were successful on the very first try.

My brother Jim tests out my American Flyer narrow-gauge model train before allowing me to play with it. Notice how he always managed to remain incognito. Like our dining room carpet?

On the off-chance that you eventually got the plane through its taxi run, and off the ground, your biggest challenge was just beginning—keeping it in the air. Since flight schools for model airplaners back then, as now, were as scarce as six-wheeled bicycles, you had to learn to fly by the seat of your pants. Roughly translated, that means you had to crash and burn about a zillion times before you finally figured out that keeping the plane in the air required extremely m-i-n-o-r movements of your wrist-operated control line. It took only a slight upward tilt of your wrist to send the plane soaring high into the sky (at least fifteen or twenty feet); one false flip downward and the plane would be on a non-stop dive to China for more rubber bands, a new propeller, and other parts.

Sharp readers of this account will deduce that there would be more things revolving during the course of a flight than the propeller. Unlike today's model airplanes, which can go up, go down, fly straight, do Immelman's, spin, roll, and generally perform in a very realistic manner, planes back then were limited to about four basic maneuvers. They could fly higher, fly lower, crash without any apparent reason—one of their favorite maneuvers—and fly around in circles until they ran out of gas, became a victim of amateur control error, or were left to their own flight rules and patterns when the pilot became so dizzy that he fell to the ground and released the line, thus freeing the plane to shoot for the second star to the right, and sail straight on 'til morning.

You don't know what dizzy is until you have spent two or three minutes focused only on a small model plane some 30 feet away that is spinning you counter-clockwise at about 12 r.p.m.s. (This was how our early astronauts got their initial flight training.) Without drifting from the circle center, and thus further endangering all wary bystanders, you had to exactly match your step-by-step revolutions to the speed of the plane, grasp some awareness of where it was relative to the ground, keep the control line taut enough to retain command of your airborne assault vehicle, and have fun all at the same time.

With practice, we learned to like this kind of flying. I think it was my brother who first figured out that if you were flying high, did a fast dip nearly to the ground, then soared into an overhead loop and reversed your wrist actions, you could actually fly the plane upside down, while rotating in a reversed, clockwise direction. Since this was completely counter to the direction it (and you) had been spinning, the effect was to undue all of the dizziness that you had been building up—so long as you didn't stay spinning clockwise for long. There was, of course, an inescapable clock ticking on the whole flight, due to the finite fuel supply, because the plane just didn't climb or even fly very well when it was out of fuel and coasting. Moreover, flying the plane upside down had its own special risks, because eventually you would have to do another loop—one that proved to be a lot harder—to bring the plane right-side up in time to taxi it to a one-piece landing.

Landings were easy. When the plane finally ran out of fuel, it would simply glide to the ground. As long as you kept the control line taut you had a good chance of taxiing the plane to a halt without having to look for a fresh set of rubber bands and a new propeller. One little lapse of control, however—say a blink of the eye—and you would be picking up pieces.

I flew the durable little P-40 for years, but today I have no idea what became of it. Did it finally crash and go to that great model airplane hangar in the sky? Did I give it away? Did it somehow snap its lines and fly off to freedom, never to circle Sonora again? It remains another one of life's little mysteries, like the sudden disappearance of my cobalt-blue, narrow-gauge American Flyer model train (with a real, working headlight), my three-rail Lionel trains, my motorized red metal model coupe car with battery powered head and tail lights and turning front wheels, my round-boxed set of Lincoln Logs, my cardboard Captain Midnight decoder ring, and my entire Davy Crockett at the Alamo set with its realistically painted tin walls, American and Mexican action figures, and tiny plastic cannon with wire-spring firing mechanisms that launched little plastic projectiles clear across the room. I know for certain that I accidentally shot one of these "cannonballs" into my mouth one Christmas morning as I was rewriting the history of the Alamo, for I did a thorough search of our living room and never did find it, but I know I was shouting something bad about Santa Anna when it disappeared. After more than fifty years of periodically recalling and replaying this tragic shooting episode, I am convinced that one of those devious Mexican soldiers had something to do with the disappearance, although I don't know exactly what. Maybe they also got my trains, Lincoln Logs, Captain Midnight decoder ring, and P-40 Flying Tiger. Or maybe it was that Japanese guy, who wrote those misleading instructions for starting the Flying Tiger's .049 engine.

Captain Midnight and sidekick. The TV show ran only two years.

Davy Crockett probably wasn't shot by a spring-loaded cannon like this one, but I'm pretty sure I was.

Probably every boy in the United States had a Lincoln Logs set in the 1950s. The company still produces sets, but they are a bit different now than they were then.

# CHAPTER TWELVE

# Peregory's Pennies

Fred Peregory must have been a poor man. Every time he came through Sonora and stopped at our store, every kid within running distance hit him up for a penny or two. After a few years, we must have drained his bank account down to zero. Fred ("Mr. Peregory" to every little beggar) was the only such benefactor most kids in Sonora ever had. But when you have a perpetual fountain, you don't need to go anywhere else to drink.

Fred was a strange man, and very tall. He was probably as tall as Walter Gibbons, the railroad worker who lived up by the cemetery and always wore dirty coveralls, but was much sturdier and stockier. Walter was sort of loose-limbed and gangly, which probably helped him get his job on the railroad gang (but that's another story). Obviously refined, obviously a successful businessman of some sort—maybe a salesman or a supervisor or a plant manager or something, Fred was the best-dressed gentleman who ever cruised through Sonora in one of the expensive, late-model cars that he regularly traded-in. It was to protect and polish these like-new vehicles that Fred paid probably tens of thousands of dollars to the children of Sonora over the years, a few pennies at a time.

Fred had a farm up in the country, about a half-mile north of Sonora, that was well off the beaten path. To reach it you had to turn off a gravel township road, pass through a wind row of trees, and wind your way through a few alfalfa, clover, and timothy hay fields or corn, then roll down a hidden hillside to the homestead. Fred and his wife appeared to be very private persons, who never attended Sonora's social functions that I remember. But white-haired Fred always had a quick, seemingly sincere smile under his white-haired bushy mustache, and a raspy, gracious greeting for all of the little rip-off artists to whom he paid his protection dollars when they came running up.

Fred's new cars never got a scratch on them when he parked in front of Jack and Alma Greiner's house at the corner of Sonora Road and Webster Street to patronize our post office or shop at our store. Every kid in Sonora knew Fred's work schedule as well as he did, and every kid in Sonora also knew that all of the others would break every bone in his body if he ever caused Mr. Peregory to cut off those pennies from heaven.

This is a Russian overhead photo that was taken in the early 1950s by a Captain Moscovite, en route to the moon by way of Sonora. At top center (west) is Fred Peregory's house. At left (south) is the Baltimore and Ohio Railroad where it curves by Frog Run (in the patch of trees). At bottom right (north) is Leonard Orndorff's farm, where we Boy Scouts searched for his son until we, apparently, found him. Ronnie Baldwin ran his two-wheeled tractor-trailer rig up and down the steep hill that is between the bare white field that looks like a flying saucer and the clump of trees. Sonora, unbeknownst to the Russians, is about a half-mile off to the top left, which is maybe why Captain Moscovite never quite made it to the moon. So near and...nyet—so far. (Sorry about that.)

# CHAPTER THIRTEEN

# The Fishermen

I got my first real fishing rod when I was about nine or ten years old. Up until then, like most other young boys in Sonora, I had cut and trimmed my poles as needed from the always-available stands of young sassafras saplings that seemed to grow everywhere you looked.

My first real rod, a gift from Dad, was made not from wood but from a greenish white fiberglas. It was just under five feet long, and came complete with a metal tip, three line guides, and a black-and-red wooden handle with circular serrations. Mounted on the handle was a chrome reel with curlicue lettering, a casting/reeling clicker that you could override if you wanted to, and a screw-adjustable drag. The reel even had a long length of twisted Dacron line, and the line even ended in a sharply barbed hook.

To complete the package, Dad sorted through his several old tackle boxes that contained at least one each of every known fly, lure, and hook in the world, including one giant that could only have been used in salt-

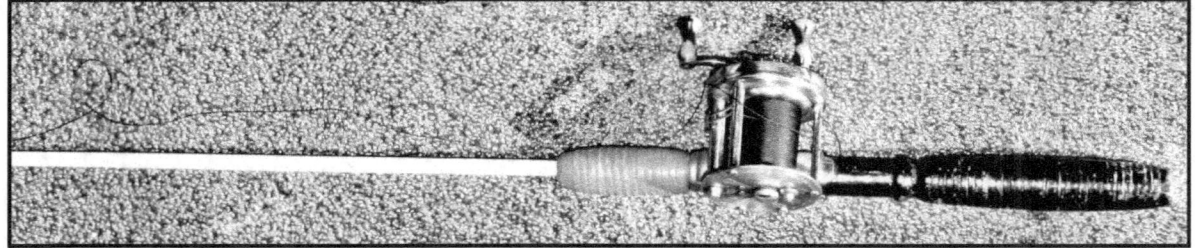

Still going strong after five decades is my first real rod, with a Ward's Sport King No. 60 6310 Model 5C reel, original Dacron line, and fiberglas rod.

water seas to fish for whales, although nobody ever told Dad that whales weren't fish, so you couldn't do that. He set me up with several round red-and-white bobbers, extra lines and leaders, and almost a ton of assorted lead sinkers, including some lead oval river sinkers that weighed more than my reel that Dad had molded himself. I was the envy of all of my fishing pals. Dad even gave me one of his battered old metal tackle boxes.

In one fell swoop, I had been outfitted with everything that any kid ever needed in order to take on the monster bluegills, sunfish, catfish, and "chubs" in the shallow ponds and small creeks around Sonora.

To most of my pals and me, fishing was a summertime sport that you took up only when you got tired of playing baseball. It was not a particularly exciting pastime, and it required a lot more effort to organize a fishing outing than to get up a baseball game. So fishing was never our first choice of all available summer activities, if a few innings of baseball could be thrown together.

It wasn't the fishing itself that was the problem, but all of the detailed planning and preparation that was needed to go about it properly. To begin with there was the unavoidable problem of bait. You could, of course, just ball up some bread or cheese on the end of a hook and attempt to lure a hungry fish that way. There were also bottled baits available, like fish eggs and gritty slabs of something that resembled pig skin pickled in salt water. But the cheapest bait, and therefore to us the best, was the common earthworm.

To get the biggest, juiciest earthworms, you had to begin the night before the day you planned to go fishing. You mixed up a pail of soapy warm water, took it out to a likely spot in the yard, and simply dumped it on the grass. Then you went back in the house to read a Marvel Comics, play a game of checkers, or watch *Beat the Clock* or *I Love Lucy*. After ten or fifteen minutes, you returned with an empty tin can and a flashlight, and easily picked up a dozen or so of the big juicy night crawlers that had slimed their way to the surface in order to avoid suffocation. The worms probably weren't particularly happy to have been interrupted in their endless underground boring to be confined to the cramped quarters of the tin can, but they certainly were clean. To help them get accommodated to their temporary new digs, we would toss in enough fresh dirt to let them burrow down and hide, but not enough to allow them to climb up and over the edge of the can. On warmer nights, this can of worms would be hidden in a back corner of the kitchen refrigerator, where fickle mothers and foolish sisters wouldn't find it and ask crazy questions like what in the world we thought we were doing anyway.

An alternative to night-stalking earthworms was to get a can, find a shovel, and dig for them just prior to leaving for the fishing hole. You could dig just about anywhere in the loomy soil around Sonora and find a few earthworms and perhaps a puffy white grubworm or two—but seldom any night-crawlers. But if you could locate an old rotting board or a concrete block that had lain so long that all of the grass under it had died and dried, it would almost always produce several juicy worms that had taken shelter from the sun in the cool dirt below. Most of the time, however, we had to slice out shovelsful of soil in some shaded corner of the yard, break the clods apart, and pick out the long plump worms that would be found there. The disadvantage of that method, of course, was that you had no way of knowing if and when you were slicing your best bait in two. And it was no big secret that one whole worm threaded much easier onto a hook than several smaller pieces of it.

If you wanted to catch bluegills and sunfish, the best place to go around Sonora was Stage's south pond. Shaped roughly like a horizontal cornucopia, about fifty feet across, it had been artificially formed by an earthen dam on its south side that had backed up the water from a small spring-fed stream to a depth of maybe ten or fifteen feet. Typical of southeastern Ohio ponds, this one was surrounded by a few scattered stands of cattails that resembled fuzzy burnt hotdogs. The banks were steep, cut clay, sprouting several stands of rough marsh grass.

As long as you fished Stage's pond in the early morning or early evening, you stood a better-than-even chance of being successful. But in the middle of the day (from about nine until five), the fish in this pond apparently had better bait to fry. Your red-and-white plastic bobber never bounced a ripple during those hours, and most of your earthworms either drowned while waiting to be eaten or died of boredom. In mid-day, the fish in Stage's pond apparently all migrated to the deepest, coolest water, and they weren't much interested in taking your bait.

A better place to fish, at any time of day, was on down the road at the foot of George Hill, in Little Salt Creek. There you could toss a line in on either side of or under the steel-and-concrete bridge that carried the paved secondary road over the creek and usually have your fishing dreams fulfilled. There were pools two or three feet deep on either side of this bridge, and they usually sheltered a hungry fish or two, particularly a day or so after a rainstorm when the rising creek waters would wash a whole new batch of fish into these pools from other holes upstream. You could also follow the grassy banks of the twisting creek eastward for about a hundred yards and find a few more pools at least worth investigating. But the best fishing spot on Little Salt Creek was several hundred yards to the west of the bridge, upstream, and was reached only by fighting your way through scratchy, head-high weeds and clumps of cutting swamp grass that hid small pockets of water that you invariably stepped in and got your feet wet.

This was a place just made for sunfish and bluegill fishing. At a bend where the creek widened to about twenty feet and the water slowed accordingly, there were a few fallen trees that angled out over the water. These trees had long before been storm-stripped of their thick jagged bark but were still gray and sturdy. When the trees came crashing down, they had shed their more-brittle branches but had retained their larger limbs, that now poked down into the water and provided choice cover for fish. From these safe havens a hungry, more-adventuresome fish could cruise out, piddle around with your bait, decide whether or not to snap it up, then take it and dart back into shelter before you even knew what hit you. By the time you saw your bobber sinking, the thieving fish was headed for home. Nine times out of ten, when you jerked a teased line taut you either came up with a bent and baitless hook or you lost the hook, bobber, and sinker, all snagged on an underwater limb.

These fish knew how to fight and run to live another day. They were some of the bigger ones that we routinely fought, because they had outsmarted us more often than other fish elsewhere. It wasn't that we took our catch home, when there was anything caught to take home, because we never fished for food. It was just that we caught and released the same fish here, day after day, all summer long, as we did at most places. We often landed fish that showed signs of having been caught four, five or even six times before. Some of them even started to recognize us. It got so bad one summer that some of these fish would curse us by our first name as we hoisted them from the water, and we had to start wearing Lone Ranger masks in order to avoid being recognized.

This hole was heavy with metals from all of the steel hooks and lead sinkers that we were forced to cut loose once they had gotten stuck. We seemed to spend most of our time re-threading sinkers, re-tying hooks, and re-attaching the few bobbers that we were able to retrieve. But it wasn't long, after we had fallen in the cool brown water a few times while attempting to rescue our entangled tackle, that we came to realize just how good a swimming hole this place could also be. From that point on, when we tired of fishing or snagged our lines, we turned from one water sport to the other, thinking that if we couldn't beat 'em, we could at least join 'em.

Perhaps the best place of all for fishing—and, most of us believed, for swimming—was several stones' throw northeast of Sonora, in the cool waters of a dizzy little creek called Frog Run. You could reach this secluded spot by leaving the paved road just around the corner from the turnoff to Leonard Orndorff's hill and hiking through a cow pasture, climbing a couple of barbed-wire fences, and fighting a field full of high weeds and thick bushes. But the preferred way to get there, because it was by far the easiest, was to walk the Baltimore & Ohio Railroad tracks. During this hike you could practice the useful skill of balance-beam walking on a hot steel rail, so long as you watched out for trains and the soles of your tennis shoes were still thick enough to insulate your feet from the stove-hot steel. By the end of the summer, the soles of our shoes often were so thin that you could see the light of a candle through them. If you were lucky enough to have a coal train come along while you were risking your very life on the rails, you could also plunk down a copper penny and get it flattened into an ellipse the size of a half-dollar under the huge wheels of the heavy, smoke-belching engine and its dozens of coal cars, box cars, and tube-shaped tankers that were seemingly filled with everything from milk to magnesia.

The B&O railroad tracks generally followed the curving course of Frog Run in this area north of Sonora, and closed to within a banked fifty feet of it in some places. At our favorite fishing hole, you could almost sit on a shiny rail some thirty or forty feet above the creek and toss your line into the water. But that would have been a terrible waste of some of the best fishing shores any of us could ever hope to have.

The Frog Run fishing hole had the priceless advantage of being located at the edge of the summer grazing grounds of a mixed herd of black-and-white holsteins and white-faced herefords. Since it was such a

good place to drink, these burping bovines patronized it often, and spent a lot of their cud-chewing snooze time on its shaded green banks. They spent an equal amount of hours cooling off in the pool itself, especially on the hottest summer days, when Sonora's temperatures could boil clear up into the humid high-nineties. What bankside grass the cattle didn't crush by tramping down, they ate. So the banks of this fishing hole were always inviting to the young fisherman who didn't much care to battle bushes and weeds, and occasionally found himself more interested in joining the cows and dozing off than in keeping a keen eye on his bobber.

## - OF FIRES AND FOGGY MORNINGS -

Frog Run was the largest non-pond fishing hole around. It was some twenty feet across and some forty feet long. Although it was usually less than four feet deep, on some days the depth could increase to more than five, depending on the amount of recent rainfall, the average daytime temperature, and how thirsty the cows were.

Unlike Salt Creek's limb-filled fishing pool, which had a sticky, muddy, clay-based bottom, Frog Run was a pond founded on a fine bottom of sand. Only one nearly-dead tree tilted out from the northwest bank and provided varying degrees of shade over the water. And only a few of its roots interfered with the smoothly banked shoreline. So there was almost no place for the fish to hide, other than deep down in the pits of the pool.

Into this remote watering hole flowed a constant supply of food for the up to eight-inch chubs that were easily caught, soon released and just as easily caught again. Upstream the creek twisted and tumbled over a  jumble of rocks and waterlogged limbs and formed sandbars at curves that first sped and then slowed the progress of the water, always keeping it roiled up. And all along its banks were wicked, barb-filled briars that weren't worth fighting to get to any fishable spot. But once the rippled water reached the wide watering hole, it slowed almost to a stop, and deposited flies, worms, grubs, larvae, and other fish food right onto the waiting tables of the lazy chubs. It was no wonder that these fish took our worm bait so gently, causing our bobbers to sink ever so slowly as they snacked at their leisure. These fish had no need for speed. They were accustomed to having their meals brought to them on a sun-silvered water platter, unlike normal fish that had to fight for every last morsel in the mainstream of life.

Not by coincidence, this pool also was one of the area's better swimming sites, and it was not unusual to have both fishing and swimming going on at the same time. And when you tired of those activities, you could just lie on the soft, warm grass under the summer sun, and sleep. The only pool rule for fishing, swimming, or snoozing was

84

to keep a constant eye out for cottonmouths—water moccasins—and copperheads, both of which were poisonous snakes sometimes seen in these very waters. While these snakes had never to our knowledge interfered in any way with anyone at Frog Run, they were often seen skimming over the pool's surface, crossing from one bank to the other. We kept an especially close look-out for these slimy snakes in the grass, because none of us wanted to be the first kid in Sonora to test Frank Nolan's alleged seventh-son curative powers. *(See Chapter Seven: "The Seventh Son.")*

We spent entire summer afternoons at Sonora's best fishing and swimming holes. Towards evening, we would often wander home with no fish, empty bait cans, damp hair, and a whole night's worth of stories about the ones that got away, which somehow were always much bigger than the ones we actually caught and released, and caught again another day. But the point of fishing always has been the game, not the score.

My off-white fiberglas fishing pole has held a number of shiny new reels over the years, has been bowed by the weight of many bigger fish, and has whipped the air in much larger lakes, ponds and rivers than Sonora's, including the Yellowstone, the Snake and the Firehole Rivers in Wyoming. But it has never fought any finer fish, nor brought any better days, than when it was the terror of its time, in the 1950s, on the cool creeks and quiet ponds around Sonora.

Pal David Bonifant helps me build a fishing boat out of boards salvaged from Bowers Monuments. We never saw anything of my brother Jim, but I put on my fireman's hat anyway. Our boat never made it to water. In fact, it never made it out of our yard; it was so heavy that we couldn't even move it.

Not everyone who handled a rod and reel in the 1950s was a fisherman. Some, like Mom, were women. If she seems to be a bit fuzzy here, well, that was just her normal condition.

# CHAPTER FOURTEEN

# Trailing Tractors

I don't remember how or when I first met Ronnie Baldwin, but we soon became good friends. Ronnie lived up in the country, about three miles northeast of Sonora. He was some years older than I was, maybe six or seven.

Ronnie lived on a farm, and did farmer things, like milking crops and planting cows. I lived in a town, and did towner things, like roller skating on the big concrete unloading platform behind the feed mill and fishing golf balls from the creeks and ponds at the nearby Jaycees Public Golf Course and trading them in for cash.

Ronnie had a garden tractor, the kind you walked behind and held onto the handles of while its two huge, cleated rubber tires clawed at the ground. It had a pin hitch on the rear, to which you could hook a variety of implements, such as a plow or a cultivator, but our favorite hook-up was a wagon—a wooden cart, really, with two small balloon tires axled under its middle and a removable standing board at its rear. The highlight of any visit to Ronnie's rural farm, which had the normal number of interesting outbuildings to explore, was tooling through the woods and fields of his acreage on the wagon, being pulled up, down, around, through, over, and about by the garden tractor.

You had to be an expert to drive Ronnie's garden tractor, because its hinged connection to the cart created a lot of technical difficulties. To begin, with the tractor didn't exactly stop on a dime. To be more accurate, it had no brakes at all. So every downhill trip became a high-speed adventure that you hoped you would live to tell about. Moreover, when you steered Ronnie's rural tractor-trailer rig, you always made wide turns—not just the common, right-hand highway trucker kind around sharp corners, but left-handed ones as well. There was a good reason for

this. The sharper your turn, the longer your arms needed to be, because the radius of the turn determined exactly how much control of the tractor that you were going to lose. As you made a sharp left-hand turn, you lost all contact with the engine's handle-mounted speed control. As you made a sharp right-hand turn, you forfeited your hold on the clutch handle. When you went beyond a certain point, left or right, you gave up any hope at all of steering the tractor, made an instant decision to attend church more often, and often had to jump ship before a corner of the cart was grabbed by the cleats of a tire and the whole bi-folded rig flipped over.

Ronnie's trailered tractor went no more than about two miles per hour, except downhill,

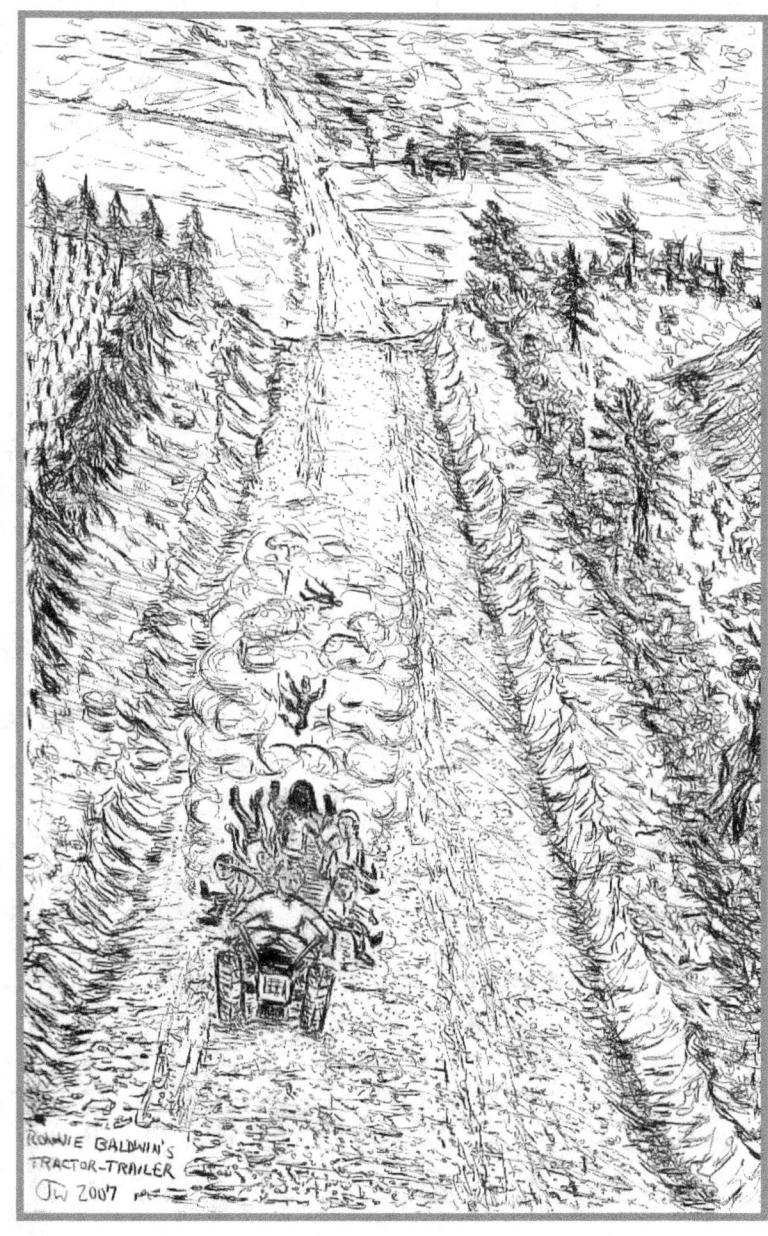

but it must have gotten 200 miles from a single gallon of gas. This fuel statistic was important, because Ronnie often puttered all the way in to Sonora with two or three kids in the cart. It had plenty of power to pull such a load on the level and even to pick up some additional weight at the store in the form of groceries or more kids. Where the little tractor met its match was on the south side of Orndorff's hill.

## - OF FIRES AND FOGGY MORNINGS -

When approached from the north, the Orndorff farm side of this hill was moderate enough that you could easily climb it on one of the era's single-geared bicycles. Ronnie's garden tractor took that side of the hill in stride. But then you had to face the bigger problem of getting down the other, much steeper southern slope without the benefit of any brakes. This problem was usually solved by having everyone on board drag their feet in the loose gravel, churning up a huge cloud of choking dust, while Ronnie steered for the biggest piles of gravel along the way down to get the most friction braking. With any luck, this braking scheme would get you down the hill in one piece in about thirty seconds. With no luck at all, you might make to the bottom in about ten seconds, but there would be a lot of wagon parts and body pieces to pick up.

When you approached Orndorff's hill from the south, you faced a climb that looked like it should have had roller coaster rails on it. It was tough for some automobiles, even shifted down into second or first gear; it was a major pull for Ronnie's little garden tractor. But you never rode Ronnie's tractor/wagon rig up the south side of Orndorff's hill. You always had to push it. All passengers and the driver had to walk beside or behind the tractor and cart and help the tires fight gravity and loose gravel all the way up the hill. The hill was so steep, and the gravel was so loose, that the cleated tires of the tractor spun furiously from the bottom of the hill to the top—once again stirring up a dust storm that was seldom seen west of the Sahara. On the positive side, however, once you had overcome Orndorff's Hill by climbing it a step at a time, you felt like you could tackle anything in the world. You had taken on an unbeatable foe and had emerged victorious. It was Sonora's early version of Outdoor Leadership School.

In his young adult years, Ronnie Baldwin played for Sonora's men's softball team. These guys were not pansies; they played for keeps, wearing real steel spikes and pitching underhanded faster than most baseball players could throw overhanded. Of course, they played only for the sport, not the money (☺). Ronnie was their catcher.

I don't remember much about Ronnie's softball career. But I do remember that it came to an abrupt and painful end one evening when Ronnie was rounding the bases, having hit another potential homer, and had to slide at home plate. Ronnie's onrushing body was met by an immovable object in the form of the opposing team's catcher. When Ronnie slid, the catcher's firmly planted steel spikes stopped him cold, and he broke an ankle. The snapped bone stuck out through the muscle and skin of Ronnie's lower leg.

## - TRAILING TRACTORS -

Ronnie lay writhing and screaming in the most pain I had ever seen anyone suffer, outside a Baptist church, while an ambulance was summoned from Zanesville, some seven miles away. Struggling to stay conscious, Ronnie was loaded up and rushed out of the ballpark to the appreciative applause of the crowd, who seldom witnessed such dramatic entertainment, for treatment at one of Zanesville's hospitals—probably Bethesda. The softball game then continued. Ronnie was replaced by a substitute catcher who couldn't hit the broad side of a barn from the inside, let alone any home runs like Ronnie. I can't say for certain, but I think Sonora lost.

# CHAPTER FIFTEEN

# Locks and Beagles

Dad's favorite fishing holes—when he wasn't pulling six-inch chubs from a few choice creek locations around Sonora—were the Muskingum River at Ellis Dam, about six miles north of Zanesville, and Salt Fork reservoir, about ten miles northeast of Cambridge. Rarely, Dad would also put his banged-up aluminum boat in at Buckeye Lake, home of a popular but poorly maintained amusement park east of Columbus. Where Dad fished depended almost entirely on what he wanted to catch at the time. Salt Fork and Buckeye Lake were fine waters for smallmouth bass and bluegill. Ellis was a dam good place to corner a mud or channel catfish.

Named after a small whistle stop on the dual parallel sets of steel rails of the Norfolk and Western Railroad, Ellis Dam stretched about 200 yards across the muddy Muskingum and created an upper and a lower pool. The Muskingum generally runs northwest to southeast from its source at the confluence of the Walhonding and Tuscarawas Rivers in Coshocton to its mouth in Marietta where it empties into the Ohio. Ellis Dam was built at a bend where the Muskingum runs northeast to southwest. Horizontally perpendicular to the southwestern end of Ellis Dam a concrete lock with two massive sheet steel gates at either end enabled modest-sized pleasure boats and commercial carriers to continue their trips up and down the river, despite the elevation difference of the two pools. Because the dam created an upper pool and a lower one, with a fall of about ten feet from one to the other, river craft traveling the river had to be raised or lowered from one level to the other in the lock, which was operated on an as-needed basis by a tender who lived in a small house about 100 yards away. Boats traveling south would pull through the opened upper gates, which the tender would then close by hand-spinning a steel wheel that was connected to huge gears. Then the lower gates would be cranked open, the upper-pool water would flow out and

ELLIS DAM

the boats would slowly settle down to the level of the lower pool. Boats traveling north would be raised to the level of the upper pool in the reverse order. While these transfers usually involved more than one craft at a time, due to the amount of time and effort that was required, many cycles saw only a single boat being escalated up or down.

Some fish obviously traveled up and down the Muskingum River in the very same manner. When either set of gates was left open fish from that pool could easily meander in and out of the lock at will. When a boat transfer happened to take place, which could be often or rarely, some of these fish would suddenly find themselves swimming in a whole new underwater environment. Migrating upstream in this particular manner didn't necessarily make the Muskingum's catfish any smarter than their trout and salmon cousins in the Northwest, but the climb certainly consumed less energy.

## - OF FIRES AND FOGGY MORNINGS -

Dropping a line into the open or closed lock pool would occasionally produce a channel cat or, less often, a broader-mouthed and considerably bigger mudcat. But this in-lock area was normally reserved for floating perforated metal buckets of bait containing silver minnows and their bigger brother chubs.

The first task of any fisherman arriving at Ellis would be to remove his multi-holed bait bucket insert from the two-gallon can full of creek water containing it and lower the snap-lidded insert some twenty-five feet from the top of the concrete lock to the lockside water level by using a reliable cord or a rope. When rebaiting, this dripping mini-fish prison would be pulled up as quickly as possible, one of the inmates would be chosen and hooked, and the remaining felons would be paroled once more to the water, where they could swim around in their ten-inch circular cell until they were brought before the parole board again.

**Dad (foreground) is joined by an unknown fisherman atop Ellis Dam lock on a very foggy morning. The best place to drop a line was right at the corner of the concrete, in the roiled water.**

Counting a quick in and out at a small bait store on North Linden Avenue to buy a dozen soft crawdads Dad and I could usually make it from Sonora to Ellis Dam in his old Chevy pickup with only a single stop needed for fresh creek water between Zanesville and Ellis. This depended directly, however, on the size and the number of chubs and minnows occupying Dad's bait bucket. The more bait we had and the larger they were, the more oxygen they needed to remain in usable condition at Ellis. It was rare that we didn't have a few floaters by the time we reached Ellis. While these asphyxiated minnows could still be used as bait, they just didn't seem to be as lively and as tasty to the big catfish as their friends who were still breathing.

Dad fished both morning and night at Ellis, but never in the afternoon. Morning fishermen would watch the summer sun come up directly over the wooded eastern bank of the Muskingum, alongside Route 666. But the usual aim was to arrive just before sunset, in order to get settled in for the night while there was still some daylight. After taking care of the bait bucket and getting our tackle rigged the next order of battle would be lowering our lines down along the steeply sloped concrete abutment that formed the river side of the lock—preferably right in the corner where the lock joined the dam. The water from the upper pool that tumbled over the dam not only gouged a deep hole at the dam/lock intersection, but also whisked breakfast, lunch, dinner, and midnight snacks into the mulls of waiting catfish. One of Dad's larger live chubs, anchored by either two or three heavy lead sinkers in the swift waters that were stirred to a froth in the plunge over the dam, could be mighty attractive to a bottom-cruising mudcat. A less-popular place to fish, when a sooner-arriving fisherman had already laid claim to the choicest spot,

was almost anywhere along the river-side length of the concrete lock, where the calmer waters made it easy for these catfish to lie in wait while their meals came to them. One frequent early arrival on the locks was an old fellow who always seemed to wear the same clothes, was always accompanied by his elderly pet beagle. and never seemed to catch anything. But he never seemed to care.

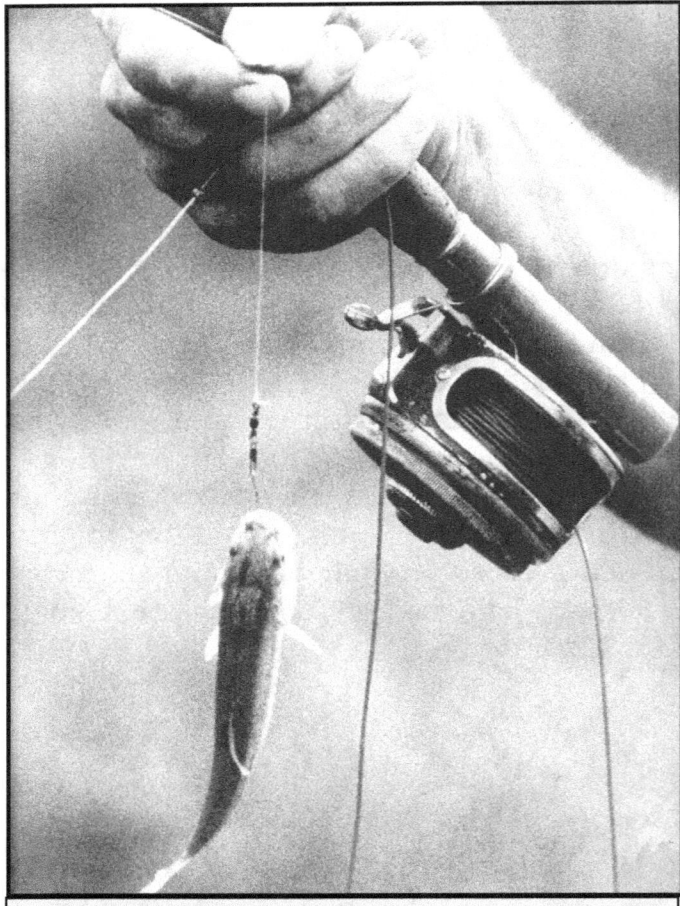

**Not one of Dad's biggest fish, but maybe one of the best, caught in a near-to-Sonora creek.**

With a baited line anchored firmly in the dam-deep water the Ellis fisherman's next task was to arrange his assorted tackle boxes, sandwich bags, two-cell flashlights, and carbide head light in their proper positions atop the concrete lock platform, so he could find them as needed during the night. Although nothing prevented any of these Ellis essentials from being knocked off the steep concrete wall and into the water during the night I never saw anyone—ever—lose a single item. That is even more amazing when you know that about half of the typical night of fishing was spent simply staring upward at the brilliant stars or snoozing flat on your back on the narrow concrete platform—usually with both of your feet hanging over the edge. Dad and I spent a lot of nights in this precarious position, along with many other fishermen (including the Sonora gardener George Smith), but I never saw anyone—asleep or awake—take a twenty-five-foot plunge off the wall into the muddy waters of the Muskingum in the middle of the night. And that included our dog, Pepi.

Equally amazing was the mysterious fact that no unattended rig was ever pulled over the edge by a hooked catfish. Rods and reels usually weren't secured in any way to the concrete platform. Thirty to 100 feet of line could be slanted down and out to the very bottom of the river. Rods often were not even held in hand but simply laid down on the platform.

It wasn't often that a singing line would signal the taking of your bait by a catfish but when the time to name that tune came around the tempo turned fast and furious. A big fish with a mouthful of your bait (in other words, all of it) invariably ran for the middle of the river, usually towards some sharp-edged rocks or sunken tree limbs that were hidden to you but well-known to the fleeing fish near the base of the dam. This was an attempt at entanglement that would snap the line and set the fish free. When this run began there was only a slim possibility that you would be able to put enough pressure on the whirring line to stop the cat's scramble for cover—doing so would almost always cause the taut line to snap immediately. Your only hope was to let the line play out until the fish stopped running, keep any slack from being created if the fish suddenly reversed its course, then see if you could slowly rewind the maybe 200 feet of line that had been unwound until you could bring your catch clear back to the base of the concrete lock. Even then a fair-sized catfish would usually have enough fight left to make at least one repeat run for the submerged trees and hidden rock piles. The key was to keep the catfish off the bottom and gradually work it up to the surface, where you could wear it out and break its spirit. Assuming you were successful in doing that the next skill test was to walk the exhausted fish along the entire length of the dock, around its end, by the closed gates and along the bank of the river until you or, preferably, an assistant could scoop up the fish in a sturdy net at the edge of the water. All of this would take place under the narrow beam of a flashlight or the dim light of a carbide flame.

Catfish landed in this way were immediately transferred onto a stronger stringer or rope, since it was running a real risk to keep a powerful catfish contained by only your thin fishing line if it didn't want to hang around. Once it caught its breath, there was no question that a catfish would attempt to make a run or two for freedom again. More than one fish fooled a fisherman into thinking that the war was over when only the first battle had been won. Only by threading a metal stringer or a strong rope through the lip of a big catfish and by tying that to the stub of a steel pipe or lock gate handrail could a fisherman be absolutely certain that he would have something besides himself and his dog to take home at the end of the night.

## - OF FIRES AND FOGGY MORNINGS -

Not all trips to Ellis took place in the early evening. Early morning expeditions would begin with Dad's traditional woodsman breakfast of scorched eggs, burnt bacon, and industrial-strength coffee before 5 a.m. After packing the tackle and the dog we would go to the small creek that ran through our five-acre farm at the edge of Sonora and pull out the bait bucket insert that contained some two or three dozen pre-netted minnows and maybe a crawdad or two from the day before. This insert would be placed in a fresh can of creek water, along with the hope that the temporary tenants wouldn't run completely out of oxygen before we could make a quick creek stop north of Zanesville to renew their supply.

In former years, throughout the Twenties, Thirties and Forties, some truly large catfish were pulled from the Muskingum River—in the order of six and seven feet long if you can believe the fish tales that were repeatedly told by the older anglers who still came to Ellis. In the Fifties, however, perhaps the biggest catfish taken from the Muskingum stretched to no more than three or four feet from its whiskers to its tail.

**Dad in his element, afield afishing.**

Of course, that record fails to take into account the one that got away from my own personal rig one foggy morning, when Dad and I were fishing on the sunrise side of the muddy Muskingum at Ellis Dam.

Those who didn't take the narrow gravel road to and through the eye-blink town of Ellis to reach the dam's northwestern end, where the locks were located, could as an alternative drive north from Zanesville on State Route 666, a two-lane paved highway that led to the basket-making town of Dresden on the east side of the river. At the dam there was a small roadside pull-off where you could park your car or truck, cross the highway and carry your two-gallon bucket of bait and water, one or two fishing poles, and one or two tackle boxes, and coax one or two dogs down a steep, spring-watered, dew-slickened bank, following some blind foregoer's idea of a well-blazed trail, through weeds and briars and fallen broken branches some 100 perilous feet to the river's edge. Once at the river, assuming you actually made it that far, the only way you could get to the concrete pier that formed the east end of the dam was by climbing up, down, over, and around rocks the size of big boats or small houses that were kept smooth and slippery by the roiling water and by a fine, fish-scented mist that completely fogged your view of the greater perils ahead.

Those who fished the east side of the Muskingum River at Ellis Dam early in the morning were a few worms short of having a full can.

Even the guy who sometimes pulled his small boat right up to the concrete pier in the middle of the river at dusk and spent the whole night drinking a six-pack of beer, angling, dangling, and dozing out there at the very edge of disaster did not dare to risk the same health danger as those who fished the east side of the Muskingum River at Ellis Dam in the early morning.

It was here one foggy morning that I threw a silver minnow into the muddy Muskingum River, and had it immediately chomped up by the largest fish I ever hope to hook, let alone catch. From the terrific tug on my line, it must have weighed a good two or three hundred pounds, and must have measured ten or twelve feet long. Europeans drive smaller cars. Some entire Asian families don't weigh as much.

This fish was a monster, and if ever I had seen it shoot through the surface of the frothy, foamy Muskingum, I'm sure

> At right is what Dad called his "white" rod, the one that he favored for fishing the Muskingum River at Ellis Dam. The rod was a True-Temper Dynamic with a cork handle. The reel was a Pflueger Akron, No. 1893. Dad gave me the outfit to settle the lawsuit that I filed against him for fishing interference under the 31st Amendment.

that my shouts of pure joy would have frightened all of its friends and neighbors clean out of the water. It almost jerked my fiberglas rod and Shakespeare reel right out of my hands when its massive, vice-like jaws clamped down on my doomed, fear-petrified bait. It ran so fast for the deep and rocky sanctuary at the foot of the dam that my 20-pound test line actually smoked as it sizzled and sang while unspooling at a rate that would have made Moby Dick jealous. It was all I could do to keep my balance on the eel-slippery rocks, while fighting perhaps the biggest fish ever to swim in the muddy Muskingum River.

It ran. I released line. It came back. I reeled in. It led. I followed. In, out, up, down, this way, that way—it was a battle that had the potential to last for hours. There was no way that this fish was going to surrender to me, and no way that I was going to give up and let it get away. This would be a scorched-earth, winner take all, balls to the wall, death to the defeated battle for the catfish championship of the civilized world.

Less than a minute into this epic struggle, Dad happened to notice that I had snagged something interesting, and suggested that, with all of his many decades of fishing experience and expertise, he likely would have a much better chance of landing this gargantuan catfish than I, who could at the time barely spell the word "catfish," let alone catch one.

"Give me your pole," was the way Dad actually put it.

"I can do it! I can do it!" I argued.

"Give me your pole," Dad repeated, using a tone of voice that I much earlier had come to recognize as the difference between Dad's business and my pleasure.

"Oh, fart," I wanted to say (but didn't), as I relinquished my fiberglas rod, my chrome reel, my Dacron line, my gargantuan fish, and probably my last, best hope of making it into the *Guinness Book of World Records*.

I don't think Dad even had a firm grip on the handle of my rod when the line snapped loudly and cleanly.

"He cut the line," Dad reported (unnecessarily), after making a brief dispassionate and unapologetic attempt to analyze the situation. "Looks like he was in the rocks. He must have pulled the line over an edge and cut it. Too bad. That appeared to be a fair-sized fish."

## - LOCKS AND BEAGLES -

With no further comment, Dad handed me back my rod, my reel, and the limp black line that now lay draped and curved across the water, turned, and went back to his own luckless line. I stood there for a while looking at the frothy brown foam, that always reminded me of a root beer float. I thought I could see the faintest outline of a huge catfish, with a satisfied smirk on its face.

"I could have done it," I said, not caring that Dad was too far away to hear me above the roar of the roiling waters. I did a rock walk over to the bait and tackle boxes near him to re-rig my tackle. "I could have done it," I repeated, this time within Dad's earshot.

"No," Dad assured me, "that fish wasn't going to be landed. It was just an accident that you even snagged it in the first place. If I wasn't there to take your rod when I did, that catfish probably would've pulled you and everything else right into the water. You were just lucky that I was here to save you."

Somehow, I didn't feel all that lucky. In fact, I felt pretty disappointed that I had not only lost the biggest fish that I had ever hooked, but so quickly had even lost my long-presumed right to lose it.

I put new tackle on my line, of course, and rebaited. I even cast a couple of dozen times to the very same spot, hoping that the big catfish would be over-confident on the heels of his easy success, and would come back to relive the victorious adventure. But I didn't get a single bite the rest of the morning. Nor did Dad. We just went through the physical motions of serious fishing for a few more hours, while the sun struggled over the eastward carpet of trees, and cast its warming rays down the treacherous hillside to our slick rocky ramparts. Somewhere around 10 o'clock, Dad said he thought it was about time to leave, so we packed up our gear, called for the dog, and climbed back up the perilous trail to the highway.

It was a long, quiet ride home. You could have cut the tension with a rock. After we got home, I got to thinking, and became more and more convinced that Dad must have violated some sort of fishing law when, by his usual intimidation, he forced me to turn over my fish to him. I stewed about it for several months, but eventually decided to be a good Christian and forgive Dad. Besides, it was costing me way too much money. I had to work all summer just to pay the first bill I got from the guy I hired to file the lawsuit. Dad must have thought it would be bad for his grocery store/post office business, and for his fishing and hunting reputation as well, because he soon offered me his favorite white rod to settle the lawsuit and keep it out of the newspapers. But I rejected that first offer flat-out. I told Dad the 31st Amendment to the Constitution prevented any interference with someone's right to pull in his own fish by someone else. Fortunately, Dad didn't have a copy of the Constitution in the post office to check that out. So he got even more worried about losing the case, and upped his settlement offer to include the franchise rights to the Marilyn Monroe bust and boom business that I was already in. (Dad didn't know that I had already set up shop in sixteen states, and was working on a deal with Pontiac to take the business global.) Just to end the arguing, and to get back to fishing again, I told Dad that I would drop the lawsuit and stop publication of the illustrated article that I had written for *The Times Recorder* if he would throw in his two best shotguns. He was kind of reluctant to part with his prized matched Winchesters, but people were starting to buy less meat and fewer stamps, and rumors already were circulating about Dad's fish-market purchase of some of the whoppers that he claimed to have "caught" at Ellis Dam. Even more threatening, a few people also said that they, personally, had never seen *any* squirrels "cut their nuts," and had their doubts about Dad's many stories in which they—allegedly—did it. Dad and I finally came to terms. I agreed to call off the lawyer dog that I couldn't afford to pay anyway. In return, I got all of that hunting and fishing stuff, the worldwide rights to the Marilyn Monroe steering wheel knob business that I was already in, and Dad's written apology (in triplicate). I think they call it plea bargaining. Worked for me.

# CHAPTER SIXTEEN

# Washday Wonders

**M**om usually did the family laundry on Mondays, starting early in the morning, just after the overnight fog cleared. The reason for this early start was directly related to the availability of her clothes dryer. When the sun didn't shine and a breeze didn't blow, Mom's wet laundry didn't get dry. So she started her washing early, to make maximum use of the day's sun rays.

In the 1950s there were very few families in Sonora with automatic washers and dryers. You could count them all without using either of your hands. The washing machines back then were all manually operated (washboards—manufactured by a Columbus company—were still in common use on back porches), and drying was done on a rope or wire clothesline in a back or side yard. Less often you would see a gauzy white curtain stretched out to dry on its own special hardwood frame.

Most of Sonora's mechanized laundry was washed in Maytags, in tub-based, motorized machines that stood sturdily on their own four legs atop grossly undersized wheels. Mom's red-and-white enameled Maytag had a powerful electric motor under a square-lidded tub that housed a reciprocating, four-bladed plastic paddle. In design, the paddle looked like it really belonged behind a ship at sea, powering it along as a propeller. Mounted atop the tub was a pivoting metal arm that contained two rubber rollers that were kept pinched tightly together by a hidden stout spring. Emerging from the bottom of the tub and hooked at the top was a drain tube made of rubber as thick as radiator hose. The hose was capped with a hooked metal fitting that was threaded to give you the option of attaching a garden hose. This drain outlet usually got knocked off right at the beginning of the wash cycle and spewed water all over the linoleum floor of the porch before you could pick it up and reattach it.

Mom's Maytag tub was filled by dumping a half-dozen or so pails of hot water into it, along with a loosely measured amount of Tide, Ivory, Fab, Breeze, Oxydol, or some other brand of powdered laundry detergent, some Clorox or Niagara bleach, and for whitening and brightening a packet of blueing. That never quite made sense to me. To get things whiter, you had to add blueing—but to get things bluer, you didn't add

Mom must have loved our back porch, since she seemed to spend so much time there. At right is her Maytag washer with the dangerous open rubber-coated rollers. Dad sits at our kitchen table and reads the Zanesville *Times Recorder*, for which I eventually worked Saturdays, summers, and finally full-time as a reporter. Just visible behind Dad is the doorway that led to our general store/post office/service station. Just right of the inset wooden shelf for our Ohio Bell telephone (452-5998) is the corner dish cabinet with lower doors that concealed pots and pans. To the right of it is the refrigerator that Dad bought in 1948. Mom is rinsing clothes in one of two hot-water tubs, stirring them with a wooden paddle that Dad made for her.

whiting; of course, being a kid, I was more of an expert at getting things dirty than I was at getting them clean. When you closed the washer's heavy lid, a switch was tripped, and the wash cycle began automatically. By wash cycle was meant that the blade simply sashayed back and forth until you reopened the lid. Unlike today's automated washday wonders, there were no timer dials or cycle sensors on the washers of this era, to tell the homemaker when a load was finished. She simply opened the lid every once in a while to check on the status of the bubbling waters, and she stopped the washer when she sensed that the load was done. Washing clothes back then was a lot like scorching a steak today on an outdoor charcoal or gas grille.

Once a load of laundry was considered washed, Mom would hand-feed all of the items through the rubber-rollered wringer, then drop them into the hot water in the left side of a two-bay galvanized rinse tub. Some of the soap would be worked out by sloshing the clothes around in that bay with a special wooden paddle. Mom's paddle, for which Dad occasionally found other uses, was two feet long, three inches wide and an inch thick. Dad had had made it for Mom (or, perhaps, for himself) out of some leftover hardwood. She would use the paddle as a hook, to lift and transfer the hot, first-rinsed load to the right side bay, where a second-rinse in still more hot water would worry out most of the remaining soap.

After another load was washed, using the original water, with some fresh hot water added to the big tub to regain the initial level, it too would be wrung out and dumped into the left bay of the rinse tub, then would join the first load in soaking in the right rinse bay. Meanwhile, back at the washer, Mom would unhook the long drain tube (onto which she often remembered to screw a garden hose) and lower it below the bottom level of the tub. This caused gravity to start the gray water flowing through the hose, which was normally snaked out our slightly cracked screen door, across the concrete sidewalk, and onto our slanted cindered driveway. Through a roundabout process of draining, channeling, and leaching this water ultimately flowed into either the Atlantic Ocean or the Gulf of Mexico, where it was evaporated by the sun, got sucked up into the sky, and came back to Ohio as a dark cumulus cloud to rain on Mom's clothes parade about every other washday. Although she never knew it, this happened to be one of America's first experiences with the new concept of recycling, and Mom would have been darned proud to be a part of it had she ever realized what she was doing. (Mom seldom realized what she was doing.)

## - OF FIRES AND FOGGY MORNINGS -

When the propeller-pounded water in the washing machine tub had been drained, and when all of the soapy water residue had been rinsed away, Mom would squeeze as much moisture as she could out of each individual piece of the original load, reverse the direction of the motorized rollers, and run the load back through the wringer, dropping the washed, rinsed, and re-wrung clothes back into the empty Maytag tub. From there she would take them to an oval laundry basket, which had been woven out of some weed that looked like it could have come right from *Ben Hur* or *The Ten Commandments,* and carry it to the back yard. At the end of three or four loads of laundry, the gray waste water would be drained with the garden hose from each of the rinse tub bays, and those tubs would be given a final rinse with more pails of hot water.

The most dangerous part of the wash/rinse operation, of course, occurred when each wet item was hand-fed through the three-inch, hard rubber rollers. There was nothing to prevent you from feeding your fingers through the rotating rollers along with the clothes. There were no shields ordered by an Occupational Safety and Health Administration, no safety switches mandated by the rules of any other governmental agency, nothing at all to provide even a minimal amount of protection for fingers that, once sucked into the spinning spring-squeezed rollers, would not be freed until someone else came to provide assistance.

The mechanical parts of Mom's clothes dryer consisted of three braided-cotton, quarter-inch rope lines, each about sixty feet long, which ran from three locust-post supports that resembled small telephone poles

near the house to the metal hooks that were attached to our backyard barn, about seven feet above the ground. Allowing for a natural line sag, and for the weight of the wet wash, this brought the horizontal rope to no nearer than about five feet from the ground—to about the same height as the top of Mom's head.

Bed sheets and blankets, shirts, socks, and all other damp items were clamped to the clothes line by wooden pins. (The earlier wooden clothes pins of a split-leg, round-headed design were succeeded by squarish, two-piece spring-clamped ones, which later were made from plastic. Today's clothes pins are probably machined from aircraft aluminum, carbon fiber, advanced composite, or some other high-tech material.) Once a whole load of laundry had been draped onto the line, Mom propped up the line in the middle with one or two long wooden poles, each having either a notch or a nail at the upper end to hook the rope.

With these poles spiked firmly into the ground, at a supportive angle, the clothes were at last ready to begin blowing in the breeze or be dried simply by the heat of the sun and an evaporative light breeze. The drawback to this drying system, which usually worked fairly well and produced fresh-smelling clothes that were softened by being snapped repeatedly by the breeze, was that the clothes did not always remain firmly

**Mom (center) takes a break from laundry to play Rook with my sister Eileen and her husband Dunkin' Dave. When Mom's toy fox terrier Skippy bit me, I bit him back. True story. You can ask anyone in our family, even my brother Jim. (Don't let him change the topic of conversation to fires and outhouses.)**

pinned to the line. Anything that dropped to the ground most likely would have to be washed again. Another disadvantage could occur with whole lines of laundry being toppled or blown away by the tornadic winds of one of the sudden afternoon thunderstorms for which Ohio was famous. More than once friends and family had to hurry to save a whole washing from being drenched in a rainstorm or to corral clothes that were being blown down the driveway by strong gusts.

## - OF FIRES AND FOGGY MORNINGS -

After an afternoon of blowing in the wind, under the hot summer sun, the week's wash would be taken down, placed in baskets, and returned to the back porch, to await ironing and folding. It was unusual for these final stages to take place on the same day as the laundry was washed. I think that had something to do with the amount of Mom's available time and energy.

Most women in Sonora had an electric iron. Some even had one of the new models with a steaming feature that never seemed to work right and forced you to still use a sprinkling bottle to dampen the clothes as you ironed them. Some women had irons that were heated and reheated on stoves—and some still had the wood-fired stoves on which to heat and reheat them. Mom was lucky enough to have both a steam iron and a helping hand, which was lent by Grandma Jones, her mother, who often came by to assist in Mom's ironing after doing her own. Most of Mom's ironing took place in the kitchen, where she could look through an open curtained door and keep an eye out for customers entering our grocery/post office/residence. She would set up a folding ironing board, grab a plastic bottle of water for extra dampening, and spend many joyous hours ironing and folding clothes. A week later, she would do it all again.

One thing Mom had that I never saw anywhere else in Sonora was a commercial grade of ironer that she seldom used and thereby met perfectly well her own definition of "labor-saving device." This was a completely self-enclosed, white-enameled appliance that, until its doors and panels were unfolded, could not be associated with any particular purpose. Once opened, the ironer had a waist-level platform, above which rotated at slow speed a padded, eight-inch canvas-covered tube, attached at only one end like a large, smooth, half-scorched paint roller. Behind the roller was a quarter-curved chrome press, containing the heating element that was moved towards or away from the padded roller by using a foot pedal. For small flat things such as wash cloths, towels, and handkerchiefs, this heavy-duty ironer seemed to work just fine. For more challenging items, such as long-sleeved shirts, it wasn't even in the running, because of the likelihood of simply ironing in the wrinkles. At most, Mom infrequently used the ironer for a sheet or pillowcase. But I soon discovered that, if you unfolded its hinged support table and turned on its little light, it made a great place to draw.

Like the self-defrosting refrigerator, the self-cleaning-oven range, and the huge horizontal freezer that eventually usurped most of our screened-in back porch like a big porcelain coffin, the arrival one day of an

106

automatic washer, with fill hoses that attached right to the hot and cold water lines and a drain hose that you didn't have to manually operate, and an automatic electric dryer—with a push-button on/off switch and a dial load timer—was greeted by Mom with open arms. I had not seen her so happy since the summer Dad built a bathroom onto the house. It had real indoor plumbing, electric baseboard heat that was adequate most of the time, except any day during the winter, and a square, door-topped chute for dropping dirty clothes straight down into the laundry room in the basement that Mom never used.

The construction of our indoor bathroom, incidentally, had been hastened by a mysterious fire one afternoon that seriously impaired the functionality of our drafty old outdoors toilet, which was particularly uncomfortable on cold winter nights. I was always (unfairly) blamed for the untimely passing of this smelly little outhouse that made you sorry just to sit down. Over the years, I have taken a lot of verbal abuse for my non-participation in this family event. It was not until recently, however, that I drew the indisputable evidence that it was actually my brother Jim who was responsible for the outhouse fire, although he somehow fails to remember it that way, and doesn't seem to accept my drawing as actual evidence of his guilt and my innocence. I told him to draw his own picture, if he doesn't like mine, and we would compare the two, like in court. So he sent me a little piece of paper with some chicken scratches on it that, if printed here, would be really embarrassing to anyone who is not so senile. Therefore, in Jim's best interest, not my own, I have chosen not to present his scratchy drawing to you, the jury, thus making my own depiction of this historical event the only—and hence the best—available evidence to be considered. So, after all of these years, there is no longer any lingering doubt about who actually burned down our family outhouse. Case closed. Listen to the fat lady sing. Anyone can look at my drawing and clearly see that I was still in swaddling diapers at the time of the outhouse fire. I did not even know what a match was, let alone how to use one. I am completely innocent. I have always been completely innocent. I will remain completely innocent until hell burns down. (Jim is working on it.) As for Jim, well, he was certainly old enough at the time of the fire to have known better. It's not my fault that he has only gotten older and more guilty every year. Actually, he should thank me for taking all of the heat, for so many decades, and make some sort of gesture of his profound appreciation, like they did in the old days of Roam and Grease. Maybe a simple sacrifice of a cow or something. Or the burning down of an altar. Yeah, that oughta do it. Jim would be good at that.

# CHAPTER SEVENTEEN

# Skinny Dipping

One of the more-popular but least-acclaimed swimming holes around Sonora was located just east of the Baltimore & Ohio Railroad tracks, off the gravel lane that led to the homes of Ray Culbertson, John Galloway, and Paul Haren. Here, a small pool had been created with a lot of effort using sticks, stones, weeds, mud, and bare hands to make a small dam that was always leaking and in need of repair.

Clothing, when swimming in this small, sun-warmed pool that was concealed from public view by distance, woods, and weeds, was optional.

Nowhere else was the creek that fed this secluded swimming hole any deeper than about two feet, even where it went under the railroad, through a bricked-around, head-high culvert at the east end of our five-acre farm. However, in this place the pool had been deepened to about four feet, with the aid of our leaky dam, at a wide run through the trees. Adding to the pool's popularity, a long grassy bank was available for sunning. Elsewhere along the narrow banks of the shallow creek, long weeds draped into the water, creating perfect hiding places for such other local swimmers as muskrats and water moccasins.

Probably every town in Appalachia had at least one of these local skinny-dipping pools in the 1950s, whether its existence and location was known or not to the town's adults. The pools weren't signed as such, but they were strictly for the kids. The adults usually had their own.

## - OF FIRES AND FOGGY MORNINGS -

The first time you visited the local skinny-dipping hole, you were surprised, if not shocked, by all of the exposed skin. It was not that you had no idea that these body parts existed. Many of us had brothers and sisters, and over the years we had gotten occasional indications of the small but significant distinctions between them and us. And, sooner or later, we had all come across those magazines that we weren't supposed to know about. There were even some classical paintings and sculptures that we were actually allowed to look at (briefly, to be sure) that clearly detailed the greatest physical differences between the two sexes. Even without parental permission, you could study all of the naked people that were stuck to the ceiling of the Sistine Chapel or view David's, um, knees, because that was regarded and appreciated as art, not nudity.

But at this swimming hole, on display for all to see, were some of our best friends and neighbors, running around without a stitch of clothes on, showing a complete lack of propriety, among other things.

And not only were there other boys here, but girls. It was more than an eyeful. It was almost too much too bare.

Into such an indecently exposed display of young humanity you took your first chary steps, thinking that your Methodist minister would have your butt for breakfast if he knew what you were about to do. Under the brief sidelong glances of the others, who had stood first where you stood now, you walked as nonchalantly as possible over to the bank where everyone's clothes were piled, and began to contribute your own. Shoes, socks, shirt, jeans, well, this is it. Do I do this or not? Do I join the ranks of all of these unnaturally bared sinners? Or, yea, do I walk through the Valley of the Shadow of Death and down the path of religious righteousness for my name's sake, and keep on my Fruit-of-the-Looms? Do I really want to show the whole world what I am made of? Or do I want the whole world to have to guess? Does it really matter to anyone else in the world if I drop my drawers? Does anyone else really care?

Nobody is watching, but everyone sees. The cotton tightey whiteys slip slowly to the ground. The die is cast. The painting is hung. It's all over but the shouting.

A cheer goes up, as you walk as inconspicuously as possible under the circumstances to the edge of the water and ease yourself in, feeling it penetrate places that you haven't had this wet since you were a babe in the woods. Up close and personal, you make some inane remarks to your friends. They joke back. You offer more observations. They see your bet and raise you one. You swim. They swim. You're all in this pool of sin together.

Under the hot sun, the evaporating water feels good on your suit-less skin. The marked contrast between the warm air and the cool water is like eating something sweet simultaneously with something sour.

On the grassy bank, a few of your naked friends have stretched out to let the sun shine on their glistening bodies. You build up enough courage to leave the water and join them, and drip over to the first free place on the grass, next to one of your female acquaintances. With only a little self-consciousness, you begin a conversation that takes your relationship with this girl to a whole new level. You see things you haven't seen before. She talks. You talk. Others join in. The sun dries your skin, and the clinging sand slowly slips off.

After another hour or so of sunning and swimming everyone dresses and goes home. The next night you see some of these same friends at a party. They seem to look a lot different to you than they did yesterday. But then, you suddenly realize, so do you

# CHAPTER EIGHTEEN

# The Music Man

When I was twelve or thirteen—there is some room for interpretation on this—Mom decided that I was going to be a musical genius. Although she was eminently unqualified to make such an assumption *(See Chapter Six: "Religious Affiliations")*, her hopeful prognostication was not entirely unjustified.

Even in my youngest years I was always the star soloist in our elementary school musical extravaganzas. Not before, and perhaps not since, was there ever a vocal rendition of *Danny Boy* that compared to mine. And Mrs. Rosalie Parks, our once-a-week visiting music teacher, who never wore less than a million pounds of bling and bangles around her wrists, and even more around her neck, knew she could always call on me to show the rest of the class how any really difficult passage should be performed. Mrs. Parks preferred to teach us highly technical but rousing rounds—*Row, Row, Row Your Boat* was far and away her favorite—to any lesser forms of music. I had also stood solo in a cramped recording booth at Buckeye Lake's amusement park and belted out the entire first verse of *Chattanooga Shoe Shine Boy* when I was so small that I had to shout up into the microphone to be heard.

With such a strong, unbroken string of sterling vocal performances behind me, Mom somehow decided that I should play the trumpet.

One day I was perfectly normal, or as close as I could be when I still lacked any formal musical instruction. The next day I was a music man, learning how to play a brass instrument with which I had no particular affinity and for which I had next to no enthusiasm. I had always wanted to play the drums. That was the main reason that I often visited the home of

## - THE MUSIC MAN -

Bobby Shirer, one of my second cousins who lived at the northern edge of Sonora. Bobby had a terrific toy set of traps. (He always thought I was there because I enjoyed his company.)

And yes, I had, on occasion, snipped off a stiff blade of green grass, put it to my puckered lips, stretched it out tightly, and tried to blow a recognizable tune (*Row, Row, Row Your Boat* had become one of my favorites). I had also, on other occasions, picked up a plastic sweet potato, metal mouth harp, or old harmonica, and imagined myself in the Country Music Hall of Fame, playing my own classical composition, *You Can't Come Home Again Arlene If You Don't Go Away First and Leave Me Here With the Sick Dog and Our Ugly-As-Sin Baby Girl George.* In my tender years, I had even owned an authentic four-valved plastic trumpet that I used mainly to drive all of our neighbors nuts. But never had I imagined that I would one day be playing a real trumpet.

On one memorable summer's day, following an unusually foggy morning, a shiny brass trumpet arrived in the mail. It was housed in its own finely crafted, red velvet-lined case, with chrome catches and hinges. The outfit included a 10-½ C silver Bach mouthpiece, a leaking bottle of valve oil, and a tiny tube of slide grease. There was even a screw-on lyre, although I had no idea at the time where it went or even what in the world it was used for.

With the arrival of my authentic trumpet, I became an instant local celebrity, a musical star in the performance heavens of Sonora, for no other thirteen- or fourteen-year-old in town even had a real guitar, let alone an actual trumpet. (David Oliver, admittedly, did have a

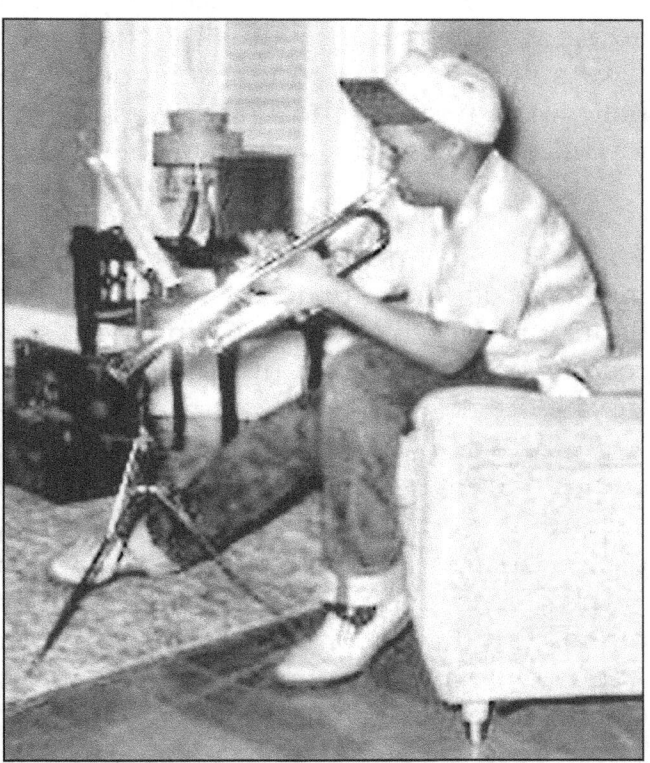

Half of the secret to playing the trumpet, I soon discovered, was finding the right leg position and wearing the right shoes. Here, I demonstrate the proper shoes and position.

113

real accordion. But back then, as now, accordions had no official or even admitted status in the world of music—sort of like bagpipes. To mildly appreciate the sound of an accordion, you either had to be polka-crazed or be named Lawrence Welk. Not for nothing did someone once define a gentleman as a man who knew how to play the accordion but refrained from doing so.) Soon, relatives came from rooms around to hear me play my trumpet; some of them even stayed. I had no sooner begun tooting on this long brass tube when I, and everyone else in the family, the neighborhood, the town, the county, and a good part of the state of Ohio, realized that I was going to need some lessons. At least half of the effort that I was putting into the trumpet seemed to escape as so much hot air. And the rest of my attempt to produce recognizable notes was so shaky that it soon prompted perhaps the most famous line that my first cousin, Bobby Jones, ever uttered in Sonora. Having initially decided to delay his participation in an important game of baseball and wait for me in our living room, while I completed a mandatory half-hour daily practice session, cousin Bobby quickly changed his mind when he heard my first few, strained notes, and exclaimed, "Jesus! I'll wait for you outside." I believe that was the first, and perhaps the only, time that I was mistakenly identified as one of the lead characters in the Bible.

It was somehow decided that I should sign up for lessons with Mr. Wade B. Fair (his actual name). Mr. Fair was a cherubic, white-haired, maestro-looking individual who operated a "music studio" on the second floor of a Fourth Street building over Eckerd's Drug Store in Zanesville. To reach Mr. Fair's low-rent, low-profile, low-everything studio you clattered up the creaky wooden steps that started at a sidewalk-level glass door and led upward to a dimly lit hallway that stretched away so far that you couldn't even see the end of it. On your left, about halfway down this second-story mine shaft, was an opaqued glass, wooden-framed door, under the first official transom that you had ever seen. On the pale-green glass of the door was neatly lettered Mr. Wade B. Fair's unforgettable name. The door opened into a tiny, putrid-green painted squarish cubicle. About two-thirds of the way across the room stood a cheap folding screen that apparently was intended to separate the parents from the performers. The screen created a coffin-sized cubicle that was Mr. Fair's "studio." To be absolutely honest, I don't believe I ever saw a single rat anywhere in Mr. Fair's studio—but I never dared to look down.

Mr. Fair's studio was where greatness was born. It was there that I, and several other luckless students that I saw coming into and going out

114

of the office like wraiths, but never talked to, was gradually to progress from a rank amateur who could just barely play the C scale in Rubank's first book of trumpet instruction, to a rank intermediate who could blow a basic tune almost without mistake, to a rank advanced musician who could passionately perform such trumpet classics as *Have a Tequila* (a Jewish-Mexican classic), *Oh Solo Mio* (an Italian piece that you always had to perform alone), and *Cherry Pink and Apple Blossom White,* the sheet music for which Mom found one day on a back-room sale rack at Glosser's Music Store on Fourth Street and purchased as a birthday gift to me, for seventy-five cents, with tears of joy echoing in her eyes.

Mr. Fair charged his students $1.50 per lesson, each of which lasted from fifteen minutes to one-half hour, depending mainly upon how long he could stand the pain and how many aspirin he had. Behind the Iron Curtain, sweating profusely in the high summer humidity or excessive winter forced-air furnace heat, you and Mr. Fair would sit on wooden folding chairs and stare expectantly at the printed sheets of your weekly assignment (that you just *knew* you should have practiced) until something awful, and perhaps even illegal, somehow escaped from your instrument. If you could encourage most of your notes to sound somewhat similar to the scales and selections that Mr. Fair had reluctantly assigned, so much the better. But Mr. Fair was usually not very particular. It was as though all of your mistakes of the lesson were forgiven as soon as you handed over the buck and a half that your parents had thoughtfully provided for Mr. Fair's getaway fund.

For nearly two years, Mr. Fair taught me everything (apparently) that he knew about playing the trumpet. Then, as I was about to enter high school and leave the foggy 1950s behind, I realized that I would never be one of the greatest trumpet players in the world, regardless of how much money my parents continued to spend on my lessons. So I quietly stopped torturing Mr. Fair, opened a bank savings account with all of the lessons money that I was continuing to receive from my unwitting parents, and eventually bought a couple of Al Hirt records for Mom to listen to. She especially loved Big Al's *Sugar Lips.* I later read in *The Times Recorder* that Mr. Fair packed up his Iron Curtain one day and took off for Texas. I was probably the only person in the whole musical population of Muskingum County who knew exactly why he, like Elvis, had eventually left that creepy building. It took him a little longer than I expected, but Mr. Wade B. Fair finally learned his lesson.

# CHAPTER NINETEEN

# The Golf Pros

The Zanesville Jaycees had an eighteen-hole public golf course about a mile west of Sonora, as the ball flies. To the boys of Sonora in the 1950s, that meant only one thing: money.

We didn't play golf—most of us didn't know an athletic cup from a hole in the ground, and the rest of us couldn't even spell it. Nor did we caddy, mainly because Gary Mizer, the young, crewcut golf pro, or his Nazi troopers, ran us off the course every time we tried. What we did was find lost balls, and rescue an occasional club when some guy who took the game way too seriously threw a wood, an iron, a putter, or his entire bag of clubs and balls into the nearest pond or creek, then didn't want to get his new spiked saddle shoes wet by making like a Labrador retriever.

We were not that picky about getting our shoes (or anything else) wet; consequently, we made a lot of spending money at Mizer's private public golf course, unbeknownst to him.

Our typical golf day began early in the morning. While most golfers had tee times that had them shooting through the foggy morning mist and walking on diamonds of dew, we would leave Sonora by eight or nine, cut through Clarence Porter's farm fields, and be searching the corn field and pastures that paralleled holes thirteen, fourteen and fifteen before ten o'clock. That would give us time to do a thorough walk-through search for lost balls before the heaviest flow of golfers began to show up on the back nine, and would also give us something to sell them.

Our search for balls that had been hooked or sliced into the corn rows or cow-patty peppered pastures was very methodical. We had learned early on that simple random wandering through the itchy rows of chest-high corn and up and down the rocky pasture hills was a complete waste of both time and effort. So the two or three of us who usually went together to the golf course spaced ourselves out evenly, and combed the search area methodically, from one end to the other. Then we would reverse course and quickly work our way back, gradually moving away from the broken down, rusty barbed wire fence that paralleled the back edge of the course and supposedly separated the paying golfer wheat from the Sonora ball-hunting chaff.

We would normally make two or three trips along this path, knowing that the farther away from the fence we walked, the less likely it was that we would find any wildly hit balls. But we also discovered a curious fact about the misdirected balls and their new-found condition. The newest balls, and the most expensive brands, seemed to be the ones that had been whacked farthest out of the fairways. Titleist 1's, the premier balls in golf, nearly always were found forty, fifty, or even sixty feet away from the fence, and they almost always were in near-perfect condition. The balls found closer to the fence, or lost among the weeds, vines, and bushes that clung to it, almost always were the less-respected, less-expensive brands like Spalding, Wilson, and Pinnacle, and almost always had more smiles than a used-car salesman.

By mid-morning, our search for lost balls normally had recovered anywhere from five to fifteen strays, some of them saleable and some of them not. All of those balls we would hastily recondition in one of the two nearby ball washers that the Jaycees had thoughtfully provided for us, and be ready to market them when the mid-morning crowd came by.

We soon learned what haggling was all about. We would show an old duffer a nearly new Titleist 1, that didn't have a scratch on it, and he would offer us a dime or a quarter for it, saying he could buy them all day long at the clubhouse at three for a dollar. That we knew to be an outright lie, to use another common golfing term, because on our occasional trip to the clubhouse to buy overpriced Cokes and overcooked hot dogs from Mizer, who had to work the snack bar when he wasn't working the matron who wanted a golf lesson, we kept a pretty close tab on the current prices of various brands of new balls. So we would come back to the old duffer with an offer to let our excellent example of a dimpled sphere go for, say, a dollar. He would then frown, and begin to walk away, while we would turn to go in the other direction. As though he had given it some real thought, and had decided to split the difference, he would soon stop us in our tracks with a shouted best and final offer of fifty cents, which we would accept with considerable reluctance, having bargained our way to the exact price that we knew the ball would bring anyway.

Lesser brands, or balls in poorer condition, fetched anywhere from a dime to a quarter. But we occasionally tossed in a few better balls with a bunch of real losers, and sold them as a group. The longer we had to carry our balls around the course, so to speak, or the more balls we found, the lower the price per ball became, until at the end of the day a golfer could pick up twenty or thirty "shag" balls and four or five playable ones from us for a couple of bucks. One real-tired-of-toting pal of mine actually paid a confused golfer fifty cents one day to take thirty or so heavy balls off his hands. The guy at first wanted a whole dollar to do it, but after a bit of haggling cut his price in half when my pal shrewdly said he would throw in a brand-new sand wedge that he had just found to seal the deal. (The last I heard, this kid had grown up to be a wealthy politician, and was making all sorts of pork-barreled laws in Congress, instead of making license plates in the state penitentiary, where I fully expected him to end up, and was very disappointed to learn that he hadn't.)

As soon as the back fields were stripped clean of lost balls, we would wander out onto the course itself, staying mainly in the wooded areas and the "rough," away from Mizer's course maintenance Gestapo agents, to complete our findings. This was not the best way, perhaps, but it was one way to learn how to play golf, while getting paid to do it. When we weren't hunting their balls, we were watching the golfers. (Somehow, that just doesn't read right.)

Once we got onto the course itself (a highly illegal practice, for which we could be—and often were—banned for life), we had to learn to think like a golfer. We had to assume that, being amateurs, most of our shots would go somewhere other than where we aimed them. The next question was where. Would we most likely screw up this shot and hook it into the left rough? Or would we blow it by slicing the ball over there into those trees? Would we take our eyes off the ball, top it, and dribble it just barely down the fairway? Or would we accidentally hit it so far that we couldn't even see it when it waved good-bye to the fairway and plopped into the pond? If we wanted to find these lost balls, we had to have a pretty fair advance idea of where they might be. And it was obvious that our guesses were at least as good as those of the guys who had lost the balls to begin with, who ultimately had abandoned their search for them. Our proudest moments came not from making a killing on any of the recycled balls but from methodically predicting where a ball was most likely to be found and then finding it exactly where we had predicted it would be.

Since there were eighteen holes on the Jaycees Golf Course, there were at least twice as many places—in the rough to the left and in the rough to the right—to search for stray golf balls. We knew the best weeds, the best creek banks, the best woods, and the best banked or marshy places at the edges of ponds and creeks to look for them. In an eight-hour day, while the average duffer was losing four, five, or six playable balls, we could pretty much cover all of the places on the golf course where he had most likely lost them. One of our favorite pastimes was to watch a guy blow a shot into some weeds or a woods, wait for him to give up trying to find it and play on, then find the ball and clean it up. A hole or two later, we would sell it back to him. In so doing, we provided a necessary service to the world of amateur golf, and you would have thought that Gary Mizer could have shown us a little more appreciation because of that. But n-o-o-o; he always regarded us an unnecessary evil.

I don't know exactly how we discovered the swamp in the woods at the fifth hole tee, but it produced the greatest number of golf balls that we ever found in one place. This was one of the most interesting and apparently most difficult tee-shots on the entire course. As you approached hole four along the ruins of another rusty barbed wire fence to your left, you had to hit the ball upslope and land it on a green that had a hillside that fell off forever on your right. Just beyond the green was a heavy woods. If your approach shot on this Par 5 was too far to the left, it went over the rusty fence and into an area that was thick with briars that was viewed as an impenetrable jungle by most golfers. Too far to the right, and your ball was likely to start rolling down the slope, and not stop until it reached a shallow creek that we had named (somewhat cleverly) China. Use too much club, and your ball would be joining the squirrels in the back woods for breakfast.

Those who successfully negotiated the fourth hole were faced with a whole new ball game at the uphill, nearby fifth tee. It was the start of a tough Par 4 that had you hit down the hill, over China Creek, and back up the next bank, aiming for a green that, most of the way, you couldn't even see. Straight ahead was China Creek. Off to the right was plenty of fairway—but all oriented in the wrong direction. Just to your left was the diabolically situated woods, wherein we found our lucrative swamp.

I don't know why, but it seemed to be incredibly difficult for dozens upon dozens of golfers to simply hit the ball straight down this fairway hill with a Number One driver and completely avoid the woods. The trees on the left just seemed to suck their balls in. We must have found hundreds of balls in this one woods, and I would not be surprised to learn that there are hundreds more in there this very day. (After all, most of us haven't been back in there for, like, fifty years.)

"Found" is perhaps the wrong action verb to use to describe the way we discovered so many of the fifth tee flub shots. While many of them were indeed just lying atop the fallen leaves in the down-sloped tree line (incredibly, since all you had to do was see them and pick them up), most of the balls were buried deep in the decomposing black muck of the small swamp. It was only about ten feet wide and fifteen feet long, but this little swamp was like a magnet for golf balls. Down on our old-denimed knees, with our sleeves rolled up above our elbows, we had to sink our hands a foot or more into the smelly, squishy, rotting muck and actually feel our way for golf balls. Many of them had been in there so long that they were permanently stained the blue-black color of the decomposing swamp soil. Most of them also retained a scent of *cologne d' septic* even after a vigorous scrubbing in the nearby ball-washer. But there were simply so many balls that had been socked into this swamp that several of them were almost new. Those could be sold at the normal price—particularly if we waited until we were at some other, less-nasally offensive place on the course to sell them.

The majority of the fifth hole swamp balls we sold for shag at maybe two dozen balls for a dollar. For the duffers who hit them—who may have been the original owners—those recycled balls undoubtedly helped to develop swings and skills in practice sessions that probably cut into our ultimate earnings. But we never gave that a thought. In the wide world of golf, you had to keep your mind on the game as you played it, not on the eventual outcome, and our immediate goal was to make the most money that we could, day in and day out, at Gary Mizer's privately protected public golf course. I don't recall ever going home with empty pockets. And as a group, we golf pros from Sonora probably made far more money than Mizer ever did. At least we were more professional.

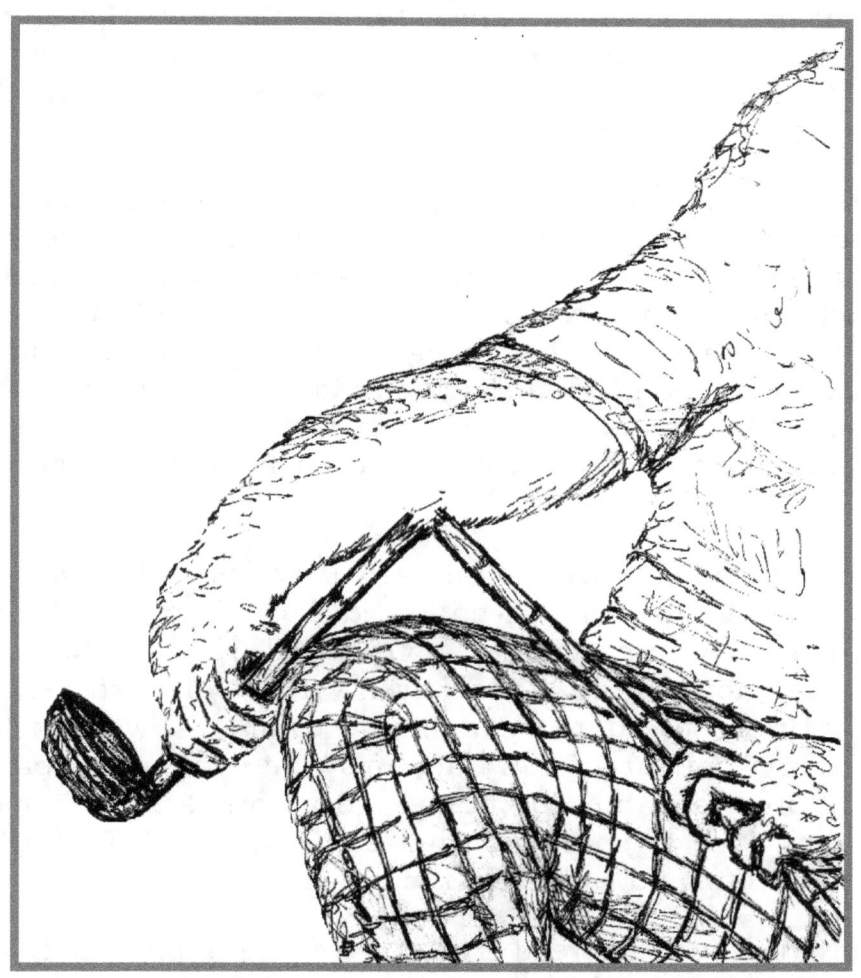

Apparently, in order to join one golf club
you have to break another.

# CHAPTER TWENTY

## The Dough Boy

None of my friends really knew Tommy Cannon. However, none of my friends ever lived in a grocery store to which Tommy Cannon delivered bread a couple of times a week. Tommy was the son of the man in Dresden who owned Cannon's Bakery.

Tommy was cross-eyed. He could watch both players simultaneously in a tennis match without ever taking his eyes off the ball. You could never tell whether he was looking at you or something else unless he addressed you directly. When you talked with him, you had to choose to look at his left eye, his right eye, or somewhere in between. When Tommy tilted his head far back and looked at you through the pair of eyeglasses that always rested on the very end of his nose, it was hopeless. You had to wonder why they even let Tommy walk, let alone drive.

"Popeye" must have been in his early twenties in the 1950s, and was remarkably thin for a fellow who could have had all of the sugar-sweetened flour he wanted, no questions asked. He was always hustling, always in a rush to get his job done, even without any extra energy boost from sugar. He appeared to be a happy camper, always helpful, and Whissel's Grocery bought a lot of Cannon's white and wheat bread, eight-packed hamburger and hot dog buns, and assorted pastries like cream-filled cupcakes (my personal favorite) as a result of Tommy's hustle, pleasant personality, and salesmanship.

Tommy had a great bread truck. It was the typical boxy affair that you still see on streets and highways today with big square windows and sliding side doors, lots of wire racks and shelves, and a sticker in the window that said he wasn't allowed to pick up passengers. When he pulled up to the store to retrieve all of the two-day-old loaves and pastries, and to restock them with a fresh supply, Tommy's truck was soon surrounded by Sonora's younger kids, not only to catch a whiff of the aromatic bread, but because Tommy often gave them "samples" of the expired products.

Only I knew exactly how great Tommy's delivery truck was, because several times each summer he would let me ride with him as he completed his route clear back to Dresden, some fifteen miles away. There was no real place for a passenger to sit (since, officially, he was not allowed to pick them up), but I was always able to squeeze in with the sweet-smelling breakfast rolls, or find an empty spot on the cab cowling that covered the engine.

Grandma Jones restrains our across-the-street neighbor, Alma (Mrs. Jack) Greiner, from taking home any more pies and pastries. At right rear is the Sonora post office. For rush, after-hours mail, there was a wood lock box (left center, under the fluorescent Meadow Gold dairy sign). We would check the rush-mail box at least once a week.

Leaving Sonora, we would head over to Adamsville Road to a small service station there that sold basic food staples, including bread. A few miles closer to Zanesville there was a similar operation, at the Pleasant Grove Road intersection, and a mile or so more would bring us to still another service station, the nearest thing to a local grocery, at the East Pike.

## - OF FIRES AND FOGGY MORNINGS -

Backtracking eastward a bit, Tommy would then re-supply Mickey's Restaurant, turn around and head back towards Zanesville, and swing in to the Greenlawn Drive-In, where they sold great novelty games that Tommy would occasionally buy me, such as one that involved stacking a pyramid of wooden rings on a pole; this game makes no more sense to me now than it did back then. Tommy's delivery route then called for a few stops in Zanesville before he took Route 666 northward to his home outside Dresden. There I would spend the next day and night stuffing myself on fresh bread and cupcakes with pink sugar icing and a fluffy sugar filling and various other free pastries, until we made a return trip to Sonora. (There was a pony in here somewhere.)

Tommy made his bread truck runs for years, summer and winter, rain or shine. He was as dependable as a postman. Nothing could stop him from making his appointed pastry rounds. Eventually, his father died, and Tommy inherited the company. It's probably unrealistic, after all of these years, but I like to think of Tommy still baking bread up there in Dresden. I can easily imagine him sitting in his front office in an executive swivel chair, with his feet up on the desk, looking out over his rising bread empire, east and west or north and south at the same time, producing whole piles of pastry, making tons of dough.

# CHAPTER TWENTY-ONE

# Sonora School

Whissel's Grocery may have been the core of our community in the 1950s, but most of the town's non-fire-watching activities took place in the building that was its elementary school. By day this three-room metal building was the learning center for the one-hundred or so local children who were divided into eight grades under three teachers, one of whom, due to both size and budgetary considerations, also had to serve as the principal. By night the building was a place for public meetings, round and square dances, sock hops, bingo parties, and films.

I don't remember much about the films. I do remember that they were usually in black-and-white, and were shown on a 16-millimeter projector. The film showings were always well attended by both young and old Sonora residents, who had few other local ways to identify with Hollywood. About once a week some nerdish guy would come in and set up his screen and film projector in the building's "middle room" and show mainly documentaries to an audience that was nothing but appreciative. Where this guy came up with his films, and how much he charged for admission, I have no idea. I do remember, however, that he was pretty good at splicing, probably because he got an awful lot of practice. Two or three times during the typical film showing he would have to stop the projector, flip on the fluorescent overhead lights and spend four or five minutes taping the broken film back together, all the while being taunted by the younger viewers in his audience for a breakdown that probably was not his fault.

Even more popular were the Saturday night round and square dances that brought out most of Sonora's adults and many of its younger habitants. For these dances they opened the folding partition wall between the middle room and another where the sixth, seventh, and eighth grade inmates were confined. The band itself was positioned on a cream-colored

creaking board stage, which was just a broad boxed platform that rose about a foot off the asphalt-tiled floor. Behind the band was a non-folding metal wall bearing a three-sectioned slate blackboard that divided the middle room from the third classroom area, where the first and second graders resided. During all dances this northernmost room served as a cafeteria, a seating area, and a kitchen. This room came fully outfitted with a sink, an electric range, a refrigerator, several folding tables, and plenty of really small one-armed writing desks that you couldn't get into without being a dwarf and couldn't get out of without using grease or a pry bar.

People patronizing the regularly scheduled dances either walked out from Sonora, which took about two minutes, or drove cars and trucks that were parked all along Sonora Road in front of the school and on the school property itself, mainly on the north side of the building or behind it on the sloped field where we played ball. There was no charge for on-site parking, and the fifty-cent admission fee for the dances also got you a ticket for a door prize drawing. The door prize was usually a large, delicious cake baked by one of the town's many accomplished cooks. If you were a pupil, you only had to pay half-price to get in to a dance, but if you won the door prize, you still got the whole cake, so it was a pretty good deal.

The entire Upper Room population of Sonora School, comprising the sixth, seventh, and eighth grades. Front row, from left (bear with me here), Tommy Russell, Bobby Jones, David Huffman, Gary Williams, Timmy Nolan, Richard Phillips. Second row, Pamela Francis, unknown, Barbara Huffman, Diane Spragg, Caroline Wisecarver, Linda Culbertson. Third row, Beverly Nolan, Regina Layton, Kay Birkhimer, Evelyn Whissel, Charlotte Harding, Marsha Whissel, Dixie White. Back row, Richard Harding, Billy Blackstone, Bobby Shirer, Raymond Gaumer, Harold West, Howard Whissel, David Oliver, Jimmy Wheeler, the author, Principal Alma McCance, David Francis, and Bobby Huffman. At least seven or eight of these kids are my relatives (maybe more). Notice, at far right, that the boys had to stand on a plank platform to be seen. Bobby Shirer and Ray Gaumer almost didn't make it.

Each dance lasted from around eight o'clock until midnight or later, and you could hear the singing and the strumming and the occasional square-dance calling both inside and out of the poorly insulated building.

## - OF FIRES AND FOGGY MORNINGS -

Most summer nights were so warm that all five of the building's doors and all of its elbow-jointed, swing-out jalousie windows had to be opened for ventilation. Even then it was necessary to keep the big brown wooden blades of the overhead fans in each of the three rooms spinning at full speed in order to keep room temperatures within reason. But come heat, hail, or high water, most of those attending were determined to have a good time. As one might suspect, there was some alcohol available at these dances, and an occasional fist fight as a result, but mainly they featured just real bad country music and a lot of dizzying dancing. My personal favorite event was the cake walk. I used to spend days on end before an upcoming dance with a cake walk practicing for it, and gradually came to be recognized as one of the best cake walkers in Sonora.

Sock hops, of course, didn't really come into their own until the late 1950s. That was when the easier-transported 45 r.p.m. records and their cheaply constructed players suddenly were everywhere, when the weirdest guys in town declared themselves to be "deejays," and all of the girls began running around with black-and-white or brown-and-white saddle shoes on their bobby-socked feet. These sock hops weren't for the same crowd as the square dances, which also featured a lot of country and western, but most adults of that era couldn't even find the parts on their own body that singers like Elvis Presley were shaking, rattling, and rolling. Some of the young ladies and gentlemen who attended the evening sock hops actually spent as much time outside the building as in it, and some of the things that they did outside would have been banned inside or anywhere else by their easily duped adult chaperons. (They certainly weren't listening to any records.)

There was no law passed to prevent them, but I think the films, dances, and public meetings at Sonora School had almost disappeared by the end of the Fifties. Our eighth-grade class may have been the last to graduate, when someone made the decision to close down the old Sonora School and bus all of

Perhaps against his better judgment, Muskingum County School Superintendent Asa O. Tom presents my eighth-grade diploma, allowing me to matrickle on to New Concord High School. The glow at left seems to be coming from my proud Mom.

128

the local kids to Perry Elementary, about four miles away, presumably to get them a better education, but probably to cut costs.

It wasn't quite necessary to open up the bi-fold partition to make room for the parents and participants who attended our eighth-grade baccalaureate/commencement ceremony. There were only eleven members in our graduating class. We got a graduation lecture from Donald Stockum, the principal of New Concord High School. Kay Birkhimer recalled our brief class history, Bobby Shirer read our class prophecy, and Regina Layton revealed the class will. Then we all sang the class song that I, as Sonora School's sole songwriter and leading musician *(See Chapter 18: "The Music Man"),* had the distinct honor and privilege of composing. I lifted the martial music from the West Point Academy song that they played on the television series, but I actually made up the lyrics. Five minutes after singing my song, not a single person could recall even one note or one word of it. Fame, they say, is fleeting.

Incidentally, while we had frequent fire drills, and an occasional real smoke alarm, the mainly metal Sonora School building never did catch fire. Despite this serious shortcoming, and often fatal fault, most of the dedicated fire watchers in Sonora still held the building in high regard.

Almost the entire eighth-grade graduating class of Sonora School. (Paul Jones must have had the day off.) Front row, from left, Caroline Wisecarver, Marsha Whissel, Regina Layton, Charlotte Harding, Kay Birkhimer, Evelyn Whissel. Back row, David Francis, the author, Bobby Shirer, and Bobby Jones. Our teacher and school principal Mrs. Alma McCance, is appropriately represented by the right rear tail fin of her Green Machine, a 1957 Plymouth Fury. The boys are all on boxes.

# CHAPTER TWENTY-TWO

# The Entrepreneurs

Sonora offered endless economic opportunities to kids who were ambitious in the 1950s. There was always something that you could do or sell to make money. Many of us searched for stray golf balls at the nearby Jaycees Golf Course, and peddled them back to probably the same golfers who had lost them in the first place. This was one of the easier ways to make money, and it didn't take much muscle or selling ability.

Some of us worked harder, however, on a few of the surrounding farms. From mid-summer through late fall, a farmer with a lot of planted acreage would occasionally find himself shorthanded, particularly when his crop of hay or straw was ready for first or second cutting, and occasionally third. Since there were only so many farm boys available in the vicinity to help with these time-critical chores, the word would go out that this farmer or that was in dire need of a town boy or two to fill in. Those who were quick to jump on the farm wagon, when compelled to do so by a lack of cash or perhaps ignorance due to age, often came to regret it. That farming stuff was hard work.

Back then, as now, farmers had to make hay while the sun shined. Once cut, their fields of clover, timothy, or alfalfa had to be raked into wind rows and allowed to air-dry for a day or so. Then the hay had to be baled and taken to the barn for stacking. All of that had to be done before even a light rain shower could wipe out the entire cutting. Every field of hay was in jeopardy once it had been cut, and it was mainly a matter of blind luck as to whether the end result of weeks of growing time would be instantly ruined by a rainstorm or eventually end up in the stomachs of the farmer's ruminants. In Ohio's high summer humidity, just a few minutes worth of hard rain on hay that lay only partially dried, even in wind rows, could cause mildew destruction in only a matter of hours. Such mildewed hay, if accidentally fed to farm animals, would soon make

MAKING
HAY
JW 2006

them sick, or even kill them (particularly horses). If stacked tightly in a hot, airless barn, moldy hay also could overheat and catch fire, through spontaneous combustion, causing one of the greatest disasters that could befall a farmer. More than one area barn met its maker in that way.

Faced with such brief weather windows to get a mature crop of hay or straw cut, dried, raked, baled, picked up, transported, and stacked in the barn, Sonora's shorthanded area farmers often were eager to pay big bucks to any town kids who were willing to help them save their precious crops. The usual farm wage of a dollar an hour could shoot clear up to a buck twenty-five.

Most rural kids in the 1950s were much stouter than their city and town counterparts. Urban kids had to lift things like baseball bats and basketballs. Rural kids had to lift things like 125-pound bags of ground feed and 85-pound bales of hay. And do it all day long. A typical cutting of hay would add up to hundreds of bales, each of which had to be picked up by its two twine handles from the ground and tossed up at least four to as high as ten feet onto a flat-bed wagon, where fifty or seventy-five bales were stacked, and maybe even restacked, before they were tractor-pulled to the barn. One bad bump in the field on an unseen rock or ground dip or an unbalanced stack could mean picking up a whole wagon load of bales and stacking them all over again. But even if a load of hay or straw made it out of the cutting field and back to the barn, all of the bales would have to be pitched off the wagon and onto a bale elevator or directly into a mow to be stacked again. A farmer's day was stacked against him.

A day of putting up hay or straw would normally start at about nine in the morning, after the sun had burned off most of the morning's misty fog and damp carpet of dew. The workday would last until five or six o'clock, with an hour or so break for a big sit-down meal around noon that was prepared by the thin farmer's big-bodied wife and his flirtatious daughters. Large thermoses of ice-cold water or lemonade would usually be brought to the fields at some point in the afternoon by those daughters,

A popular pastime for those who were not working was to bounce a baseball off the nearest set of concrete steps, in this case at the home of Dick Phillips. His neighbor was Cora Gibbons, whose house (later owned by my sister Eileen and her husband, Dunkin' Dave) is at left. At near right is one of our favorite ball fields. At right center is the five-acre farm where Dad built barns and eventually a new house.

and would quickly be consumed under a hot sun. By the end of the day, six or seven hundred bales of hay might be moved from the field to the barn.

Putting up hay was bad. Putting up straw was worse. With either crop there was always a lot of dust floating in the air to irritate your eyes and clog your lungs. You became adept at holding your breath when the worst wind gusts blew the dust in your direction and in sneezing and coughing out any small particles that lodged in your lungs and nasal passages. But no matter what you did to avoid it, you would always go home from a day of putting up straw with your nose, throat, and lungs full of the fine black dust that was inevitably created when the motorized balers chopped and chunked the dry, raked, cut straw into bales, and the wind whirled the chaff your way. Up in a straw mow, the heat and dust was stifling, as bales were bounced from one place

It really is a small world. In the 1950s, I used to sell Cloverine salve. In 1984, my wife and I moved to Jackson, Wyoming, with our three kids. In the late 1990s, I discovered that Cloverine salve was being manufactured for MedTech, Inc. of Jackson, Wyoming. However, I don't sell much of it any more.

to another, causing even more dust to be circulated than in the open air. A bandana didn't really help much to filter out the dust, because it just added to the heat, and it was hard enough to breathe in a mow without a bandana; exhaling your humid carbon dioxide breath onto its mouth-side surface just caused the fine black powder to clog the bandana's cotton threads, adding asphyxiation to your potential health problems.

Those Sonora kids who had the most brains didn't work in the hay or straw fields. Instead they went door-to-door and sold things like Cloverine salve, magazine subscriptions, New Testaments and newspapers. My cousin Bobby Shirer was envied by everyone for the big bucks that he pulled down from his daily *Times Recorder* and Sunday *Times Signal* paper routes. I myself sold *Grit*, a less-newsy but far more interesting little tabloid that earned me a nickel every time I sold one for fifteen cents. Bobby had an income advantage over me, since his newspapers were produced more often and were local, and thus had an inherent attraction to those who looked for such news. The *Grit* was a national weekly that most people could easily do without, so I actually had to learn to sell it, like the guys in television commercials.

One of the most interesting ways to earn money as a Sonora kid in the 1950s was to carry a punch card. Those were postcard-size pieces of cardboard. On the front of the card there were usually ninety-nine small, perforated circles and one big one about the size of a dime. The small ones were numbered, and were punched out by whoever picked and paid for them and wrote their name on the corresponding numbered line on the rear of the card; the large one concealed the winning number. The front of the color card also showed just the cutest little doll, or an 80-band radio that contained a flashlight, compass, emergency whistle, handy-dandy writing instrument, and five or six other practical devices that you just couldn't live without, or some other prize that you, as a super-salesman, could assure all of your friends and neighbors that they would probably win if they would just part with a mere quarter. This ever-popular little lottery was most likely illegal in not only Ohio but every state in the Union in the 1950s (but I viewed that possibility as just another unenforceable provision of the law, much like the one that allowed thirteen-year-olds to ride their Whizzers on Ohio's highways). Many punch-card players, to increase their odds of success, would pick and pay for two or three numbers. After all of the numbers had been punched, the big front circle would be ceremoniously uncovered and the winning number would be revealed. For your efforts in collecting about three times as much money as the declared value of the prize, and about ten times as much as it was actually worth, you received the same prize that you would present to the lucky winner. You then usually turned around and immediately sold your unwanted baby doll sales reward at a reasonable discount and an exorbitant profit to one of the card-punchers who had really, really, really wanted to win that doll but didn't.

Cloverine salve was a much smoother sell, because virtually everybody needed and used it—for something, I guess; New Testaments somehow sold when virtually *nobody* needed a new one. Every house in Sonora must have had at least one or two copies of the King James Bible gathering dust in a remote corner—Bibles which obviously contained both an Old Testament and a New. But I never had much difficulty in selling the separately published New Testaments. Apparently there were an awful lot of doubting Thomases in Sonora, who had a continuing and desperate need to know if anything had changed since the last time they picked up and read a Bible.

Magazine subscriptions were always the most fun to sell because you could offer both men and women literally dozens of reading choices, and sign them up for various numbers of issues, ranging from a few weeks to a full year. They would receive extra added issues absolutely free at no charge for buying even more. It was almost impossible for a reluctant subscriber to deny having a passing interest in at least one or two of the subjects that were covered colorfully and enticingly in your broad selection of magazines. So you almost always walked away with cash in hand for at least a trial subscription. If they later decided to cancel the magazine it really didn't matter, because you would be back again in a couple of weeks with a whole new selection—and an even better deal. If they just couldn't afford to buy any more magazine subscriptions, you could try to sell them a tin or two of Cloverine salve. Already way overstocked with Cloverine salve? Well then, ma'am, have you seen the latest punch card? Already have more cutie-pie dolls than you know what to do with? Well, maybe I could interest you in a New Testament today, with all of the latest changes?

# CHAPTER TWENTY-THREE

# Feed and Grain

Sonora's biggest building, in height, width, depth, and profit dollars produced, was the three-story Keystone feed and grain mill at the town's southeast corner. Half of the west-facing front of this building had an elevated planked dock with a ramp at the north end. Here such farm necessities as mixed feed, feed additives, and blocks of salt could be offloaded from commercial trucks and loaded on to the trucks of area farmers for a middleman's profit. Most of the dusty bags of ground feed that farmers packed into their pick-ups and larger trucks had minutes before been whole ears of corn that they had trucked in.

One of the main reasons for the existence of a feed mill is, logically enough, to provide a grinding facility—a mill—for farmers. It is where they bring such crops as ripe ear corn to be mashed up and mixed with certain other nutrients and turned into heavy bags of feed for their livestock. Most of the raw field corn at the Keystone mill was dumped into a steel-doored grated pit at the rear of the building where you drove up a dirt ramp and across a concrete platform that covered an area about half the size of the building itself. The level of this platform was flush with the floor of the railroad boxcars that were shoved alongside it one or two at a time on a special siding to the east. In earlier decades, this convenient railroad access contributed significantly to the mill's success, much more than it did in the Fifties, when commercial trucking was growing in popularity, or in the Sixties, when the old mill's truck luck ran out.

Pulling their trucks over the grated platform pit, farmers would dump complete loads of corn into its mechanical maw, where whole ears would be crushed by the rotation of powerful steel teeth. The mangled corn solid mash then would be augured through a complex network of metal tubes, and eventually would be blown into one of several large circular bins that funneled downward until, at waist level, the feed finally could be removed through square chutes with sliding metal doors. Onto

This drawing contains a fair amount of Sonora history. In the middle foreground, Dad has parked his 1954 Chevy and has hung a canvas outgoing mail bag from an arm near the tracks where the bag will be pulled in to the nearly stopped train of both freight and passenger cars. At the left is the home of Billy Blackstone. At top left is the general store operated by Eldon and Elsie Spicer. On the rear concrete platform of the feed mill, a few kids roller skate while a farmer dumps corn into a hopper for grinding. At right, the popular smoking weed patch is not burning.

the horizontal lips of these chutes you hooked an empty cloth or woven plastic bag that was capable of holding more than one hundred pounds of feed, pulled the sliding door towards you, then choked on the mist of powdery corn dust that saturated the air while you filled the bag.

Each of these bags was tied with a special knot, using a standard length of a soft cord. This bag-tying process took anyone who knew the secret about two seconds flat. My best time was just under four minutes. The knot that was always used to tie the bags of feed was known, appropriately enough, as a "miller's knot." It was actually more of a wrap and a twist than a knot, having been devised for both easy tying and easy release. To tie a "miller's knot," you were supposed to grasp the foot-long string at a particular place, and hold it about three inches down from the top of the feed bag, while you formed an open loop. You then bunched up the top of the over-filled bag until you could grasp it entirely with the hand holding the string. Then, using your free hand, which was normally your right, unless you were left-handed (which I was), you wrapped the string twice around the bunched bag, over itself, under itself, through itself, in one ear and out the other, up the creek without a paddle, hooking and looping, and holding and stretching, and twisting and tightening, and pulling this into that, and hooking this end over that one, until you accidentally upset the bag, spilled half of the feed all over the floor, got yelled at by your dad, and had to sweep it all up and start all over again.

Once tied, by a tier who actually knew what he was doing, the bags of ground corn were then loaded two or three bags at a time onto hand trucks, or placed several bags at a time onto little wagon-like carts, with long steering

The three-chute feed bin that Dad built in our main barn. He then built a wood and metal rolling screw elevator, which would lift unbagged ground corn to the top of the feed bin. When you pulled open any of the three metal slides, more often than not a dead mouse or two would drop into the plastic buckets at no extra charge.

arms, and rolled out to the front dock, where you stacked them in your truck and took them home. At home, the heavy and unwieldy bags would be wrestled one at a time into the barn and stacked again—sort of like bales of hay or straw. Eventually, the bags would be opened and their contents would be dumped into troughs to be eaten by your livestock.

At our farm, Dad had made a motorized screw elevator to augur unbagged feed up about twelve feet above the concrete floor in the main "feed room," where it was spewed into a big tongue-and-groove yellow pine board bin, similar to the metal one that it had come out of. Dad's bin had three tapered board bays that each had its own sliding metal door at the bottom. When you slid open one of these doors, gravity poured the ground corn through the opening and rapidly filled the five-gallon plastic paint bucket that you held directly under the bin. When you closed the slide,

chunks of hardened feed or a dead mouse that had died with a full stomach and a smile on its face usually clogged the opening and stopped you from shutting down the outflow completely, so that several hundred pounds of feed frequently ended up on the floor (at least for me). At the mill, any feed spillage problem was taken care of by having a bar-grated opening in the floor directly below the chute, where any feed and dead mice could fall or be swept in and recycled back to the bin. At our barn, we shoveled up the spilled feed, sifted out any mortified mice, dumped the overflow feed back into the motorized elevator, and sent it back up the tube to the top of the bin. It was from long experience with this recycling operation that I realized just how much of their time farmers have to spend doing the same thing over and over. No wonder they have to begin their day at 3 a.m. and work until the following midnight. ("Hurry up and milk them steers, Mildred. We still got all of them goatherds to castrate.")

From the standpoint of most kids in Sonora, the best thing about the Keystone feed mill was its fairly smooth concrete interior floors that were by far the best places in town for roller skating. Much rougher were the exterior ramps and platforms. Several of us had the popular, one-size-fits-all roller skates, with metal wheels and noisy bearings, that you leather-strapped over your shoes and fell out of every five feet or so, causing major pain to body parts that you didn't even know you had.

The big concrete platform at the rear of the mill had a few sloped sections that added interest to your otherwise monotonous skating trips around and around it. The scrub grass and weeds that grew from the dirt in the expansion cracks of the concrete also helped to keep you awake. At the north end of the mill, two large garage bays not only housed an old dump truck that belonged to the mill but also, when the truck was gone, made a great indoor skating rink, where you could glide from one room to another and back again in relative safety, as long as you remembered to watch out for the ceiling support poles that were hard to see in the dim light and could have been padded a lot better.

North of the feed mill, clear over to Center Street, was almost a whole block of dead and dying weeds, "snagbark hickory" briar bushes, and smelly sassafras saplings. Most residents probably viewed this as one of the worst areas of Sonora; most of us kids saw it as one of the best. We must have had a couple of dozen well-worn paths weaving through the scrub, which was up to seven or eight feet high. These tall weeds allowed us to play all sorts of games involving hiding, seeking, smoking, wheezing, and coughing. The tall weeds routinely hosted their smaller, better-known relatives with such names as Pall Mall, Chesterfield, Old Gold, Marlboro, Lucky Strike, and other fine tobaccos, always illicitly obtained. The tall weeds also tended to catch fire frequently, with maybe half of the block going up in smoke and flames before a fire could be brought under control. Apparently nobody ever made any connection between the routine weed patch fires and the common smoking of cigarettes by Sonora's pre-teen puffers.

Like the customer traffic at Sonora's two grocery stores, patronage of the Keystone mill gradually faded with the urbanization of the surrounding areas and the loss of more and more farm acreage to creeping suburban civilization. For whatever reason, late one night, when most Sonorans were at home or in bed, the old feed mill suddenly burst into flames, and soon set a brand-new and probably unbeatable Sonora fire attendance record. Whole families quickly showed up—some still in their bedclothes—to admire the solid sheets of flame that started at ground level and flashed forty feet or more up into the night sky. The entire building was burning at once. You could read a newspaper by the mill fire's light half the town away. Arriving volunteer fire crews took one look at it and decided not to even waste their water trying to put it out.

The feed mill blaze burned so long into the night that some entrepreneurs were able to set up small booths on

Flames leap from a former grain mill at Sonora during a fire which destroyed the landmark early Sunday. Flames were visible for miles during the height of the fire which was fought by firemen from three volunteer departments. (Photo by Fred Whissel)

## Sonora Fire Destroys Former Grain Mill

By FRED WHISSEL

Sonora's oldest landmark, a building which formerly housed a grain mill, was destroyed by fire early Sunday.

Firemen from Perry and Washington townships and Adamsville were unable to save the frame, three-story structure. Flames had engulfed the building before the first firemen arrived at the scene about 1:30 a.m.

Intense heat kept firemen from getting nearer than 50 feet from the structure for a time. Flames leaped high into the air and were visible several miles. Falling embers threatened to ignite a dry, bushy area

just north of the mill. Firemen sprayed water on a grocery and dwelling, both several hundred feet from the mill, to keep them from catching fire.

Perry Township Chief Jim Miller said the mill was owned by James B. Dull of Connelsville, Pa., and was partially insured. Dull used the mill to manufacture grain products which he trucked to several feed outlets in Pennsylvania before the mill was shut down several years ago.

A dump truck parked inside the mill, and large grain storage tank were also destroyed by the fire.

Cause of the blaze was not immediately determined, but Miller said some children were

believed to have been playing inside the building before the fire was discovered.

Mrs. Martha Nolan of Sonora was the first person to telephone firemen. She called about 1:23 a.m.

All that remained of the building yesterday was part of the stone foundation. A former owner, Clarence Wheeler, said the mill contained about $70,000 worth of usable machinery when it was closed. Since that time, however, the contents were severely damaged by youngsters playing in the building.

The 70-by-100-foot mill was built in the late 1880s and early 1890s by Harry E. and William G. Hanes.

See the by-line? It is proof positive that everything the author has written in this book is absolutely, positively true. (Sort of.) I wrote another story about my brother Jim when he burned down our outhouse, but they decided not to print it. They said he probably had enough problems already.

Sonora's street corners, where the fire-watching crowd could buy things like hot sandwiches, cold pop, and assorted souvenirs, like Zippo lighters that had cleverly been engraved with a good likeness of the mill and the adjacent weed patch and the words "Gone But Not Forgotten." There were also individual packs and even whole cartons of the popular cigarettes for sale, as fully representing the probable cause of the feed mill fire. In full recognition of the historical significance of the occasion, I was asked to go back home and get my trumpet and play *The Star-Spangled Banner.* But I had to decline Mom's

MAR. 31, 1958

### New Norwich Volunteer Firemen.

My brother Jim, who burned down our outhouse, eventually got so good at fires that he was recruited by the Norwich Volunteer Fire Department a few miles from Sonora. Today, big corporations hire guys with special computer skills to help them tighten up their security measures. Jim is in the plaid shirt in the back row, second from the right.

musical request. I reminded her that the show had already started, and said the next piece would likely be performed by some fat lady singing *Gone with the Wind.* Soon a reporter from the Zanesville *Times Recorder* started taking notes and pictures. The next morning, Sonora's feed mill fire was front-page news. The brief, by-lined story included a three-column black-and-white photo of the building, fully involved, with tall white flaming fingers turning Sonora's oldest landmark into smoldering wood embers and alkalinic ashes. I was very pleased to notice that they had not only spelled my name right, but had printed the story just as I had written it and the photo just as I had taken it.

# CHAPTER TWENTY-FOUR

# Fair Enough

In the 1950s, the biggest event in Sonora, in August of each year, actually took place about ten miles away, in the city of Zanesville. It was the annual Muskingum County Fair.

The people who organized that week-long agricultural exhibition, the county fair board, probably would have told you that they always spent a whole year making the million arrangements needed to bring each fair off without a hitch. The kids of Sonora probably would have told you that they spent at least an equal amount of time in preparation for the fair.

Our planning for the next county fair started with a study of the fair that was then under way. You had to know the current cost of a week's worth of rides, games, souvenirs, and food in order to make some estimate of how much you would need to budget and earn for the following fair. Moreover, if you were planning to submit some sort of display, or enter one of the hundreds of competitive events that involved arts and crafts, science and industry, or animal husbandry, you had to know exactly what your peers were doing now so that, next year, you could go a step or two beyond that and beat their pants off.

None of the kids of Sonora, to the best of my knowledge. ever had a project on display at the county fair, in any category. Exhibit items included horses, pigs, rabbits, chickens, mice, guinea pigs, goats, cats, and dogs, such farm crops as corn, hay, oats, wheat, rye, barley, and sorghum, and harvested home produce like pickles, peas, potatoes, tomatoes, corn, carrots, gourds, and umpteen other blue-ribbon candidates from the garden. All of those things were of far less interest to the kids of Sonora than they were to our country cousins, who belonged to such civic organizations as the FFA (Future Farmers of America), the FHA (Future Homemakers of America), and the 4-H (Head, Hands, Health and Heart). If you lived in the country, where your nearest neighbor usually lived so far away that you couldn't even hit him with a thrown stone, you apparently had to belong to some sort of organization. We town kids prided ourselves on not belonging to nothing, and instead chose to perfect our performance arts abilities—playing the midway games.

Our preparation for the Muskingum County Fair required only two things: assembling a cash stash adequate to make it from the Monday morning opening through the next Sunday afternoon closing, and honing our gaming talents to take home our fair share of prizes in the midway contests. All year long, from early September through the middle of the next August, we set aside a part of every penny we earned for the fair. Throughout the same period we concocted close approximations of the many midway games and practiced them diligently, to improve our chances of beating the odds that we knew before we started were clearly stacked against us.

## - FAIR ENOUGH -

Most midway games involved some kind of ball—baseball, softball, basketball, rubber ball, ping-pong ball—and since we were constantly hitting, tossing, and shooting those round objects all year long anyway, according to the season, as part of just being kids, we had acquired a sort of natural adeptness in those events. A few other games required dart-throwing sharpness or nerves of steel, like pulling up a pop bottle that was sitting on a slightly tilted, highly waxed stand with a springy pole-and-string, to which was attached a wooden ring that you slipped over the neck of the bottle. We tossed darts almost daily at cardboard Reese's Cup inserts, which we lodged in the bark of the nearest maple tree, and made our own pop-bottle set-ups to prepare for those events. The remaining games of chance we usually avoided, since we could find no easy way to sharpen our skills at them, and increase the potential pay-off, without using up a lot of our limited supply of luck.

The Muskingum County Fair, in the 1950s, was exactly what every county fair in the country should have tried to be. Although the grounds were located within the city limits of Zanesville, both adjacent to an industrial area and bordered by boxy, look-alike homes, you never got the impression that it was an urban affair. When you turned off Pershing Road near Brighton Boulevard, and entered one of the two available gates in the circumferential fence, you became countrified. In an instant, you passed from the uninspiring housing neighborhoods of a typical old midwestern city to an earlier, simpler world of farm sights and smells, rural sounds and feelings, woodsy arts and crafts, and homemade everything.

The "upper" gate of the fairgrounds led to a large grass parking lot atop the only hill on the fairgrounds, the sloped west side of which was shaded by ancient maples and hickories. This steep hillside was perfect for viewing every venue of the fair, from the midway at the foot of the hill to the grandstand hundreds of feet away. Although steep, the hillside was an easy climb for fairgoers of all ages who needed to rest their legs, catch a few winks, put down a blanket and have a snack, or engage in more personal activities before heading back to the excitement below. Anyone who needed to look could often see teenagers or young adults with blankets both under and over them, while twenty or thirty feet away there would be a whole family having a late-afternoon picnic or a full evening meal. When you got tired of resting, it was only a few paces back down the hill to the rides and the games, and the screams of the thrilled and the chilled were always beckoning you back.

## - OF FIRES AND FOGGY MORNINGS -

Entering the main gate, where general admission tickets were purchased from a window-framed person in a little stone gatehouse or someone else standing off to the side with a fistful of dollars and a waist pouch full of change, your vehicle was usually motioned around to the right, past the open tent with the poorly attended talent show and the much larger and better patronized farm implements area, and through a gate in the white, boarded fence that protected the very heart of the fairgrounds, the huge grass infield that was surrounded by a half-mile oval dirt race track. In the evenings, you would sometimes have to wait for the dozen or so horses in a harness race heat to trot or pace by before a gate keeper would let you cross the track. On Saturday nights, the perennial favorite daredevil auto wreckers could cause similar short delays by using a long back stretch of the track for a tension-building run up a rickety board ramp with a concealed explosive that would be remotely detonated into a ball of fire just as they reached the top. During most daylight hours, you could cross the dirt track without any delay. Once you reached the inner grass area of the oval ring, you could park pretty much anywhere you wanted; even spaced oddly there was probably enough room there to park a thousand or more pickup trucks.

At the middle of one of the oval track's two straightaways, on the infield side of the track directly opposite the covered grandstand and its wings of open wooden bleachers, stood a white covered stage on a cement block foundation. Here, both name and nameless show business entertainers, country and western music artists, and even an occasional local wannabe, performed rain or shine. Here, also, the winners of the Sunday horse show, the Saturday morning horse pull, the several evening harness races, and certain other competitions received their just awards. Under the grandstand, there were a couple of dozen commercial booths, food stands operated by volunteers from civic groups, a short-lined rest room for men and boys, a long-lined rest room for women and girls, and always one fast-talking fellow who sold expensive sets of beautifully bound encyclopedias to people who would never in their life use them but seemingly couldn't leave for home without them.

Nearly surrounding the oval track, which was kept in top racing form by huge tractors pulling chain-link drags and water tank trucks that dribbled their loads lap after lap, day and night, were several fan-ventilated horse barns, animal show arenas, display barns, cavernous exhibition halls, and lesser sheds and maintenance buildings. Over the years, all of these sturdy structures had been brushed with so many coats of white, lead-based paint that the paint coats themselves could have stood without the supporting inch boards. A blacktopped road ran around the entire outside circumference of the track, paralleling the white picket fence and the midway stands and booths. This broad thoroughfare provided a mud-free, reduced-dust path for the thousands of fair attendees who paraded around each year.

As viewed from the hill, there were always many open-sided food tents operated by service groups and auxiliaries to your left, as the paved road curved towards the grandstand. To your right, at the end of a similar curve, there was always a giant Ferris wheel that appeared to have been built from a super-sized erector set, and a tinkling, thumping merry-go-round. Its crashing cymbals seemed to symbolize galloping horses. At the center of the merry-go-round was a big bass drum that boomed a beat from morning until midnight. Each evening, the fluorescent-lit spokes of the Ferris wheel joined many other fared rides in an always successful effort to outshine the star-bright sky, and the wheel's chugging diesel drive engine added to the loony-tuned merry-go-round, to the other roaring ride cacophony, to the clapping, oohing-and-aahing crowd in the grandstand, to the not-unexpected screams of the thrilled and the terror-seekers, and to the acrid gunpowder-powered snap-snap-snapping at the bare-boned rifle shoot booth, where you never had anything to win, but always had everything to prove.

The whole east end of the paved oval midway, from one dirt-track straightaway to the other, was bordered by dozens of dusty canvas tents with gaily colored, wind-flapped flags that made them look like a long used-car lot. Intermixed with these small sanctioned gambling casinos and stump-sites for over-promising political candidates were rubber-tired trailers with swing-up sides of painted plywood that were set up on the fair's horse-show Sunday and taken down seven days later. Closely clinging to the dirt track's white picket fence line, the game tents, booths, and trailers were operated by an endless number of identical grimy gamey attendants, who loudly hawked their wares, shouted irresistible challenges to gullible male passersby, and made lurid remarks to any unattached female who chose to keep her distance at very close range.

There were always a few tattooed lady attendants behind the booth counters, with smoking cigarettes hanging from their crooked mouths, who invited you to try your luck and join them in the good life. You could toss all of these game attendants into a barrel, reach in and grab anywhere, and pull out the same one, no matter who you came up with. They were interchangeable, booth after booth and year after year, and you sometimes thought you saw the same attendant at four or five game booths in a row in the span of a few minutes. These carnies obviously lived a very tough life, constantly trucking from town to town and county to county, forced by their chosen employment to spend most of their waking hours in less-than-sterile outdoor operating rooms and most of their sleeping hours on the highway or in some cramped corner of their multi-functioned trailers. After about the second stop they must have become so embittered and cynical at their low-paid lot in life that they began to look forward to foisting from you, the luckier opposition, every dime they could get. In my half-dozen years of confronting these road-hardened game runners many times a day during fair week, I never met a single one who I thought would play by the rules if the rules could be broken.

When you stepped up to the plate, to stand up soda pop bottles, you knew that the small square platform had been slickened with wax or polish and slanted slightly, that the top rim of the green glass bottle had been sanded smooth, that the wood curtain ring had been chipped, and that anything else that could be done had been done to make the ring slip off the bottle and make the bottle roll off the platform to end your game. It looked so easy; it was actually so tough. If you wanted to have any chance at all of pulling down a stuffed panda bear or a purple poodle, you had to reconnoiter each of the eight or ten platforms in a booth before playing. You had to know which way each of the seemingly level platforms was leaning, which bottles were rolling suspiciously fast towards the sawdust, where others were occasionally winning, and where nobody ever won. If

you failed to do this required pre-play reconnaissance, perhaps due to greed, haste, or obvious inexperience, the quarter you plunked down to play was as good as gone. It was only by analyzing each game thoroughly before handing over the price of fame and glory that you would have any hope at all of evening the odds and—perhaps—walking away with a major prize.

Standing up a small Coke bottle with the string-lined stick was my specialty. It took nerves of steel, a feather touch, and a steady hand. You had to pay no attention to the helpful advice from the loud-shouting huckster behind the rail (who, after all, did not want to lose). It took unceasing concentration and frequent fine adjustments, and you had to sense exactly when the bottle was ready to pivot to an upright position, just when to give it a slight final jerk, and how much help the bottle needed to overcome the tilt of the platform and stand erect without toppling on over.

It took years of practice and careful study to acquire my skills in setting up pop bottles, but I eventually got so good at it that I almost always walked away with "a major prize" on my very first quarter. One memorable day I was even banned from a booth at the operator's request by Fair Board President Scott Patton himself when I won five top dogs in less than an hour. To all of my pals, and to a large crowd of onlookers, who were both amazed and temporarily entertained by my run of good luck, I was an unexpected and unlikely war hero. To the losing-money guy behind the wooden sucker rail, I was a pain in the posterior. To President Patton, it all seemed to be pretty funny.

I became equally adept, after more years of practice, at knocking over pop bottles. In this game, two identical Coca-Cola bottles, of the small size that disappeared when all of the soda pop bottlers opted for eight ounces, and doubled the price, were placed side by side on a square platform just above the ground level. Here you had to pitch a beat-up baseball underhanded at the intimidating soft-drink duo, hit both bottles simultaneously at just the right point, and not only knock them over but roll them completely off their platform. The trick was to notice that one of the bottles was situated slightly farther away from you than the other. So, when you stood straight-on to the little bottles and tossed the baseball at them, you invariably made contact with the closer before the farther, which drained the ball of enough energy that it would carom off the first bottle and hit the remaining one more head-on, thus causing that bottle to scoot backwards but not fall over. To overcome this deceptive placement, you had to quickly determine which bottle was farther back, before the operator could observe that you were on to him and reposition the bottles, then shift your stance in that direction so that your natural inclination to hit both bottles evenly would make them tumble over at the same time. Eventually, even some amateur fairgoers figured out the winning formula, and frustrated operators began to use baseballs with so little sawdust stuffing in them that even Whitey Ford couldn't have knocked over both bottles. When the game reached the point at which few stuffed prizes could be pulled off the rafters, it all but disappeared.

Less fruitful were my few attempts to fit an overblown basketball into an undersized rim at the three-balls-for-a-dollar shoot. I never could understand why the high school varsity basketball stars, who were otherwise deemed to be nearly normal, were never observant enough to see this almost unbeatable combination. Yes, the grossly over-inflated ball actually *could* be slipped through the smaller-than-standardized hoop—*if* it made absolutely no contact with the springy, loosely bolted rim. The odds that anyone but Dead-Eye Dick or Annie Oakley could sink three shots in a row—which was necessary to win one of the undersized stuffed animals—must have been incalculable. Only the occasional shooter who was clearly under the influence, and thus completely off his game, seemed to get any stuffed rewards at all, and that was only after he had spent at least ten times on the attempt what an identical animal would have cost him to purchase from a vendor only fifty feet away. This guy's female friend for the evening always stood near by, using her mere presence to egg him on, apparently fully aware of the fact that, one way or the other, she was going to walk away from the basketball booth with some kind of animal.

Properly dressed for the Muskingum County Fair, with cousins Oscar (the tongue) and Bobby Jones. We had to look long and hard to find those hats.

All of the dart games, of course, relied upon pinpoint accuracy, and sometimes speed. Whether you were simply bursting balloons or adding up tough-to-figure combinations of numbers, the trick was to throw the dart hard enough that it didn't bounce off the board or the balloon but flew straight enough to go where you intended. I seldom took a shot at the dart numbers game, because the prizes never seemed up to the challenge. (How many cheap plastic combs does one person need, anyway?) The balloon bubble burst when I learned that you had to accumulate points by playing game after game and keep trading up from trinkets to toys in order to take away the teddy bear that you thought you were going to win in the first round but never did.

Most other midway games relied upon pure chance, not practiced skill, like the one where you rolled a ball down a sloped runway and it bounced on dividing rails until gravity and good or bad luck directed it into a numbered slot that, when added to four others, was always too low or too high to win a prize. (We called these the Goldilocks games.) Or you tossed a table tennis ball into a sea of globular glass bowls that were filled with colored water until it bounced away or plopped into one containing a tiny goldfish that would be cat food before you even got off the fairgrounds. Or you gave a sturdy toy car such a hefty shove that it was railed back and forth by rubber-banded bumpers until it finally stopped between two nails alongside it that appeared to mark the big winner but actually got you the cheapest whistle that it was possible for modern Chinese technology to produce.

I don't think I ever picked up the greasy wooden mallet and pounded the hard-rubber bumper to see if I could catapult the heavy weight high enough on the railed tower to ring the bell. The reward for doing that was just a cheap smelly cigar that made more than one of my older friends sicker than a dog. If I wanted to get sick, I soon decided, I could simply stuff myself with ketchup-coated hotdogs and go on one of the rides that whirled you every which way but loose. But I didn't do that, either.

At least twenty thrilling rides were available for the undertakers each year at the Muskingum County Fair, but I undertook to ride only a few of them. I was never into any transparent attempt to impress an acquaintance of the female persuasion in my age group with my fair daring-do. And I couldn't see the point in subjecting myself to such bodily punishment for any other reason. Besides, I could just imagine myself seat-belted securely in a colorful pastel-painted cockpit that was shaped like an egg as it broke loose from its retaining arm and hurled both me and my less-than-fortunate companion clear over the midway, across the white picket fence, and under the steel shoes of a herd of galloping horses as the last harness race of the evening just got underway. ("No, thanks. I'm on my way now to the rifle gallery to borrow a gun and shoot myself.")

## - FAIR ENOUGH -

It was more fun, and far less painful, to patronize the penny arcade, where for a few cents you could get your fortune told by a real shrunken gypsy lady who lived in a glass booth, take your own picture with a good fair friend in four different poses, buy a handful of black-and-white pictures of scantily clad women, Hollywood stars, or other show business animals, direct a swinging claw or a sandlogged bulldozer to put a plastic trinket worth about a dime a dozen in your possession, or fire a real light-shooting rifle at the taunting tin rabbits who rolled back and forth between painted-metal bushes in the glassed-in gallery that was always too high to see from the wooden box that was provided.

One thing I always did at the fair was take a tour of the show buildings. I never failed to marvel at the amazing talent and outright ingenuity on display in the arts and crafts hall. I walked through the commerce hall aisles only to see how many 37-inch yardsticks and printed balloons I could receive from the politicians as an unregistered pre-teen voter. I visited the animal exhibits just because they were there (when you've seen one pig, you've just about seen them all). And I spent a fair amount of time in the horse barns scouting out the likely harness race winners.

## - OF FIRES AND FOGGY MORNINGS -

I don't know exactly when, but I somehow got hooked up, in a fair way, with Jack Greiner. Jack and Alma had the house across Sonora Road from our grocery, and I used to spend a lot of time bothering Alma as she sat in her front porch swing and carefully watched the world go by. Jack spent most of his days with his dogs, a handful of baleful 'coon hounds that used to ride in the back of his old maroon pickup, barking wildly behind the doors of a custom-made wooden doghouse that occupied the entire truck bed and hung out over the sides. On many summer evenings, Jack would tie one or two of his dogs alongside his truck and run them for miles up into the country, at a reasonably comfortable pace, just to keep them in 'coon-hunting condition. Today Jack would be reported immediately by some concerned interfering do-gooder to the Humane Society of the United States or to the SPCA, and would be charged with animal cruelty. Ironically, I can't remember anyone in Sonora who took better care of his dogs. Is the world really such a better place today?

The last American Indian in Sonora. Across Sonora Road, next to my right ear, is the porch where Alma Greiner spent many hours in her swing.

Jack loved to watch the harness races at the fair, and he was personally acquainted with many of the owners and trainers of the highly skittish horses that were entered there and elsewhere. He had been around racetracks long enough to acquire a running reputation. When Jack placed a bet with one of the unofficial bookies who set up shop trackside, it had some horse sense behind it. Jack generally won, because he knew the horses, and he played the odds.

Since Sonora was nine or ten miles from the county fairgrounds, one of the biggest challenges for kids in our community was finding daily rides to and from the fair. My cousin Bobby Jones and I eventually found a solution to this tough transportation problem on several nights by riding in with Jack Greiner when he went to the horse races. It wasn't long, as Jack talked about horses and horse racing on the drive in to the fair, before I started hanging around with Jack instead of Bobby. And it wasn't long after that, as I developed a halfway decent horse sense of my own, that I began to bet on those races.

## - FAIR ENOUGH -

My first bets, of course, were with just with Jack. He had the insider information, but I had a certain amount of intuition, and the question was which was more useful. Jack was blessed by hearing all sorts of behind-the-horse-scenes talk in the stables, which he always toured immediately upon his arrival. I was handicapped by having to actually see the horses trotting or pacing on the track in their warm-up laps before I could make a reasonable guess as to which horse was stronger, faster, better driven, or least likely to break stride. Even the fastest and strongest horse can come in dead last if it suddenly loses its pace, has to be reined in, and can't regain its footing. Unfortunately, there's no real way of predicting when that is likely to occur, but a horse with a history of breaking stride is highly likely to continue the practice. It was that kind of insight that Jack had, being around pacers and trotters and their trainers and drivers at various other tracks, and I did not.

Still, over the several races of an evening I could just about match Jack's winnings, which were never more than eight or ten dollars, and I usually walked away with enough cash to support at least the next day's fair game and food requirements. My cousin Bobby, on the other hand, who seldom played the horses, usually rode home from the fair flat broke, having spent all of his money foolishly on mere food and fun.

Win, lose or draw, we always looked forward to the Muskingum County Fair. Because it came just before the start of the school year, it was our final fling of the summer, our last chance to cut loose before

returning to our far-less-interesting, prescribed path of public education. It was a fun time for kids of all ages. It was the best show that Sonora didn't have to offer. If we usually spent far more there than we finally took home, that was fair enough. We still had our pockets full of memories.

# CHAPTER TWENTY-FIVE

# The Squirrel Hunters

Dad spent many late afternoon and early evening hours on summer days fly-fishing in the small creeks around Sonora for three- to six-inch "chubs." He fought these mini-fish with a three-sectioned bamboo rod that had a Shakespeare wind-up spring reel that spooled a brown waxy line that might have restrained Moby Dick if put to the test. On to the heavy line he tied a thin monofilament leader about four feet long, using a special knot of his own design that applied some formula that combined both geometry and magic. On to the leader he hooked a fly that no fish in its right mind ever would have fallen for. But Dad was very successful with this unlikely tackle. He pulled one chub after another from hidden pools wherever awoods or afield he went.

In the narrower, shallower straits of the remote fishing holes, where the small creeks were rippled by large rocks and stones, Dad went after the chunky chubs and their even-smaller relatives with a seine, scaring them out of their hiding places along the weedy banks with pokes and jabs from the two square wooden upright poles that held the current-bowed net. Every ten feet or so he would lift the seine, lay it flat on the grass by the bank and sort through an amazing conglomeration of victims that included silver-sided minnows, hard-shelled crawdads, and other freshwater denizens that you normally never saw or even suspected as living in the water. All of those candidates that Dad selected for further consideration as bait would be tossed into the multi-perforated liner of a water-filled bucket and taken home. There they would be confined temporarily in the creek that bisected our five-acre cattle farm at the edge of Sonora. That night or the next morning they would become most of Dad's bait (and be supplemented with a dozen "soft craws" that were purchased on the way through "town") as he fished for catfish from high atop the Ellis Dam locks on the Muskingum River north of Zanesville. *(See Chapter 15: "Locks and Beagles")*

The five-acre farm on which Dad (and I) built barns and finished the house at rear. Sonora School was straight across Sonora Road from the driveway. The property is now owned by my brother Jim.

When he wasn't fishing, Dad was often "sighting-in" the scopes of his guns, "up in the country," alongside a gravel road, in one of Clarence Porter's back fields, or in our own lower pasture next to the railroad, where he would stake out paper targets against an earth-banked background, precisely so many paces between the target and the "business end" of one of his high-powered rifles. While these printed targets promised so many points for putting a bullet through the solid center eye, and lesser scores for hitting between the eye and the first ring, first ring and second, or second and third, the numbers had little relevance to the process of zeroing-in a gun's telescopic sight. The aim, so to speak, was not merely to score points— although the closer the shots were to the center, the better—but to achieve a tight "grouping" of shots. For that reason, Dad's sighting-in was always done on a couple of long cloth bags that he had filled with

The bankside backstop for the targets that Dad erected when sighting-in his rifles. At right center is the B&O railroad. My brother Jim still mows the grass twice a day and once on Sunday.

sand. The bags provided a solid, easily modified rest for his rifle, so that when he lined up the cross-hairs on the center of the target's solid black circle, took a deep breath, released some of it, and slowly squeezed the trigger, Dad stood an excellent chance of putting a sharp-nosed bullet exactly where the cross-hairs indicated, time and again. If he could get a good grouping of two or three shots—say, close enough together that you could cover them all with a quarter—he could then adjust the vertical and horizontal hair reticules of the scope to move the next grouping even closer to the center of the target. By shooting consistently, with the gun braced solidly on the sandbags, Dad could eventually have every shot hitting the black eye—with the hole from one shot shared by the others.

Sighting-in the scopes of high-powered rifles was a necessary though painstaking task for serious shooters that was often repeated. Even a slight accidental jolt could throw a scope out of alignment, and a whole day's hunt could depend upon pinpoint shooting accuracy. Since a bullet usually tended to go where the gun was aimed, it was critical to have the scope's cross-hairs precisely aligned with the spiral-scored bore of the barrel. The ultimate embarrassment for a hunter was not to miss what he was shooting at but to be aimed at one thing and shooting something else. Sighting-in a scope was intended to prevent such disastrous and unsportsmanlike occurrences, and usually did.

The sighting-in process was complicated by the fact that the trajectory of a high-speed bullet is actually not a straight horizontal line but a rainbow-like arc that has the bullet starting at or below the apparent position of a distant target, rising well above that target, then falling back down to intersect it at some point that is precisely X distance from the muzzle of the gun. When using the barrel-mounted front and rear sights of a rifle it was difficult enough to determine that distance. (Most

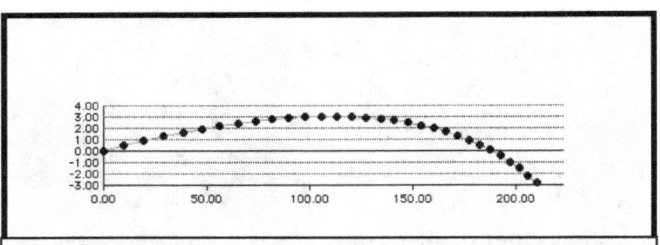

**The trajectory of a rifle bullet rises above the aiming point before falling below it.**

rear sights have long been click-adjustable to account for the known-to-be-forthcoming nose dive.) When using a telescopic sight it was even more difficult, because the magnified glass sight's accuracy fell off dramatically if a target was somewhat nearer or farther than the distance the scope had been set for. Unless the hunter had excellent depth perception, knew exactly the distance for which his scope had been sighted-in, and had a fair knowledge of bullet trajectories, which changed according to the

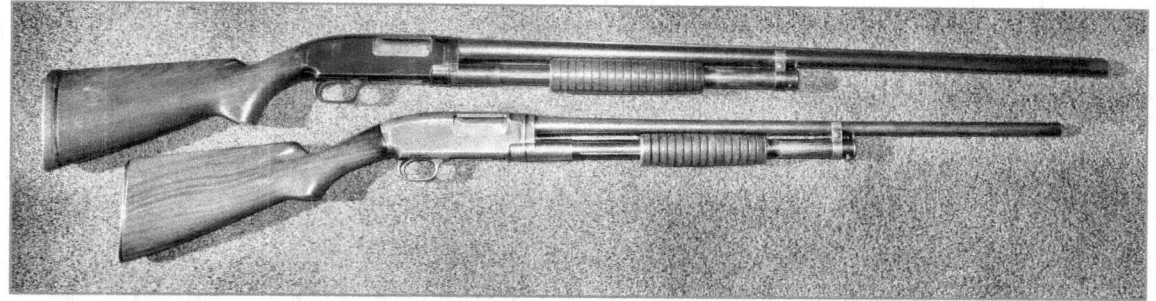

The seldom used Winchester Model 12 12-gauge (top) and the Winchester Model 12 20-gauge that Dad almost always took to the woods for squirrels

weight of the bullet, its shape, and the burn characteristics of the powder load that pushed it, the odds of his hitting any long-shot target he aimed at were in actuality pretty poor. Dad picked up a lot of his shooting knowledge by reloading his own ammunition, which allowed him to control the size and shape of the bullet and the amount and combustibility of the burn load. The rest he learned by spending probably the equivalent of a whole year of his long life in the woods.

Dad had accumulated an arsenal over his decades of hunting that would have outfitted the typical Ohio National Guard unit quite adequately. Among his proudest possessions was a Winchester Model 12 20-gauge shotgun that was matched by a Model 12 12-gauge. For bigger game he had a Winchester Model 94-30 .30-.30 rifle, and for the biggest of all he had a Remington 30.06 rifle that would remodel your cheekbone and blacken your eye if you failed to keep it snug when you pulled the trigger. One thing you did not want to do, when firing this personal cannon, was put your eye too close to its scope. For lesser game, Dad had lesser guns, including a Reising .22-caliber pistol that he kept immediately accessible for shooting anything or anyone one at any time for any halfway good reason, such as interrupting his nap on our dining room daybed as he re-energized for his next work shift at the glass house.

Made for rising to the occasion?

Each fall Dad hunted Ohio's gray and red (fox) squirrels. When winter fell he trapped muskrats and hunted rabbits. Every couple of years or so, in the middle of the winter, Dad joined a work buddy or two for a car trip to northwestern Pennsylvania to hunt whitetail deer. In the off-seasons, Dad read tons of magazines like *Field and Stream, Outdoor Life, Sports Afield,* and *Modern Detective.* He was the consummate outdoorsman.

Dad was known by both nearby neighbors and far-and-wide fellow hunters as a crack shot as early as the 1920s, when as a young adult he gained a reputation as being the one guy in Sonora that you didn't want to challenge to a turkey shoot. Even in his sixties, Dad could remove most of George Washington's profile from a quarter at a hundred yards with an open-sighted .22 rifle—and give you twenty cents change. Whenever he went into the woods to hunt, many of his most perceptive victims just dropped over dead when they saw him coming, realizing that it was all over anyway for them, and thinking that they may as well try to preserve their pelt for posterity.

Dad's hunting philosophy was based on the principle of first-come, first-served. He had the same philosophy when it came to fishing, trapping, camping, and every other activity that involved fields, forests, food, the woods, and water. To beat him at almost anything involving the outdoors, you had to get up pretty early in the morning.

Dad's definition of "early" in the morning didn't mean eight o'clock, seven, six, or even five. To Dad, during squirrel season and always, "early" meant rolling out of bed at 4:30 a.m.—well before any sensible rooster was even starting to think about leaving the coop to crow.

Dad raises his hunting knife to begin skinning his latest Pennsylvania whitetail deer, while I check to see if the deer still has a heartbeat. Probably not. That's our apple tree.

The wake-up alarm on Dad's electric clock was permanently set to sound precisely at Ungodly Hour.

The reason you had to get up so early with Dad was to get to the woods and be settled in to some position that only he could determine well before daylight. You had to find a particular spot at the foot of the right tree, and keep a close eye on all limbs and branches above, while you waited for the sun to rise and the woods to wake. If you failed to arrive in the woods until after daybreak, you lost your edge, because all of your intended victims would hear you coming, see you stalking, and take cover. But if you could sneak in and get squatted down before they even began to stir, you could surprise them. In the woods, I soon learned, surprise was nine-tenths of the law; the other tenth was who could shoot first and ask questions later.

Daybreak was when the squirrels "cut their nuts." I never quite figured out why they needed to do that (or even how it was accomplished), but you almost never heard a sound from a squirrel unless it was "cutting its nuts." Assuming you were determined to shoot such a squirrel—and unless you made that assumption you felt pretty dumb, just sitting in the woods and holding innocent trees hostage with a shotgun—you had to see it. If you wanted to see it, the best way was to hone in on the sounds of it "cutting its nuts." This obviously personal, apparently painful  male squirrel ritual could take place far up in the trees, which were usually white oaks or butternut hickories, or it could be done anywhere from the ground to the sky. In our neck of the woods, you had to keep an eye out all over the place, because a nut-cutting squirrel was just as likely to be perched on a fallen tree, feasting on an acorn, as it was to be high up in the branches, seemingly safe from such perils as some half-awake, pre-teen hunter with a .410-gauge shotgun aimed at putting an early end to its lowly nut-cutting life.

It was bad enough having to roll out of bed at 4:30 a.m. to go execute some innocent, unsuspecting, life-loving little squirrel, but Dad would never let that happen on an empty stomach. Stumbling down the stairs, not yet even half-awake, I would soon be assaulted by the smells of shell-hard fried eggs and smoking burnt bacon wafting from our kitchen, where Dad was exercising his culinary rights. To her credit, Mom usually had more sense than to arise with us at this untimely hour and make a hunter's breakfast. Despite my repeated tries, I was never able to sidestep Dad's camp cooking by making a case for cold cereal or even hot oatmeal; apparently there was some unwritten rule against walking through the woods on a foggy morning on an empty stomach or on any other energy but burnt breakfast bacon and over-fried eggs.

The real secret to squirrel hunting, other than getting there fustest with the mostest, as the Civil War's General Burnside might have said (and probably did), was to know the right landowners, who were typically farmers. As a courtesy, you normally wanted to get permission from these people before you trespassed on their land and began shooting at targets that could easily turn out to be one of their favorite farm animals. Also, as a landowner, they had first rights to threaten, maim, murder, or otherwise manhandle with extreme prejudice any non-farm animal that had wandered into their woods. As might be expected, few prime hunting woods and fields were situated within the uncharted limits of the little town of Sonora. But since Dad was Sonora's fourth-class postmaster, in charge of rural free delivery routes that ran far out into the surrounding countryside, he had automatic hunting privileges in just about any woods that he wanted to visit. This unchallenged hunting privilege seemed to have something to do with how quickly and how frequently certain rural landowners received their Sears Roebuck catalogs and other mail.

Not every group of trees was a likely home for the fox and gray squirrels that we hunted in Ohio. It took the right combination of remote location, abundant food supply, adequate shelter, and certain other elements to turn an ordinary stand of trees into a full-fledged squirrel housing project. The best woods were the ones with the oldest trees, where generations of squirrels had lived and died, climbed and cavorted, and, presumably, "cut their nuts," all in the interest of perpetuating and evolving the science of hunting. Year after year, we returned to the same woods, sat at the foot of the same trees, kept watch on the same nests, and listened for the same nut-cutting sounds. After a few years, even the squirrels began to look pretty much the same.

A three- or four-mile drive into "the country," on a maze of dusty graveled roads, would bring us to the same place we always parked, usually a well-worn lane leading off the main road to a run-down gate that fenced in a pasture or a cornfield. In the pre-dawn, dim light we would feel through the unlit trunk of the car, removing my .410 popgun and Dad's 20-gauge cannon, along with his canvas hunting coat with the bloodstained rear pocket that we anticipated filling. To keep from blowing out our own brains on the bumpy country roads, and to a lesser degree to comply with state law, our shotguns were always transported with empty chambers. Once on-site, Dad would expertly slide a number of shells into his side-loading shotgun, while I would struggle to "break" open the breech of my single-shot .410 and load either a green "short" or a red "long" shell. The length of each .410 shotgun shell—and thus the total amount of shot and gunpowder it contained—determined how far the dozens of internal lead pellets would fly before they scattered far enough apart to be useless. It took keen judgment to determine, maybe an hour in advance, whether a long or a short shell would be needed to bring down a squirrel that was, at the time of first-loading, still only imaginary. The under-powered pellets of a short shell often barely limped by a nut-cutting squirrel, maybe causing it to wonder if the wind was beginning to pick up, while the over-powered pellets of a long shell that were fired at a closer squirrel could produce a bloody mess that was not even worth retrieving. It was not until years after Dad bought me the .410 that I was strong enough to break it open without wedging it between my legs and struggling for several minutes to get it to knuckle under. This, incidentally, was to be the only instruction that I ever received from Dad about the birds and the bees. It was one of the reasons that, ultimately, I felt compelled to join the Boy Scouts.

Once loaded for bear, or at least for nut-cutting squirrels, we headed off through the inevitable mid-Ohio morning mist—which on some autumn mornings was a full-fledged fog—to our happy hunting grounds. Over hill, over dale, even over dusty trail, it didn't much make any difference whether you snorted, sneezed, talked, whistled, or even took care of certain personal problems that were caused by Dad's gas-generating breakfast cooking. But once you reached the edge of the woods, the word was silence. Every whisper, every twig that you snapped as you strode cautiously along, could give away your presence to the wary squirrels. After a damp night, the heavy dew atop fallen autumn leaves helped somewhat to cushion your footfalls. But the same damp red, yellow, or brown broad leaves that covered the ground also hid desert-dry twigs and branches that, when stepped on and snapped, time and again got me into big trouble.

To be a successful hunter, you must learn how to set your feet down toes first, very gently, very quietly. This is especially important when you are hunting with an accomplished old woodsman like Dad, who was always ready to brain me instantly for each and every little mistake I made. I didn't need any loud, unexpected explosion from a rifle or a shotgun to learn the definition of shell-shocked. Almost every time I went in the woods with Dad, I got cuffed or yelled at for disclosing our presence to the nut-cutting squirrel world by accidentally stepping on and snapping apart at least one dead twig.

The thing about snapping a dead twig is that, in the dense, heavy morning air of a southeastern Ohio autumn, the sudden sound would  carry across the woods like it was transmitted through a speaker wire from tree to tree. As long as you were two or three miles away from your intended target, and a day or two early, snapping a dead twig or two didn't much matter. Any closer or later than that, however, and you gave your sharp-eared prey enough time to pack up and move to the next county. There seemed to be nothing worse, so far as squirrel hunting was concerned, than to be only a few hundred feet from your destination tree and have a misplaced foot blow your whole stalk. At that point, you had about two options: you could either continue walking clear to the other side of the woods, where you might find another leaves-and-twigs nest in some un-scouted tree, or you could just sit down and remain perfectly still, both in sound and movement, for the next full hour or so, while any suspicious squirrel in the neighborhood forgot that you were there and resumed cutting its nuts.

# - THE SQUIRREL HUNTERS -

One thing you had to be aware of, when creeping up on any particular squirrel's nest or nut-cutting domain, was that this squirrel was fair game for not only you but possibly somebody else. It wasn't like you filled out a reservation form and had exclusive title to stalk a single tree and any squirrel that was in it. Chances were, the same tree had been scouted earlier by or was known to at least one other hunter. Who got the squirrel often came down to a matter of who could see it—and shoot it—first. Sitting in silence at the foot of a concealing tree, peering up at a nest while waiting for a squirrel (possibly) to appear, we often spotted some other fellow sitting at the foot of some other tree, peering up at the same nest from his own vantage point, hoping that the same squirrel would show up on his side not ours, thus giving him the first opportunity to blast it. On rare occasions, you would both fire at exactly the same time. It was pretty much a moot point at such times as to who had fired first. The squirrel that came tumbling down through the limbs and branches probably wouldn't retain enough meat to even argue about.

A successful hunt often produced three or four squirrels by eight or nine o'clock, more often of the gray variety than the fox  These would all be tucked under the back flap of Dad's venerable canvas hunting coat, which seemed to have warmed, protected, and helped hide him on every hunt he had ever undertaken. Once at home, the first order of business would be to skin the squirrels. A special spike for that purpose had been nailed to one of the exterior walls of our backyard barn, about six feet above the ground.

I never much cared for skinning squirrels, skinning rabbits, skinning muskrats, or skinning anything else, for that matter. Some persons probably found these hospital-grade home disembowelment operations fascinating. They always made me extremely nauseous.

A typical squirrel skinning began by using a sharp knife (Dad's knife was *always* sharp) to make a slit in one of the rodent's hind legs, between the knee and the ankle, between the tendon and the bone. This would allow you to hang the squirrel upside down on the nail. Then you would circumcise the skin around both legs near the ankles, and run a slit parallel to the leg, until you came to the torso. Slicing the torso from tail to neck would allow you to skin the hide all the way from the back legs to the front, where you once again cut around the bone to free the skin, which you could then peel on down to the neck. At this point, you simply decapitated the victim with a firm chop of the knife, and the skin (along with the head) would be released. Next, using the knife and a couple of fingers, you would eviscerate the animal—which sounds a lot better on paper than it smells in person. The entrails always had some special appeal for any dogs or cats that had been sitting patiently by. The squirrel's tail—particularly that of the fox—was chopped off and normally preserved for flying on automobile radio aerials or dangling in the wind from your bicycle's handlebars. At this point, the squirrel, rabbit, or muskrat was nothing but a mass of muscle and bone, ready to be taken in to the kitchen sink, cleaned of any embedded shotgun pellets, and soaked in a salt water brine for several hours, until it would be cooked (usually boiled).

I don't believe I ever actually ate a squirrel or a rabbit, although I certainly shot my fill of them. I haven't been hunting for any animal, except when armed with a camera, in over forty years. I still have my own K-Mart-cased collection of guns, along with some of Dad's, and much of his old ammunition, cleaning kits, and ammunition reloading paraphernalia. (If our Jackson Hole, Wyoming, house ever catches fire, no volunteer fireman who knows about my explosives armory would dare risk approaching within a thousand yards.) Despite retaining all of these periodically cleaned but never used weapons, and a large pile of related accouterments—mainly for their memory value—it turns out that I never actually was much of a hunter. In fact, after some fifty years of denial and simply sidestepping the issue, I would have to admit that I just went out hunting with Dad for the hell of it. Unfortunately, due mainly to those damned noisy twigs and Dad's quick temper, the hell of it was usually all I took home.

# CHAPTER TWENTY-SIX

# A TV Guide

Dick Phillips bought either the first or one of the first home color televisions in Sonora. He probably wrote it off on his income tax return as a business expense. Along with Al Schoeppner, who lived next to our school, Dick was one of the two individuals in Sonora who claimed to have more than a basic understanding of electronics. Both Dick and Al proclaimed themselves to be radio/TV technicians. They both had all sorts of test equipment, leather tool cases filled with various wrenches and screwdrivers, and box after box of little glass filament tubes with designations like GBX14R, ILIKEIKE, and U2BRUTE? So, Dick and Al must have known what they were doing.

We were fortunate that Dick and his family (a wife and four boys) lived right next door to us at the intersection of Sonora Road and Webster Street. Richard, Carlos, Ronnie, and Russell provided good competition when we played basketball outdoors all summer long and inside their unheated garage/shed during the winter. We also wasted many hours batting a plastic whiffleball nowhere in their backyard, occasionally running our innings so far into the night that we had to turn on a porch light just to see who was still playing. Dick was also good for a few bucks one afternoon when he decided that his new TV and radio repair business would pull in more customers if he had an outdoor shop sign, and hired me to paint it.

The main benefit of having the Phillips family living right next door was their color TV. Every once in a while, one of the boys would invite me in to watch it with them, although Dick usually did not allow them to turn the set on during the day, to avoid wasting any programs. So I spent most of my viewing hours standing outside their TV room window, watching Dick's color TV at night.

I remember the first program I ever stood in the dark outside Dick's window and watched. The world was just becoming a wonderland of color and Walt Disney was wielding the paintbrush. In a starburst of color, a tiny yellow-haired pixie with a magic wand named Tinkerbell, wearing a green, woodsy, one-piece bathing suit, invited me to help Walt host a feature presentation from Frontierland, Adventureland, Tomorrowland, or Fantasyland. I think we went first to Frontierland, where Davy Crockett was born on a mountaintop in Tennessee and kilt him a b'ar when he was only three. Davy soon grew into a man that big Mike Fink, the real Ohio River pole-boat pirate who later died in Wyoming, didn't want to mess with.

Dick's color TV was amazing. Although it was a bit short on volume, it could reproduce apparently every color under the sun. NBC had a peacock that unfolded its tail into at least eight separate colors. And when *Bonanza* came on, you could almost feel the flames as an old paper map of Ben Cartwright's Ponderosa ranch was burned to pieces. This was a great improvement over watching a black-and-white film about rainbows and having to use your imagination for the colors.

It was only a couple of years after Dick Phillips led the way to TV modernity in Sonora that Dad broke down and bought us our own color TV. I can't remember whether it was an RCA, an Admiral, or a Zenith, but those brands were about all of the choices that we had to begin with, and Dad would not have known one from the other. Our new TV required a high-tech aluminum antenna, which had to be properly positioned atop a 50-foot, tri-masted galvanized aluminum tower that was braced by long woven "guy" wires. Such a huge antenna was needed in Sonora to pick up the weak broadcast signals that were traveling a whole seven miles from Zanesville, from the only station that was then available. *WHIZ-TV* was an NBC affiliate. It wasn't long, however, before the development of stronger transmitters allowed us to pull in programs from Columbus, some

168

60 miles away, on *WTVN*, *WCBS*, and *WRFD*, the latter of which seemed to have a lot of farm-oriented shows.

We soon were watching Milton Berle, Ed Sullivan, Abbott and Costello, Jack Benny, Bob Cummings, Burns and Allen, and even Roy Rogers. We tried to *Beat the Clock*, enjoyed *The Life of Riley,* and put out a *Dragnet* for Groucho Marx, who tried to get us to say the word on some duck that hung from a string. We said *Howdy Doody* to *Captain Midnight*, and listened to *Your Hit Parade* as we blew the *Gunsmoke* off Spring Byington, who was our *December Bride.* We absolutely loved Lucy, joining apparently everyone else in the country in doing so.

Even the commercials were usually interesting (and, unlike today, they were not repeated three times every five minutes). Most of the commercials seemed to encourage us to smoke a certain brand of cigarette, such as Old Gold, Pall Mall, Chesterfield, and Lucky Strike ("Lucky Strike Means Fine Tobacco"). But there were also helpful hints on choosing the right brand of dishwashing liquid, the most-flavorful chewing gum, and the most-powerful car to drive. Although we were urged to see the U.S.A. in a Chevrolet, Dad usually picked Pontiacs whenever he went

to Zanesville, Cambridge, Duncan Falls, or Newark to buy a new car. He never cared much for any of the commercial announcers, and seldom bought what they were selling.

The best thing about having our own color TV was that we could watch it whenever we wanted, while standing up, sitting down, lying on the floor, or hanging from the ceiling, without having to watch through a window—and it even had sound. We could stretch out in front of our open fireplace, curl up on the couch, as Mom usually did, or even view it long-distance from the dining room, which was Dad's preferred daybed location. The only problem with Dad's dining room daybed spot for watching TV was the square wooden stand that Mom placed at the edge of the archway that divided the two rooms. This stand, with a table-like platform that was topped by artificial flowers, was just high enough to block Dad's view of our TV from his daybed. So he soon moved it. And then Mom moved it back. The battle went back and forth for days, during which the stand racked up more mileage than our car, and the eventual outcome was always in doubt. But the war finally ended when the stand mysteriously disappeared one day and never showed its face around our house again. Mom bought some more artificial flowers and put them somewhere else, and Dad never had a problem after that seeing the TV.

Dad always seemed to know when the Grand Ol' Opry was cranking up or one of the other country music shows that he enjoyed was coming on. "His" shows invariably were timed to begin exactly halfway through one of the programs that Mom or I liked to watch, so we attempted to "forget" that one of "his" programs was starting. That ploy worked for a couple of days, but broke down when Dad became a self-made expert at decoding the symbols in the new *TV Guide*. With that viewing manual in hand, he would abandon his couch position to come into the front room, and plop down in an armchair to watch "his" program. Sometimes he was there an hour before the beginning of the show that, we knew, he really wanted to watch, destroying our viewing pleasure of not just one but maybe two or three programs. We had no doubt that Dad was far less a fan of *Playhouse 90* than he was of Lawrence Welk's champagne music or of *Bowling for Dollars*.

Dad's early arrival strategy worked. Even after we got our own color set, I still spent many hours watching Dick Phillips's TV. The color on Dick's set certainly was spectacular—far better than it was on ours—but the sound on Dick's TV left a lot to be desired. And, it got pretty darned cold standing outside Dick's TV room window, in the dark, in the winter.

# CHAPTER TWENTY-SEVEN

## Winter

In Sonora, in the 1950s, winter always fell from the sky.

Spring sailed in on the crisp, cool winds of March and April that whisked our rag-tailed, plastic-coated paper kites high up into the heavens after a running start down the leeward slope of Clarence Porter's hill.

Summer began with the sharp bat-cracks of Little League baseball practice, and lasted just as long as the county fairs and family reunions held out.

Fall drifted in with our back-to-school blues, and fluttered around aimlessly in the autumn air until Halloween, when the warm days and cool nights brought down the last of the oak and maple leaves, and we awoke each morning to a thick and crunchy carpet of frost on the ground.

Winter, always the last season to arrive, usually crept into town quietly, in late November, accompanied by dwindling hours of daylight and near-teen temperatures, and lingered patiently in every corner of the community while awaiting some sign of snow.

Winter never officially settled in Sonora until the first few snowflakes fell silently from the sky.

We would usually be sitting at our custom-carved wooden desks in our elementary and junior-high classrooms, listening to still another boring lecture on some useless subject such as English, arithmetic, geography, or history, watching the last of the late-autumn leaves dance down from the big sugar maple in front of the school and fall on our shiny steel sliding board, when a single solitary snowflake would slip from the sky.

It was never missed. There was always at least one pair of eyes standing sentry against winter's welcome invasion, and the word would spread quickly around the school rooms.

"Did you see it?" someone would whisper.

"See what?" another would reply.

"It's snowing!"

"Yeah, right. It's not even cold enough yet."

"I tell you I saw a flake fall."

"The only flake around here is you."

"Okay, just watch. Look! There's another one!"

"He's right. It *is* snowing."

"IT'S SNOWING! IT'S SNOWING!" several in the class would shout.

"Children! Children! Settle down! It's only snow!"

Only snow. They never understood. In all our years, from the first to the eighth grade, I don't think we ever had a teacher—principals and substitute teachers included—who fully appreciated the world-changing importance of the winter's first snow.

This was not just the misguided flake or two that it seemed to be. This was what we had been waiting for since the day school started in September. This was the unavoidably approaching "snow days," when the school's double-doors would have to remain closed because of snow that was too deep or roads that were too slick. It was Christmas vacation, sledding all day Saturday on our Flexible Flyers, tobogganing on Heagan's Hill, ice-skating at night on Stage's frozen pond, snow forts and snowball battles, warm homes full of winking colored Christmas lights, open wood or coal fires toasting our cold, wet feet, the fir woods perfume of fresh-cut, long-needled pine trees, tons of tightly wrapped, rapidly opened presents, Santa Claus handing out stale fruits and covered two-pound baskets of tooth-sticking chocolates at the Methodist church, early evening off-key *a capella* caroling from house to house, caramel-covered apples on a pointed wooden stick for twenty-five cents at the store, and the simple fun of following the tracks of dangerous dogs, cats, moles, mice, birds, and who knows what other wild and ferocious animals over the snow-covered deserts of darkest East Sonora Africa and through the Sleepy Hollowed forests of Walt Disney.

Only snow?

We could hardly wait until recess. When the bell finally rang, all three classrooms emptied even faster than usual. Grabbing our wool and cotton coats, we ran for the exits, forgetting our gloves, never slowing to see if an unfortunate teacher had somehow failed to clear the runway. If she got splattered in the ensuing stampede, that was her problem; we had more important things on our mind.

The normal pattern of a recess in Sonora School called for all of the boys to go one way, all of the girls to go another. It was a natural segregation, with the boys having important things to do, the girls having unimportant boys to talk about. Whenever possible, most of the boys would go to the slight slope behind the school to play baseball, softball or football, or maybe even fly a kite, according to the season. Baseball could be—and usually was—played year-round. More than one white baseball would be lost in the snow every winter, not to be seen again until the next spring. Tackle football didn't really get popular with us until late October, and fizzled out when the snow got so deep that it was hard to run without falling down. But by that time we were dodging sleds and snowballs anyway, so it was time to switch sports.

Our outdoor basketball court—two steel backboards, two steel rims, no woven nets (or any others), some forty feet apart—was situated on a court of limestone and cinders. As long as you didn't fall down, it wasn't a particularly bad game. But with ten or fifteen guys on a side, and other non-players forever meandering through the playing area, it sometimes got a little confusing. We never played shirts and skins, even in summer, so it was sometimes a real challenge just to remember who was on your side. We always chose sides based on an unwritten formula that considered family income, house location, dog's name, vehicle models and number owned, and similar status symbols, including whether or not you felt like getting the snot beat out of you if you overlooked or shafted certain guys who held grudges and had time to take you out after school. But we usually played basketball only when baseball or football couldn't be played.

With fifteen minutes for morning and afternoon recess, and only one hour for lunch, during which most of us ran home for a hot meal, it was tough to get in more than a few innings of baseball at a time. We would return to the classroom with scores of 37-3, 49-5, 20-1 or something similar. The same group of guys would always be on top, and the same group of other guys would always be on the bottom. The outcome of any game was never in doubt; we could almost tell you the final score of one of our abbreviated mismatches as soon as the sides were selected. We knew who was going to hit the home runs over the metal roof of the metal school building, who was going to strike out each and every time, and who was going to catch deep fly balls or miss easy grounders nine times out of ten. Like in professional baseball today, it was not the score that mattered, but the game.

To participate in "the game," guys had to have bladders of sponge and bowels of steel. After all, one of the reasons for recess was to permit you to attend to certain bodily functions, and if you disregarded that opportunity to play baseball you could miss a whole section of Silas Marner during the next class period, or in your absence be appointed next week's road-crossing guard. (One of those consequences was, admittedly, far worse than the other.) It was always a gamble to raise your hand to be "excused" by some teachers, particularly the grumpy ones like old Alma McCance, who thought one run a month up the beaten path to the smelly boys' or girls' two-holer during "school hours" was more than adequate. If I remember correctly, Mrs. McCance (which is not what we normally called her when she wasn't nearby) kept a black, spiral-bound, simulated leather notebook in which she duly noted everyone's most personal habits from the beginning of the year to the end. Every so often she would summon us individually to her desk and show us our name in this book with gold, silver, or red stars beside it, along with hand-drawn squares that blocked out your whole year's bathroom history. With an index finger pointing to the starred evidence of your most intimate activities, she would pause and wait for you to come up with some explanation, or she would compare your stars with someone else's, and theirs were always better. It was not until many years later that I figured out that the color of the stars had nothing to do with grades or attendance. Some kids, particularly those who were highly susceptible to dysentery, seemed to get no stars at all, and learned very little, if anything at all, about Silas Marner, while others, who often were seen sitting at their desk with gritted teeth and crossed legs, had whole strings of gold and silver stars, and knew everything there was to know about good old Silas.

Regardless of our normal recess routine, it all went out the window when the first snowflakes fell. Every single kid would be standing around outside, mouth opened wide to the sky, trying to snare snowflakes before they reached the ground. It was from this neck-wrenching exercise that I learned endurance, precision, persistence, and absolute futility. I cannot remember ever having enticed a single snowflake to land anywhere near my mouth. The closest I ever came, personally, was to feel a flake or two fall cool and wet upon my cheeks, only to instantly melt and disappear.

In Sonora, it seemed like the first measurable stick-around snow of the season never fell before December. November was mainly a month of cruel temptation—snow, melt, snow, melt. December was a month of gradual accumulation, when you knew that most of the new falling snow would add to the amount that was already on the ground. You monitored each and every new inch, until there seemed to be enough to go sledding without having to be unduly concerned about frozen cow patties and unremoved rocks in the hillside cow pastures.

By early January, a few of the more adventuresome sledders would be tempted to check out the vehicle-packed ice on George Hill, but the main problem there was the sand and salt that was applied as-needed by the county highway department. George Hill was on the main road into Sonora, and the sand and salt was necessary to keep the balding tires of cars and trucks from losing their traction, which would cause some vehicles to slide back down, or even skid into Little Salt Creek at the bottom. On Heagan's hill, which was a fenced-in cow pasture just south of Sonora, there were far fewer cars. All you had to watch out for there (besides rocks, tree limbs, and frozen cow patties) were the individual members of a herd of heifers. Heagan was a dairy farmer first, a provider of hills for community sledders second.

The great thing about Heagan's hill, from the sledding standpoint, was that it was available either day or night. It was a long walk up, but a fast and fun ride down. We tended to favor a zig-zag downhill course, with a few forgotten moguls that ended with a broad right-turning sweep at the bottom next to a small creek that was occasionally frozen over. On moonlit nights, you could almost see where you were going, and the fast ride could get fairly interesting. But the best rides of all came when it was so dark that you couldn't tell a rock from a hard place or a cow from a coat rack; on such nights you always had to wear a lot of extra clothing, not so much

NIGHT SLEDDING ON HEAGAN'S HILL JW 2007

to protect you from the cold, but to cushion you against bumps and the collisions that you knew would be coming. Heagan probably wondered why he constantly had so many crippled cows, especially in the winter.

Ice-skating was an after-thought in the Sonora of the 1950s. I remember only a few nights when someone would build a bonfire on the spit of land between the two legs of Stage's north pond, and a dozen or so people would gather there to test the newly frozen ice. It was only in the coldest years, and then only in mid-January, that you felt very safe in ice-skating on this pond at the edge of Appalachia. However, we played many games of winter hockey on the shallow creeks around Sonora, where the ice was more solid but our "puck" was always as hard as a rock.

Winter was a time for fun, in the Fifties, but also a time for work. In Sonora, most of the houses were heated with coal, and that meant making two or three trips to the coal yard during the winter to haul home tons of the shaley bituminous black stuff that southeastern Ohio was famous for in energy circles. It was not the world's hottest-burning coal, but it was far and away the dirtiest, which you found out as soon as you got it home and began shoveling it out the back of your pickup truck. In a stiff wind, you often felt a strange desire to burst out in a baritone voice with the first full verse of *Old Man River.*

Many homes had a small perimeter door in the foundation that could be opened to allow coal to be shoveled down a coal chute and into a basement bin that was the closest thing to a black hole east or west of Calcutta. From there coal was carried to all of the several fireplaces and stoves in the average home, bucket by bucket. We had a stone basement, but it was more of a root cellar, with a concrete-blocked laundry room that probably seemed like a good idea at the time when Dad built it but almost never got used. In one corner of this laundry room there was a chicken-wire cage, framed with wood, which Dad had constructed with the intended purpose of capturing all of the soiled laundry that was tossed down from the bathroom above. It might have worked, if Mom had ever bothered to use it.

Cold, dark, and dank, the cellar itself had been hewn from a sandy shale stone. It made a great place to store Mom's home-canned fruits and vegetables and certain cold-preserved stock for our first-floor grocery store. Eventually, Dad built a huge bin in the basement out of one-by-twelves and two-by-fours, to hold the bushels of potatoes that we grew each year in our garden. Throughout the winter, Mom could count on these potatoes to provide a reliable foundation for any meal, and at the end of the winter we would always have some potatoes left over to be the "seed" for that fall's next crop. These potato leftovers, having had a perfect storage environment, would often have thick white sprouts two, three or even four feet long by the end of the winter. Just before harvesting our seed potato crop, we would break off the sprouts and let new "eyes" grow a quarter of an inch long or so. When the actual time for planting came, Dad and I would carry out bushel baskets of these potatoes, and cut them into pieces, each having at least one "eye". Each piece, in the cool, dark Ohio dirt in our garden, would magically turn into a full-fledged potato plant, grow green all summer, turn brown and shrivel up in the fall. When dug up, each tuber plant would have anywhere from two or three to eight or ten usable potatoes. The larger of these would go back in the bin to start the process anew. The smaller ones would soon take a trip to the table. Some we even sold in the store.

Our coal was stored in a backyard shed. A hinged side door placed well above the bed level of a pickup truck would open outward to allow us to shovel into the shed about two truckloads of coal. Since Dad always heaped a load of coal higher than the pickup truck's tailgate, there was never any way to start shoveling it without lowering the tailgate and spilling a good part of the load all over the ground, a negative result for which I was inevitably held responsible. (I'm thinking about doing a new drawing in which the blame for this, correctly, is placed on my brother Jim.) Dad was always the one who got to use the big aluminum scoop shovel. I was always tasked with picking up the coal on the ground, and was given the special challenge of tossing lumps through the shed's window without getting hit in the back of my head by Dad's swinging aluminum shovel.

Once the coal had been confined to its quarters, the next chore—at least twice a day, every day—was to carry buckets of it to our screened-in back porch for further transfer, as needed, to our kitchen stove and living room fireplace. This was how I developed my broad shoulders, strong back, and long arms, each arm gradually being lengthened by the repeated lugging of fully loaded buckets of coal. Some people used plain five-gallon metal or plastic paint cans to carry their coal. We had the official coal-carrier's bucket, a peculiar aluminum or sheet-metal design with one longer lip that allowed you to shovel ashes into the bucket, after the coal was consumed, without floating more ash dust around a room than was absolutely necessary. Coal in, ashes out, coal in, ashes out. Day in, day out. Winter after winter.

Winter was also a time for hunting and trapping. Dad did both, according to the official season, and it was apparently my solemn duty, as the only remaining son at home, to carry on some long-standing family tradition and accompany him on these outings. Lacking a certain amount of enthusiasm and ability for this enterprise, I myself should have been the first victim of any season. But when all of the shots were fired, and when all of the traps were sprung, I somehow survived to walk away relatively unscathed.

You could hunt rabbits pretty much any time you felt like it in Ohio in the Fifties, but the best time was in the winter. You didn't even have to go outside a settled area to find them. Sometimes, early on a foggy summer morning, you would see a rabbit or two cavorting on a dew-covered lawn or feasting on the still-rising proceeds of a local gardener's hard labor. In the clover and alfalfa hay fields just outside of town, they were rife. Among the cattle in pastures and amidst the briar bushes, they were a dime a dozen. But on any given day in the winter, they were almost nowhere to be found. At any other time of the year, you

178

had to try really hard not to notice a rabbit or two nearly everywhere you went; during the winter months, you actually had to hunt for the hearty little hares.

A winter hunt for rabbits was usually accompanied by dogs, in general, and by beagles, in particular. I don't know why beagles made such good rabbit dogs, unless it was because they are so low to the ground and are generally so clumsy that they will trip over a rabbit if it's anywhere within a country mile, the exact distance of which I was never able to determine. Beagles also have an excellent sense of smell. Take out of your hunting coat pocket anything that resembles food, and all of the beagles in the area will beat a path to your doorstep. When it comes to smelling out rabbits, beagles always win noses down.

When it's fairly cold, or on a blustery, snowy day, you won't find rabbits wandering around all over the place. They either hole up, backed in to a pile of logs or hidden well under the snow-loaded branches of bushes, or they make a "squat" out in broad daylight, in even the smallest clump of weeds or dried grass. And there they stay. You can almost step right on a rabbit in an open field in winter without spooking it. Even a barking dog can get within a few paces of a squatting rabbit without sending it scampering. Most rabbits seem to have been dealt a sixth sense. They have a pretty good idea of whether it's time to hold 'em, or time to fold 'em. And if they decide to fold 'em, they are going to light out like they were shot from a cannon, and run like a rabbit. I never saw a beagle chase down a rabbit, even with a head start. But that's not the dog's purpose. It's there to howl up a storm as it follows the sometimes imagined scent of a rabbit, until it gets so close that the rabbit finally gives up its warm seat in the snow and runs for its life.

For most rabbit hunters, that is when the real action begins—when the rabbit is well on its way to another day of rabbitting. You aim your shotgun—only a fool or a city slicker would use a rifle—in the general direction of where you think the rabbit might be in two or three seconds, and blast away. If you call the shot right, the rabbit will turn in the anticipated direction, will be saturated by a tight pattern of high-speed pellets, and will drop dead in its tracks. If you call the shot wrong, the rabbit will turn in the other direction, and you will stand there with a silly look on your face, having just murdered your best dog. Or you may suddenly have second thoughts about your manhood, having just been outsmarted by a hare-brained fugitive from hunting justice with four lucky rabbit's feet.

## - OF FIRES AND FOGGY MORNINGS -

Dad was seldom outsmarted. He typically had a rabbit spotted twenty yards away, had removed the safety on his shotgun, and was hoping his yelping beagle would just keep its cold wet nose out of the way long enough for him to get a shot off. I saw Dad do that time and again, but I never saw a squatting rabbit before he did. Most of the time, I couldn't even see a squatting rabbit when Dad pointed it out to me. Granted the honor of firing first, I would simply aim the barrel of my shotgun at what I thought *might* be the particular clump of grass Dad that claimed was sheltering a rabbit, close my eyes, pull the trigger on my .410, and pray to God that our two beagle warriors, Spike and Teddy, had thrown in the towel on all of this nonsense and had decided to run back home. We once walked right up on a rabbit that Dad had seen from a distance and had revealed to me, so close that I almost stepped on it before it leaped up and took almost ten bounds before Dad sent it heels over head with a blast from his 20-gauge. He could have downed it sooner, but he had to let it get far enough away to save some of its meat for the table.

Dad also hunted whitetail deer in the winter, but never (so far as I know) in Ohio. That probably explains why whitetail deer are so numerous in the state today. He always accompanied a friend or two to some other hunter's hideout near Dubois, Pennsylvania. About half the time, he drove back home with a buck deer draped over the right front fender of his car. When he didn't, he was quick to spread some cock-and-bull story about having had the biggest deer in the world in his sights when this little old crippled lady carrying a sick baby swaddled in a Red Cross blanket suddenly appeared out of nowhere, and he had to shoot between her legs in order to avoid hitting the blind man behind her, and just as he was about to shoot there was a rare total eclipse of both the sun and the moon (at the same time), and so he just missed the deer by the skin of its teeth. Or some equally unbelievable concoction. A big part of being a crack outdoorsman, apparently, is knowing how to explain the ones that got away.

When Dad wasn't hunting, in the winter, he was trapping muskrats. Just north of Sonora he had bought a five-acre cow pasture in the 1940s. There was one little creek bisecting it and another making a triangle out of its northeast corner and running under the higher Baltimore & Ohio Railroad tracks that bordered the pasture's eastern edge. This second shallow creek flowed into our property from Clarence Hanes's much larger field of weeds, having sprung from a spring at the foot of King's hill and flowed through Bob and Verna Shirer's farm. After leaving our pasture

180

and tunneling under the elevated train tracks, the creek wound through a stand of scrub brush and small trees that sheltered Sonora's number-one spot for individual and group skinny-dipping.

All along this winding little creek, thick weeds had draped down into the water, creating natural porticos for the several muskrat homes that had been dug back into both banks, and the water was cool, clear and quiet enough to provide good homes for whole families of muskrats.

Into this prime trapping grounds walked one of the most knowledgeable woodsmen Sonora has ever known. I have often wondered if Daniel Boone and Davy Crockett ever would have become so famous if Dad, too, had lived back then. But perhaps he had. (I'll have to ask Shirley MacLaine if she knew or knew of him.) He certainly shared their woodsman credentials.

So far as the muskrats were concerned, it was no contest. It is said that, in order to kill or capture an animal, you have to be able to think like that animal. Dad was the smartest muskrat that ever lived. He seemed to know every move the muskrats were going to make, hours or even days in advance. He would set a trap in some off-the-wall location that, I thought, had absolutely no chance of ever being visited by a muskrat, and the next morning there would be one in it. He could hide a steel trap in clear water so well that a muskrat who had lived all of his soon-to-be-shortened life in that water could not see it. He knew before a muskrat whether its next trip up or down stream was going to be on the high bank or the low. Any muskrat who decided to match wits with Dad went to war outgunned and outnumbered.

As Dad's only at-home son, I was apparently supposed to carry on his great tradition of woodsmanship. But first I had to be properly trained. So about every afternoon in the early winter Dad would take me down to the water to make me drink of his devine trapping knowledge. He would carefully instruct me on where to set a trap and how to hide it, which imparted critical information that I would immediately forget. We would trudge up and down the creek, in it and along it—probably in plain sight of our intended victims—and place ten or fifteen traps in what he judged to be locations of likely trapping success.

Next morning, with Dad accompanying me or not, I would have to get up well before my eyes were open, pull on some rubber gum boots that weren't warm and some heavy clothes that were still wet from the day before, and "run" our traps, checking them for innocent victims.

As often as not, I would find a trap either completely untouched or sprung but without an occupant. Such tripped traps would have to be reset, repositioned, and rehidden among the mud, weeds and cold, cold water.

Even worse, however, was when one of Dad's guesses was right, and there was a muskrat in a trap that we had set.

Most of today's computer-generated kids could not tell you how a steel trap works, or even what it looks like. It is a two-jawed contraption (sorry about that) with a round flat trip release in the center, all based on a curved hinge of steel that forms a strong spring. The whole apparatus is connected to a chain about eighteen inches long. When a victim, in this case a muskrat, steps on the trigger, the jaws snap shut, and tightly pin its trapped leg. The trap does not kill the animal, and is not actually designed to break a leg, but simply keeps it from escaping. When a trap is set, it is covered over with mud, leaves, or weeds, and the chain is secured by a sturdy, inverted tree branch, poked deep into the ground.

The best place to locate a muskrat trap is in water just deep enough to force the trapped animal to swim. Since it can't swim away, it eventually tires and drowns.

A less-preferred location is one where the trap will be stepped on by a muskrat as it leaves or enters its den or climbs up a bank to find something to eat, which is why muskrats like to live in pastures. Once snared, the animal soon realizes that it has nowhere to go, is in great pain because of the pinching steel jaws, and decides to chew its leg off to both stop the pain and make the escape.

Sometimes the muskrat will simply pull its pinched leg out of the jaws and go on living its newly lame life, until it is trapped again. That usually explained the sprung traps.

Often you will come upon a swimming muskrat that has fairly recently been trapped or a muskrat that has not completely finished chewing off its leg. These are the ones that you are forced to murder. The traditional method for murdering muskrats is to beat the animal over the head with some sort of club (a baseball bat works great) until it is dead.

With enough practice, you can kill a muskrat with just one whack, if it is properly aimed.

Back home, the morning's muskrats are skinned, stretched fur side in over long thin boards that are rounded at the top, hung on a barn or shed wall, and left to cure (dry). After a couple of weeks, the skins are sorted for size, boxed up, and sent to a buyer, who sells them to someone else, who does something useful with them—make hats for modern mountain men maybe—and you are sent a small check for your efforts. In the 1950s, each muskrat skin was worth a dollar or two. I had no trapping competition from my friends.

Sonora winters ended when all of the sledders were bored, all of the hunters and trappers had exhausted their renewable game resources, and everyone else was just sick and tired of slogging through all of the mud and slush.

Eventually, the snowflakes stopped falling from the sky, the ground's smoked white blanket washed quietly away, and the day and night temperatures rose, signaling the trees to begin their leaf-growing process and the flowers to bloom.

In a few months, it would happen all over again, Spring would be sprung, summer would come and go, fall would fall upon us, and winter would creep back into town once more, to await the first few snowflakes that would drift down and cover everything in sight with a cold but warm comforter of white. In the 1950s, Sonora never changed.

# CHAPTER TWENTY-EIGHT

# Radio Daze

I have always been interested in wireless communication. There is something fascinating about having the ability to converse without wires. With a walkie-talkie keyed to transmit you can make yourself heard miles away, by anyone with another unit that is set to receive. By using an amateur "ham" radio, you can extend your reach clear to the other side of the world. (Where another "ham" radio operator has the "cheese"?) And if you have access to a radio-telescope, which of course we all do, you can send signals way out into space, to be detected and decoded by some green horny alien in about a billion gazillion years. You can even use radio waves to travel back in time and listen to deep-space stuff that, we are encouraged to believe, ended ten minutes before it even began. Don't tell me that science isn't wonderful.

In the 1950s, I wasn't trying to set any long distance records for radio signal broadcast or reception. All I wanted to do was hear something besides static.

I got my introduction to radio electronics with a crystal diode radio kit, an entry level product like the kits that had befuddled kids of all ages over several decades of trial and error. The gift of this do-it-yourself radio followed hard on the heels of a purely mechanical erector set, and came just before I received a complete fold-up chemistry lab one Christmas. That pro lab included a real microscope, a number of precision tools, and several cork-capped glass vials of exotic powders like sodium chloride, dried and double-dehydrated boriskarloff, refined sulfur gesundtheit, and one of the most alliterative chemicals ever discovered, acetylsalicylic acid, which I would later be very disappointed to learn was nothing more than common aspirin.

After the erector set, which was basically all screws, nuts, wheels, and girders, with its own little wrenches to put it all together, I felt ready to take on more challenging assembly tasks. So my parents presented me with a box of parts and pieces that the instructions claimed could, after a certain amount of dedication and considerable time and effort, be turned into a radio. I had my doubts. For one thing, every radio that I had ever seen had included a speaker, which I thought was an extremely useful device for any audio instrument to have. My kit, instead of having a speaker, came with a little round thing that was attached by a plastic-coated wire to a plug at the end. The instructions said you were supposed to stick this round thing in your ear like a hearing aid. It had a hole in it, and the idea, apparently, was that any sound that traveled through the plug and the wire, by some means unrevealed and possibly yet to be determined, would come out the little hole and go into your ear, again by some means not specified. To get any sound through this thing, you first had to locate the proper hole to stick the plug into, making sure to put the plug in an "out" hole and not an "in" hole. It was all pretty complicated. What this thing actually did was anybody's guess.

Normal radios also had a numbered dial to spin to change from one station to the other. My kit had a two-inch tube of thin cardboard about the size of a quarter, around which you tightly wrapped a fine copper wire, placing its insulated loops as closely together as possible. You tuned in stations with this wired coil by sliding a ball bearing back and forth between two rails. While that sounds completely stupid today, back then it *also* sounded completely stupid. This part of my "radio" seemed to have a very close connection to crystal balls. There was no volume control, apparently because there would be no volume, after assembly, to be controlled. But there were several other parts and pieces that were identified in the instructions as "resistors" and "capacitors," along with a single D-cell flashlight battery. To make the manufacturer of my radio kit feel that he had not completely wasted his time, I found a place for nearly all of the parts and pieces that he had thoughtfully provided.

Having assembled this "radio" shortly after Christmas, I got my first chance to test drive it the very next Sunday afternoon when my older brother, Jim, dropped in for a visit. Jim considered himself to be our family expert on radios, since he had owned one for years. His was a compact model, some eight inches wide, five inches high and four inches deep (when the lid was closed) that he had purchased with his very first paycheck from Pollock's Jewelry in Zanesville. It had been manufactured by Zenith, who had stamped it with a small lightning bolt to let you know

The actual 1948 Zenith 4G800Z radio (No. B411165) that my brother Jim purchased with his first paycheck more than five decades ago. Apparently to atone for burning down our outhouse (for which I was always blamed), Jim gave me the radio a couple of years ago. You may remember seeing this radio sitting on the dock at Lake Tahoe in the movie, *A Place in the Sun*. It attracted teenaged bathing beauties like a magnet. I am restoring it as quickly as I can, and have high hopes that it will still work.

exactly what you were getting yourself into before you got yourself into it. Unlike my do-it-yourself model, Jim's radio had come already assembled, in a black plastic case that had a flip-up door that revealed a shiny brass grill, on which there were two flat serrated-edge knobs, one at the left, one at the right, one to control volume, and one to tune the stations. Surrounding these knobs were both lines and numbers, so you could determine just where in the radio world you were at any point in time and how loud to set the volume. In the center of Jim's set, concealed behind the shiny brass grill, was a large (3") speaker. Jim's radio had no power knob, because it switched on automatically when you flipped up the front door and allowed a spring-loaded button to rise. It did, however, have a retractable carrying handle, made of a plastic that spiraled around a springy metal band. There was an AC power cord to plug in, but you really didn't

need it because Jim's radio contained *both* a 1.5-volt D-cell *and* a 67.5-volt battery, and if you wanted to you could take this radio to the beach to listen to it. Lacking a beach, you could probably take it somewhere else, but beaches seemed to be the preferred listening sites in the newspaper and magazine advertisements of most radio companies back then. You apparently got better reception near a large body of water, or music sounded better when you were listening to it while surrounded by shapely teenaged girls in swim suits, or the water acted like a liquid crystal antenna, or something. I never quite figured it out. But I suspect that it was the possibility of attracting all of those shapely teenaged girls in swim suits that ultimately convinced Jim to buy one just as soon as he got the money.

In any event, Jim quickly became an expert with his ready-made radio. He could tune in *WHIZ* ("We're Here In Zanesville") day or night. He could tune in *WILE* ("We're In Little Emerica" –spelling didn't seem to be their strongest suit) in Cambridge, which was clear in the other direction and even farther away. Jim's radio could even pull in a station or two out of Columbus, which was more than sixty miles up Route 40 to the west. And if the wind was blowing in the right direction, and if the moon was in the proper phase, some weak signals might drift in after sunset from a few other radio stations across the state. A couple of times I heard someone talking on Jim's radio to someone else called "Bubba" and say "y'all," so I was pretty certain that it could get stations from the Deep South, perhaps from as far south of Ohio as West Virginia.

Jim became so good with his Zenith AM lightning-bolt radio that he could adjust the volume with one hand tied behind his back. He could even tune in stations with his eyes closed. It was many years before I discovered how he was able to do that. (He didn't need to actually *see* the numbers on the dials; by simply aiming his ears in a certain direction he could determine exactly how much to rotate the tuner knob to get the station he wanted. Jim always was pretty sharp.)

With such radio expertise in my very own family, I was pretty certain that Jim and I could get my new kit radio working, regardless of the number of parts and pieces that I had left out, unbeknownst to Jim.

We fiddled with the ball-bearing slide tuner for several minutes in my second-floor bedroom, but were not able to pick up anything but static. I was about ready to give up and go back to my less-complicated erector set when Jim said he thought we needed a longer aerial. A smaller relative of our tall TV mast antenna, the "aerial" for my radio was a thin wire about three feet long that you stretched out and pointed at a right angle to the direction of the radio station that you were trying to receive. The theory was that any radio waves that were flying through the air over the no man's land between you and some station would somehow be spotted by this little wire, would be shot at and forced down, and would be marched back across more-friendly lines for decoding and interrogation. Frankly, I was more inclined to believe that our failure to hear anything from my radio had less to do with the length of the aerial than with all of the parts and pieces that I had not yet installed, both in the interest of expediency and to save time.

But Jim was the family radio expert, and if he said we needed a longer aerial, who was I to argue? I was a rank amateur in radio, and was still wet behind the ears when it came to shapely teenaged girls who had been beached in skimpy bathing suits. The problem we faced was where to find a longer wire. While Jim went downstairs to the kitchen and searched through the sliding catch-all drawer in Mom's bread, silverware, and condiments cabinet, I decided to go ahead and install some more of those leftover parts and pieces. I didn't have enough of them left over to build anything else anyway, so I figured they might as well be placed where the instructions advised. You never can tell, when you're assembling kits like this, when you might get lucky by following the directions. Jim finally found about twenty feet of insulated bell wire, all tangled up and knotted into a ball, which seemed to be the normal condition for any wire or string that was found in Mom's catch-all cabinet drawer. While Jim unraveled the wire rat's nest, I rosin-soldered in the radio's final parts and pieces.

To achieve maximum reception sensitivity of the kit radio's wire aerial, the instructions called for it to be strung out horizontally. This was fine with a three-foot length of wire. It was a major mathematical enigma when you had a 20-foot length of wire to lay out flat in a 10-by-12 bedroom. Jim, our family radio expert, quickly came up with the idea of feeding the longer wire out my opened bedroom window. That solution would have worked pretty well, except for the fact that the wire then dropped straight down, two full stories, and was thus oriented vertically instead of horizontally. Jim soon solved this new problem by locating some additional wire, splicing it onto the end of the first piece, stretching the whole wire over to Dick Phillips's house, and wrapping it around one of his wooden porch posts. Since Dick was even more of a radio expert than Jim, I figured that some of Dick's vast radio knowledge might be absorbed by the wire and give us even better reception, so I went along with Jim's latest hare-brained idea. (Since Jim had earlier been responsible for burning down our family outhouse, my confidence in his constant schemes had all but disappeared. Somehow, I had gotten blamed for that unfortunate fire, which at least had prompted Dad to build an indoor bathroom.)

## - RADIO DAZE-

Back in the bedroom, we began to hear static as soon as we started sliding the silver bearing back and forth across the wire coil. Or at least Jim did. Since there was only one thing to stick in your ear, and since we had almost four ears between us, some of us did not get to listen to our own radio immediately. This seemed to be a recurring phenomenon between older and younger brothers in our family. Finally, after carefully tuning the ball-bearinged coil for the maximum signal strength, Jim turned the earplug over to me, with a grin on his face that obviously indicated some major positive development.

Unbelievably, there was something there.

"What the heck is that?" I questioned.

"It's the Naval Observatory Station," Jim replied.

"In Ohio? I didn't even know we had a navy. All I hear is some clicking. Tick-tock. Tick-tock. Tick-tock."

"That's the time."

"What do you mean, 'That's the time'? If I wanted the time, I could just look at my watch. I don't want the time. I want a radio station."

"Fred, this isn't that kind of radio. You can't get regular stations with this kind of radio. This is a short-wave radio."

"Well, how do we make the short waves longer?"

"You can't do that," Jim said, with a hint of his growing exasperation. "It only tunes in the short-wave band, not AM."

"Well...can we get anything besides this ticking and tocking?"

"Not without a longer aerial. Besides, we don't have enough power."

"Maybe we need a bigger battery."

"That wouldn't work. It's the wrong kind of power."

"Where do we get the right kind of power?"

"We don't!" Jim replied, sounding even more frustrated. "The whole radio would have to be rebuilt! The time is about all you are going to get with this radio."

I pondered our predicament for a while, thinking that I wasn't much interested in listening to a radio that could only tell time. A few seconds later, however, some guy came on the air and said the time at the tone would be three-twenty-five. There was a tone, and then the tick-tock-ticking resumed.

"What time do you have?" I asked Jim. He glanced down at the watch that was strapped to his left arm.

"It's three-twenty-seven."

"Well, either your Mickey Mouse watch is wrong, or this guy doesn't know what he's talking about."

"My watch must be wrong. He's with the government."

And that's how I learned that the government is always right.

We spent some additional minutes tuning the coil and readjusting the amount of droop in the aerial wire. Suddenly, I heard some Spanish music drifting in and out, and another fellow's voice came on.

"Hey!" I immediately notified Jim, "We've got something else. Now there's some guy speaking Spanish." I passed the earplug to him, and he held it up to his ear.

"It must be coming from Mexico," he said, in his expert opinion, "or Cuba."

"In either case, that's pretty far away," I informed him. "It's a lot farther to Cuba than it is to Zanesville. Your fancy radio won't reach to Cuba. It just barely picks up that guy Bubba in West Virginia."

"I keep telling you, Fred, this is a short-wave radio."

"Which means what? Seems to me like I have a better radio than you do. All you can pick up with yours is teenaged girls at the beach in swim suits. Mine will reach all the way to Cuba, or maybe even to Mexico."

## - RADIO DAZE-

"It's not better, you idiot. It's just different. I have a better radio."

"Just because it has knobs and a speaker? Who needs a speaker? I can hear just fine through this dumb little thing with a hole in it. You think yours is better because you can take it to the beach? How often do you go to the beach in the winter? If your radio won't even reach to Cuba, I'd say mine is better. And what if you need the correct time? You couldn't get it on yours. I can get the correct time every minute of the day, right from Ohio's very own navy."

Jim just stared at me, with reddening cheeks and a wild, funny look on his face, and shook his head. He must have decided that he was fighting a losing battle, because he said nothing else and soon went downstairs to watch TV with Mom and Dad, which was always a clear marker for a devastating defeat or outright desperation. I continued fine-tuning the coil on my radio, and eventually came across another station, with a husky voiced woman. She appeared to be a blue-eyed blonde in a black silk dress and red patent-leather shoes, wearing a string of white pearls around her neck and no wedding ring on her finger. She was speaking something that sounded like German. At least she was saying words like "dees" and "ders" and "doze." She also was using words that took up most of the line in a yellow notebook tablet, like "ooberammerglauben-steadermachen-whatshisface." Germans, I had already discovered, always used a lot of incredibly long, hyphenated words. This woman definitely wasn't from West Virginia, nor from Cuba either. She was probably a spy who was transmitting to or from Germany. Germany, I had just learned in geography class, was almost halfway around the world. If my radio could reach clear to Germany with just a single D-cell flashlight battery, I thought, how far could it reach with real house current? Probably all the way around the world, maybe even to the moon or the sun. I could become world-famous for receiving the first radio signals from outer space. They would name electric companies and maybe even cars after me. I would study myself in history books, and have to go on lecture tours around the world. Was longer radio communication merely a matter of putting more pedal to the metal? Rigging up an old AC power cord to the battery contacts on my kit radio, I decided to find out.

When I plugged the thick brown AC power cord into the nearest open wall socket, there was no question that Jim had the better radio. All I had left of mine now was a pile of smoking parts and pieces. My bedroom smelled so bad that I had to sleep downstairs for the next two nights, haunted by the nightmare of a big bang and a blinding flash of light that was even more exciting than the blue-eyed blonde from Germany. I had instantly lost her, the guy from Cuba, the correct time from Ohio's very own navy, and even all of the static. The small hole in the tiny plastic earplug had been fused completely closed, which I thought went a long way towards explaining why my left ear felt like it was on fire and my normally horizontal hair was singed, smoking, and standing on end.

THE BURNING PORCH POST
JW 2006

I went over and fully opened the single window to air out the dense black smoke in my bedroom. Over at Dick Phillips's house and radio/television repair shop, I immediately noticed, they were putting out a fire. One of Dick's wooden porch posts had somehow burst into flame, apparently having been struck by some freakish winter bolt of lightning or something. (The incriminating wire between his porch post and my bedroom window had instantly disintegrated.) Dick was standing in his front yard looking up at his flaming porch post in confusion, stunned that such a fire could break out in mid-winter without any apparent reason. All of the others around him were trying to put out the fire before it could spread from the porch to the house. As the smoke cleared away from my bedroom window, I could see other faces around Dick's burning porch post that I recognized, including my brother Jim's. It was a good thing that Jim had rushed over there to help, I thought. Jim was an expert on fires. He had been building fires for years.

## - RADIO DAZE-

Once the smoke had completely vented, I closed the window, and went back over to my scorched and smelly pile of parts and pieces that used to be a radio. Since Mom and Dad seldom entered my room, I felt confident that I would not have to come up with some kind of story to explain what had happened to this particular Christmas present. But the acrid odor from the fried electrical components was going to be something else; the fumes would soon permeate the entire house, and I had a real and growing concern for the continued health of Mom's caged yellow canary downstairs in the kitchen. Would it soon succumb to the toxic fumes, like one of those condemned test canaries in the coal mines? There was no doubt that those vicious vapors would soon drift downstairs and cause a real sticky wicket for me. Dad was already starting to get suspicious about seemingly hearing the engine of his Marilyn Monroed Pontiac Star Chief running in the garage during his daytime pre-workshift naps, when he (apparently) had the only set of ignition keys.

And then there was the outhouse fire. Always the outhouse fire.

Suddenly, I knew I had the way out of this one.

Who had come up with that crazy idea in the first place of using a longer aerial wire to extend the range of my new clock radio?

Not me.

And who had looked for and finally found all of that longer wire in Mom's kitchen catch-all drawer?

Not me.

And who had extended that now disintegrated wire out my bedroom window, had stretched it clear over to poor Dick Phillips's house, and had wrapped it around poor Dick's now destroyed wooden porch post?

Not me.

So who was *really* to blame for this latest conflagration that had already caused so much property damage and would probably produce an extremely fatal respiratory illness for Mom's caged yellow canary?

Not me.

Time to get out the old drawing pad.

193

# CHAPTER TWENTY-NINE

# The Lost Dog

The search began in mid-morning. It was unusual for this dog to be wandering around anywhere alone. It was highly unusual for that to be happening on a cold winter's day.

A quick search of the neighborhood was fruitless. There were a lot of tracks, and many fresh dog turds, but nothing to indicate unquestionably that Pepi had been there.

It was not that Pepi could not protect himself. Many times over the years he had gone into a dogfight equally matched, or even out-numbered, and had emerged victorious—bloodied to be sure, but clearly the victor. And he was not likely to investigate the deadly piles of poison that were sometimes mysteriously placed around the neighborhood by ill-tempered property owners who didn't care for dogs, didn't care for cats, and didn't care much for you either, when it came right down to it. No, it was not likely that Pepi had been poisoned.

So the dog's disappearance remained a mystery. Never before had he wandered away from home and stayed missing for hours. Repeated whistles and calls by name proved to be a waste of time; if Pepi were within earshot, he certainly would be coming home. He was neither.

By early afternoon the situation had gotten critical. A new winter storm was closing in and the temperature soon would be dropping. Exposed overnight to the worsening elements, the dog could die, particularly if he had been running hard and had gotten overheated. And the deeper the snow, the more difficult it would be for him to travel the—what? miles?—to get back home.

## - THE LOST DOG-

The solution was obvious. The dog had to be found, and that had to happen before the night set in. He bundled up, grabbed his dad's old binoculars, told his mom where he was going and set out in mid-afternoon. As best he could, the young boy followed various sets of slowly fading footprints in the snow, hoping that one of the paths would lead to the dog, but fearing what he would find. In an expanding pattern he searched every nearby trail, then decided to head up the hill. Perhaps Pepi had gone off into the woods, had gotten trapped in some barbed wire, had fallen and couldn't get up, had broken a leg or something. Perhaps he could not return home even if he wanted to.

A likely set of footprints went straight up the barbed-wire fence line towards Ora and Minnie Reed's hilltop house, then veered off into the woods to the north. He followed this descending trail as it wound pointlessly among the briar bushes, amidst the maples, oaks, locusts, pines, elms, and hickories, down across the frozen creek, and on to the west. This dog—the right one?—had not stopped, nor had it even slowed to investigate such temptations as rabbit squats and sprinklings and droppings—the spoor of other animals. It had simply meandered across the hills and valleys, in and out of the woods and harvested cornfields, through briar patches, and over small fallen trees, seemingly without purpose. Where was it going? What was it after? Was there any pattern to its wandering?

He followed the dog tracks in the falling snow for hours, and what seemed like for miles. On the highest points of the hills, he would pull out his dad's old binoculars and scan the surroundings, but he never once saw any dog, nor even any wild animal, other than an occasional flitting starling or puffed-up sparrow. It was as though winter had concealed all of the animal life that he knew must be there under a big blue-white blanket.

The night was coming on. In defeat, he decided to head for home. Maybe he would cross the dog's return path along the way. Maybe Pepi would be waiting, warm but chastened by the living room fire when he walked in. Maybe he had simply gone down the street and visited a lady friend, and was now curled up by the warm coal stove with a silly smile on his face, recalling the day's amorous adventure.

The snow fell more heavily as he trudged along, feeling the increasing cold and dampness soak through his leather boots and cotton socks, work its way up the legs of his denim blue jeans, and penetrate his whole body. He was suddenly very cold. No normal person, he thought,

195

would be out here in this snowstorm, going up and down these hills, in eight or ten inches of snow, looking for a dog that probably hadn't roamed more than a few hundred feet from home anyway while he, in vain, had roamed for miles.

He missed the dog. He missed it badly. The dog had been a member of the family for many years—it was now past middle-age, which was who knew what in dog years—and it had always been close by, in the house, in the yard, in the garden, in the fields. The dog had gone everywhere with them in the front seat of their various vehicles, perched attentively and imperiously while it peered through the windshields and windows at life of lesser station, particularly at the other dogs and cats in the neighborhood with whom he had gotten acquainted over the years. Pepi was more than a family pet; he was a best friend.

Night had almost fallen by the time he walked in the back porch door, stomping the frozen clinging snow from his wet boots and stiff blue-jeans. An empty coal bucket was waiting on the porch to be filled, so he took it to the shed and shoveled it full of coal before carrying the bucket back to the house.

His mother was in the kitchen, cooking supper on the Westinghouse electric range when he entered. He could tell by her expression that Pepi had not returned.

"See anything of him?" he asked, already aware of the answer.

"No one has seen any sign of him," she replied. "I've asked everyone who's come into the store today. Your dad has been out looking for him in the truck three or four times, but he hasn't been able to find him either. Pepi's just gone. Maybe somebody picked him up and took him."

He had thought about that same possibility, and several others, while searching the surrounding woods and fields. It didn't make any sense that someone would want to steal an older dog for a pet. And Pepi certainly would not have been kidnapped as a hunting dog. But if the pet had in fact been picked up, at least he might end up in a good home, and would soon adapt to a new owner. Pets were fickle that way. They could live their whole life with one person, and then switch loyalty to someone else almost overnight. They were quick to adopt whoever fed and cared for them, freed them from pain, made friends with them. It was not the best possible outcome, but it was a far better end result than having Pepi freeze to death or die alone, in pain or poisoned. He would at least survive.

# - THE LOST DOG-

It was not a very pleasant night. After a tasteless supper, the usual hours in front of the fire and TV were filled with thoughts of the dog not the warmth and the programs. When it came time for bed he was still distracted; he had checked the back porch and sidewalk a half-dozen times during the evening, firmly convinced each time that he had heard a scratching, but of course he hadn't. He was still thinking about the dog as he drifted off to a troubled sleep.

He awoke the next morning with Pepi still on his mind. He had decided, in between his dreams and his nightmares, that he was going to go through the same search pattern as yesterday again, first covering the yards and streets and alleys around home, paying particular attention to all of the open sheds where an injured dog might have taken shelter overnight, then search the same fields and woods once more. If he couldn't find Pepi alive, maybe he could at least find his frozen body and give the dog a decent burial.

Dejected, and knowing that all of his further efforts would probably be futile, he rolled out of bed, and was instantly chilled by the cooler air. Removing the top and bottom of his cotton pajamas, leaving only the cotton briefs from J. C. Penney's, he pulled on a long-sleeved shirt, a fresh pair of white cotton socks, and some clean denim jeans. And then he sensed it. Something in his bedroom was not the way it had been when he had gone to bed. Something, somehow, was different. He looked around. The bedroom door was still closed. The early morning light slid dimly through the curtains that covered the single window. It had to be something else.

At the foot of the bed, on the rag throw-rug, was the dog, sound asleep, apparently very tired, but seemingly none the worse for wear. Nothing looked broken; there appeared to be no blood stains; his white fur was noticeably unruffled. Considering his good condition, the dog could have spent the whole day yesterday indoors. He leaned down and petted Pepi's head gently, knowing that he did not have to "let a sleeping dog lie." This dog would not bite him, even by accident, even if stirred unexpectedly from a sound sleep.

Pepi's eyes opened slowly, and revealed a feeling of guilt mixed with foolhardiness. Without a doubt, the dog knew very well that he had caused everyone considerable grief, but only he would ever know why.

But the boy didn't care. He didn't place any blame on the dog, and he wasn't going to ask any difficult questions. It was more than enough that his friend had come home, safe and sound. He sat and watched the dog return to the sleep of sheer exhaustion for several minutes, while the tears welled slowly in his eyes.

**Pepi –The Lost Dog**

# CHAPTER THIRTY

# My Sister's Wedding

In the 1950s, I had one older brother, Jim, and two older sisters, Eileen and Pat. Even today, more than fifty years later, I still do.

All three of my siblings were much older than I was in the Fifties, and probably still are. Having moved from Ohio to Wyoming more than twenty years ago, I seldom get a chance to see them. When I was just beginning my education at Sonora Elementary School, they had already completed theirs at New Concord High. Our kids are now young adults; their kids matured long ago. Not much has changed.

Even in the 1950s, I had only occasional contact with my brother and sisters. They seemed to be much like the customers who drifted like wraiths in and out of our store. They would be around, and then they would be gone, and everything would be pretty much as it was before they came. We never had the close sibling relationships that would have developed with all of our ages being closer together. They were closely born. I always had the sneaking suspicion that I was the result of some sort of accident, showing up as I did several years after all of them had left the building even before Elvis.

Jim, following high school, had entered the Army, and had been sent to Korea to fight in a war that some people said didn't really exist. He returned home in 1951 with a non-existent hearing problem caused by the non-existent pounding of the non-existent guns that he was firing in a non-existent self-propelled artillery unit. He soon married the daughter of a grocer in nearby Norwich, Carol Morgan, and they went off to start a new life together. My younger older sister, Patricia Lou, had found her true love only a couple of miles down the East Pike, at the farm home of Harmon and Beulah Brock, and had eloped early one Sunday morning with their tall son, Herbert. My older older sister, Eileen, after first

working in Zanesville for Vance's women's clothing store and Best's Jewelry, had somehow gotten attached to a former Zanesville Golden Gloves champion from one of the rougher and tougher neighborhoods in Zanesville. One day Dave and Eileen also decided to get married.

It must have been one night in the winter that Eileen's wedding was held, in the South Zanesville home of the Rev. George Wraith. At some point Dave and Eileen moved in to a big frame house on Market Street in Zanesville, where Greenlawn Avenue Y's with Market Street, at what used

**The only known photograph of the four children of Carl A. and Edith D. Whissel, probably taken by Mom with her Kodak Brownie Hawkeye in our living room just before Christmas in the mid-1950s. Pat is at left, Eileen at right. In the middle is my brother Jim, who burned down our outhouse and fricasseed a front porch post at the home of our neighbor, Dick Phillips. (*See Chapter 28: "Radio Daze."*)**

to be Adornetto's Pizzeria. I remember very little of my sister's wedding, but I have a much better recollection of the reception that followed in Sonora at our home.

There were, of course, a lot of happy people mingling in our front living room and our adjoining dining room, but their faces are now but a blur. I don't really remember who was there. I have a stronger impression of the music which was coming from the one-at-a-time square box record player that was set atop the long chest of drawers that was made of the same genuine mahogany veneers as our sturdy dining room table. At either end of this big, two-doored, four-drawered piece of furniture, in the exact center of stiffly starched doilies that Mom herself had crocheted, stood the ugliest unintentional art deco lamps that anyone in the civilized world up to that point had ever seen. Not only did these lamps hurt your

eyes even to look at them, but they provided only a dim amount of usable light in our darkened dining room. Mom must have bought them with some misguided intent of using them to achieve a certain amount of romantic ambiance in the room. All I can remember is that, when only these two ugly lamps were lit for room light, it was kind of hard to see.

I don't know exactly where these two lamps had come from, or precisely when they had arrived, but they haunted our house for decades. Made of cheap cut glass, as fake as a three-dollar bill, each of these lamps had a many bubbled base, like it was made out of marbles. The upright center shaft of striated glass hid a brass conduit, inside of which were the dual Siamese-twinned strands of an electrical cord that ended at a low-wattage bulb in a globe-type top—open to the heavens—that took the shape of a tulip. All around the lower edge of this tulip, which was appropriately tinted a purplish red, hung long, sharp, clear, crystalline daggers (or at least that's what they most resembled), each hooked to the base of the tulip with a twist of tiny wire. When the wind blew, these hanging daggers swayed up against each other and tinkled, revealing the apparent real purpose of the ugly lightless lamps as wind chimes. Unfortunately, there never was much wind breaking in our dining room, except after one of Mom's heavy holiday meals, so the lamp chimes usually had to be manually operated. In order to hear them tinkle, you had to jiggle the whole lamp or the daggers by hand.

Between the lamps at this evening reception, an invisible Gene Autry sang such all-time favorites as *Frosty, the Snowman* and *Rudolph, the Red-Nosed Reindeer* on a red-labeled 78 r.p.m. (Columbia?) record that we had owned for a couple of centuries. Since we played this ancient Gene Autry record only during the winter, especially around Christmas, my recollection of Eileen's wedding being at this time of year would seem to be pretty sound.

**Pepi and Uncle Dave. (Uncle Dave is at rear.) Photo by my sister Eileen in Laredo, Texas, when Dave was in the Air Force.**

After he punched his way into our family, my brother-in-law, Dave Steinman, a chunky, crew-cut sort of individual, went to work for Saup's Roofing in Zanesville. Uncle Dave liked wearing black Wellington boots, driving sporty cars like a 1957 Bel Air Chevrolet and a Ford Thunderbird convertible and getting me down on the floor and tickling me until I either peed my pants or cried, whichever came first. At the roofing company, he rose quickly to something like a foreman. Either before or after this job ascension Dave spent some time in the Air Force, and served mainly at the base in Laredo, Texas, where he and Eileen acquired a small, sickly pup named Pepi that they brought back to Ohio with them when Dave exited the service. This completely white dog, a mixed breed with a natural stub of a tail, was instantly adopted by Dad, nursed back to robust health, and went everywhere he did for many years afterwards. Pepi was the smartest dog we ever had in our family. He barked in only two languages, but he understood about five, and he could always be seen sitting beside Dad in his old truck as he went down the highway, helping

202

Dad with his driving directions and making sure that all of the other neighborhood dogs and cats—particularly the cats—stayed out of Dad's way.

Dave was the only person who ever seriously tried to drown me.

Whenever we went to Cutler Lake, a favorite swimming hole some miles southeast of Zanesville, Dave would always try to goad me into deeper water than I could handle, then dunk me. This would have been fine, had I known how to swim, but it was absolutely terrifying, when I didn't. Every time I turned around Dave would be there trying to dunk my donut. I washed down so much water during these occasional outings that they had to refill the lake after we left. But that wasn't so bad, until I started to receive water bills in the mail. Then they began to include an extra charge for missing fish, since you could both swim and fish in Cutler. At that point I just stopped going there. I didn't even like to eat fish; I certainly wasn't going to pay for them—particularly when they weren't even cooked.

Dave's constant dunkings left a deep psychological scar on me, and it was years later before I forcefully taught myself how to swim—in a shallow pond, on my own, well away from any potential dunkers. I was willing to go anywhere else with Dave—we often went in to Zanesville's Municipal Auditorium to watch the professional wrestlers fake it—but not to any place with water, like a lake or a pool. I had paid more than my fair share of water bills to the people at Cutler Lake, and enough was enough.

## - OF FIRES AND FOGGY MORNINGS -

At some point, Dave and Eileen moved to a small house in Sonora, about a block away from our store. I have no idea what prompted him to do it, but he somehow became the coach of our sorry school basketball team. I can't remember ever winning any basketball games, but we all chipped in and bought Dave a thank-you pair of tennis shoes anyway.

Dave also was the only person who ever called me by my real first name, William (after the paternal grandfather that I never met), and I think he did it more out of meanness than the novelty. He knew I didn't like the name, so he tossed it around whenever he could, sort of an epithet, calling me William instead of Fred at every opportunity.

We finally got rid of old Dunkin' Dave. For reasons that probably had nothing to do with me, or to Dave's dunkings and his constant name-calling, Dave and my sister Eileen divorced after some years of a childless marriage. Dad and Mom were sorry to see him go. I

Uncle Dave gets new tennies from the ace Sonora b-ball team. From left, David Francis (partly hidden), the author, Harold West, Bobby Jones, Paul Jones, Tommy Russell, Bobby Shirer, and Harry Filkill. Little Harry, for some reason, was our center. In this photo, taken by my sister Eileen, Harry appears smaller here than he actually was.

wasn't especially overjoyed about it, either, because Dave and I actually had a relatively good relationship, except for all of the tickling, dunkings, and name-calling. At some point we learned that Dave had finally taken over the roofing company, and was running it successfully.

After Dave and Eileen's divorce, I never saw him again. I was reading the Zanesville *Times Recorder* one day and noticed a short story near the bottom of a page saying he had suffered a fatal heart attack while playing golf at a course near Newark. It was a shock to the system that someone so close to us, while no longer a titled member of our family, had passed away, and we would not even have known about it if I had not accidentally read the brief item in the newspaper. We discovered the notice of Dave's death too late to attend his funeral, so we did not have a chance to pay our last respects to him in person. In Dave's honor, however, I immediately placed the newspaper on our kitchen table, went over to the sink, drew a full glass of water, and took such a huge swig that I almost choked on it. I'm sure old Dunkin' Dave would have appreciated the gesture.

IT IS NOT TRUE THAT I ONCE SANK A BASKET FOR THE OPPOSING TEAM. AS I RECALL, THAT WAS ACTUALLY MY BROTHER, JIM.

# CHAPTER THIRTY-ONE

# The General Store

In the 1950s, there were two general stores in Sonora. Eldon Spicer's big brick building was located on the northwest corner of the southeast intersection of Main and First Streets. Whissel's Grocery was on the southwest corner of Sonora Road at the Webster Street intersection. The two stores were not just diametrically opposite, but differed in business character as well.

Spicer's General Store carried a line of wares that was nearly the same as ours—canned goods, meats, cereals, candy, soda pop, ice cream, cigars, cigarettes, fresh fruits, vegetables, baked goods, household bleaches and cleansers, snack items—the usual home goods and merchandise that one would expect to find in a general store in a rural setting. It even had the tall square globe-topped gas pumps out front that every rural store had to have at the time, apparently in keeping with some unwritten rule. (Spicer sold Texaco products; we sold those branded Standard Oil.) But to all of the neighborhood kids, there was one clear distinction between Spicer's store and ours. They stocked comic books, and we did not. For ten or fifteen cents you could get enough *Superman* or *Red Ryder* entertainment at Spicer's to keep you occupied for a whole afternoon. There was nothing better on a hot summer day than to climb up into a cool leafy apple tree, like the one in our backyard, with a comic book in one hand and a cold Coke or Pepsi in the other, find a good safe perch in its gnarly limbs, and imagine yourself saving the world as some comic book character; there was nothing worse, however, than falling asleep while doing so and tumbling out of the tree.

I always thought Spicer's store was a bit stuffy. We really didn't know Eldon and Elsie Spicer all that well, at least we didn't have much social contact with them. Eldon was a tall man, built nearly like the sturdy but lanky Fred Peregory *(See Chapter Twelve: "Peregory's Pennies")*; Elsie was thin and short (like Mom), and always seemed to wear a hair net. Whenever I entered their store, almost always, the atmosphere seemed cold and impersonal.

An interior view of our grocery/post office/service station store as it would have been in the 1950s, from a 1979 colored pencil drawing by the author. Dad is at the main counter, Mom is sweeping the pine-board floor, Grandma Jones is entering. At top right is the highly secure Sonora Post Office. To the right of Mom are racks of pastries and bread, with our ice cream case behind them. At the bottom left are glass candy cases, with a potato chip rack between Dad and Mom and a rack of Burpee's seeds over her right shoulder. The left (north) wall contains cereals, soups, canned fruits, canned vegetables, Jell-O, catsup (and ketchup), cake mixes, cooking oils, canned milk, coffee, cigars, and cigarettes. (We apparently sold a lot of stuff that started with the letter "c".) The home of Jack and Alma Greiner is visible through the window, as is the author on his Whizzer, coming up Webster Street. Not shown is our outhouse, which Jim burned down.

Either Eldon or Elsie was always in their store—but seldom both—but they never seemed to say very much, or try very hard to help you find what you came in for. I generally just bought a comic book or two and left, without making a whole lot of conversation.

Whissel's Grocery, on the other hand, was as close to a community center as the Sonora of the 1950s had, other than the elementary school, where general meetings were a bit more organized. Not only was it fully stocked with the same wares as Spicer's, and not only did it have the mandatory gas pumps in front, but it also housed the fourth-class post office that provided a vital government service to town and country residents for miles around.

Pre-1950 photo of our store.

Dad had been Sonora's postmaster since he opened Whissel's Grocery in the 1940s, and in 1945 took over the local postal duties from Al Banyai (later Bane), who also ran Sonora's post office from his home, across from Charlie and Edna Huffman's up by the church. (Al Banyai had been Jim's scoutmaster—and Jerry Ramsey's; turns out I was following in Jim's footsteps, since Mom also took him in to Bintz's for his

During the early 1950s.

uniform, in the late Thirties, and he also endured a tough winter campout at the same Camp Whatchamacallit, which he identifies as Camp Zane. Small world.) I have no idea exactly why and how Dad became a government employee, for I never asked him, but it turned out to be an act of marketing genius. Sonora residents could get their gasoline and groceries anywhere they pleased, including Spicer's General Store, but they could pick up their daily mail only at Whissel's Grocery. While they were picking up their mail or buying their stamps, they could not help but

208

notice all of the other household goods that they needed to buy, and they didn't have to walk clear down to Spicer's or drive all the way in to Zanesville (at least seven miles) to do their shopping.

Dad's official government day began early each morning, with only Sundays excepted, when he met the westbound mail train at the wooden platform south of the old Keystone feed mill, on the southeast side of the tracks. A small train station shed, on an elevated platform, with eaves so long that they made the building look too small for the roof, had been built right next to the rails, halfway between Clarence Wheeler's house and that

Dad, right, hands rural carrier Charlie Oliver a Post Office Department certificate allowing him to retire. Behind them are the 99 glass-fronted pigeon holes that held mail for Sonora residents. Our box, No. 84, always held a lot of mail. The post office no longer exists, but the pigeon holes are possessed by my brother Jim, who burned down our outhouse, set fire to a porch post owned by our neighbor, and may have had something to do with the disastrous Keystone feed mill fire.

of Mom's aunt, Ida White. Attached to the platform on the railroad side was a tall pivoting arm, on which Dad hung our locked bags of outgoing mail. As the mail train slowed to a near stop, a mechanical grabber on a special mail car would snatch the suspended bags from the arm, while a mail handler inside the car would toss off bags of incoming mail. At certain times, such as the spring days when cardboard-boxed pallets of chicks and ducklings needed to be given special handling, the train would come to a complete short stop while the outgoing and incoming parcels were exchanged.

The heavy canvas bags of mail that were picked up and delivered by the train were always sealed with a tough leather strap that encircled their neck. The strap was then secured with a thin, multi-riveted lock (stamped "U. S. Post Office Department") that was looped through a metal hasp eye.

One-half of the actual sign that used to hang from the porch roof in front of our store. (The other board said "Sonora, OH" or, much later, "2545 Sonora Road.") I never knew the post office sign was still around until a few years ago, when it was given to me by my brother Jim, who said he was not even present at these fires: Frank Nolan's house, Russ Francis's house, Keystone feed mill, John Galloway's barn, Carl Whissel's outhouse. He seems to have no recollection at all of setting fire to Dick Phillips's porch post. He does claim partial responsibility for training the Perry Township Volunteer Fire Department, which was formed when Jim took forever getting Norwich's 1941 tanker truck to Ora Reed's nighttime house fire. My uncle, Dunkin' Dave, had already run in to the burning house and rescued a guy who had caught fire while replacing a countertop. My sister, Eileen, rushed him to the hospital in their 1957 Chevy. Jim, incidentally, believes he is still in the U.S. Army (at age 78). When he left the service in 1951, with an honorable "separation," he says he needed four years of inactive duty to get an honorable "discharge." Unfortunately, before he got that discharge the *records office burned down* (Jim claims he had nothing to do with it). So the Army apparently listed him as AWOL, and must still be looking for him. Now that they know where to find him, I guess Jim will soon be reporting in. I sure hope his field artillery captain knows what he's doing when he orders Jim to "FIRE!"

There must have been a universal unlock code for these mail bag locks since Dad's single key opened every bag that was thrown off the trains, and someone else in the first-class office in Zanesville must have been able to do the same with all of Sonora's bags.

Once he brought the mail bags to the store, Dad would unlock them and pour their bundled contents all over a sorting counter in the ten-by-twelve area of the store that was officially designated as "U. S. Post Office, Sonora, Ohio." For years, nothing else demarcated this government-leased section of our store except a wood-and-glass pigeonhole structure, where postal patrons could see their glass-fronted numbered box among the ninety-nine that were available, and know immediately whether they had any mail. As an extra added benefit to curious Sonora residents, they were also able to peer into everybody else's box, and maybe even determine the sender by the color of the envelope, or see a return address. Thus the fires of gossip were fueled by noting who was getting mail, who was not, and where it was coming from. At ninety degrees, and next to the "boxes," there was another wooden sorting table, this one with a closed-back bank of pigeonholes, where Charlie Oliver, the rural mail carrier, could sort his RFD post and parcels into the routes that he would run up through "the country." Charlie was the one, each spring, who delivered peeping chicks.

Big-city progress came to Sonora in the latter half of the Fifties when Dad was instructed to make the post office area more secure. He erected a wood-framed, chicken-mesh screen around it, and installed a Dutch door, which he made from pine one-by-sixes and secured with the smallest size of sliding-bolt door locks available. This tight security system meant that any passing felon would have to use a pair of dull wire cutters or accidentally lean against the top Dutch door in order to break in to the post office after hours. Of course, that assumed that any would-be burglar would be inept enough not to think about smashing one of the large glass windows that made up virtually one whole wall of the post office—and the entire front of our store. It also assumed that there was actually something in the post office that the crook would be interested in stealing. At about the same time that Sonora's post office became "secure," by Dad's definition,

Coffee, tea, and me. Open for business close to Christmas.

211

the government awarded it a "zip code," namely 43785, although I don't think that was equally a matter of national security.

Mom and Dad, in one of their more romantic poses. (I had to keep asking them to get closer, get closer.) Mom was often dressed as above, for church, bingo, and other life-threatening events. Dad wore his only suit maybe once a year. Before he would dress up for this photo I had to give back the two shotguns and fishing rod he gave me to settle a lawsuit. *(See: Chapter 13: "The Fishermen.")*

Since Dad was often going on or coming off a second-job shift in Zanesville at the Hazel-Atlas Glass Company as a quality-control bottle checker, the daily job of sorting Sonora's mail often fell to Mom, who was the office's officially designated assistant postmaster. When Mom was busy waiting on customers in our store or service station, and as I got older, the mail sorting job sometimes fell upon me, although I had no official government designation whatsoever, that I know of.

Whoever was sorting mail faced the open bank of glass-faced, pigeon-holed boxes, provided by the Sadler Publishing Company in Baltimore, Maryland ("U. Post Office S. Supplies/*Not Every Description*"). In the late 1950s, the fewer than 100 boxes available was more than adequate to accommodate the entire town's mail-receiving population. Our family box number was 84, simply because that's where the W's fell when the boxes were set up alphabetically for each family in Sonora. As the mail sorter stuffed the boxes with letters, checks, newspapers, advertisements, and who knows what other important mailed missives, he (or she, to be both accurate and politically correct) would often see the faces of the potential recipients peering through the glass-faced boxes from the other side as they attempted to determine the name of the return addressee. Some envelopes, like those long brownish ones that contained Social Security checks, were instantly recognizable, and much in demand. Others, such as the plain white ones from the Internal Revenue Service and pesky law firms, were far less popular, and were sometimes refused delivery. Often, when time was critical, or when someone's mail apparently had come straight from the Pope or the White House, you would be urged to interrupt your sorting duties to hand over a recipient's accumulated box contents. Once the mail was "in" or "up," there would be a steady stream of postal patrons throughout the day, picking up their mail and  dropping off more, buying stamps, and posting packages.

Selling stamps was a fun part of being a paid or unpaid postal employee or non-employee, because the colorful stamps were always changing—in both design and denomination. In addition to a broad assortment of somewhat straightforward standard-issue stamps in one-cent, two-cent, three-cent, and so forth denominations, the government regularly issued new 100-count sheets of commemorative stamps that featured colorful locales, popular personalities, and all sorts of other interesting subjects to dress up a plain white No. 10 envelope. By August 1, 1958, first-class stamps had skyrocketed clear up to four cents each, and we got a lot of postal patron complaints about the size of the government and how much money it was wasting. Standing on one of the lowest rungs of the post office ladder, we didn't have a lot of influence on the politicians in Washington who were probably responsible. But we felt it was our civic duty to help avoid another American Revolution if at all possible. (Remember the Stamp Act?) So we spent a lot of time assuring

The most famous wall clock in Sonora. For more than 30 years, this timer ticked away on the only available wall in the Sonora Post Office for all to see—including generations of kids who waited for the morning school bus to New Concord High School (later John Glenn High) or, when Sonora School was abandoned, to Perry Elementary.

everyone that President Eisenhower was working on the problem, and would be coming up with a good answer in the very near future. Although Dad was a staunch Republican, he had even less contact with President Eisenhower than Vice President Richard Nixon did.

The worst part of playing post office, in my experienced non-employed opinion, was the quarterly report, which told the government exactly how much money you had taken in for postage and other services over the past three months, on a day-by-day basis. The dollars-and-cents amounts for these quarterly reports were (supposedly) entered each day in pencil in a columnar journal, at the close of business. But the postal inspector, who occasionally popped in without any forewarning to review the office records, wanted to see those figures in ink. (He was a very doubting Thomas, who seemed to ask a lot of questions. I tried to sell him a New Testament, with all of the latest changes, but he wouldn't buy it.)

So, once a calendar quarter, Dad and Mom sat down at our kitchen table or at the front counter of the store with a hand-cranked adding machine, and went over all of the penciled-in numbers for the past ninety

214

days, both to check them for accuracy and to "bring them into balance." Then it was necessary to ink over every penciled digit, and erase all of the original entries.

The inking and erasing job was such a tedious task that it was often assigned to me, who obviously occupied the very lowest rung on the government ladder, and I sometimes went to bed with visions of becoming a first-class forger. I was getting really good at duplicating Mom and Dad's hand printing, and thought it would be really easy to transfer my skills to bank checks and legal documents. But I always had to think twice about that idea when I passed by the dozens of "**WANTED—BY THE FBI**" posters that Dad posted periodically on our official government business cork bulletin board, as part of his duties as an official government agent. I didn't want to see *my* picture up there along with those of guys who had robbed banks, committed murder, and done other despicable things, like making long-distance telephone calls without paying for them. I was already pushing the legal envelope by riding my Whizzer motorbike without a learner's permit or license on Ohio's highways.

Being Sonora's postal center, our store had a constant and steady flow of patrons/customers, from its opening in the morning at 6:30 a.m. to its nightly closing at six o'clock p.m., only Sundays excluded. But the store attracted almost all area residents, in an endless, steady stream, for other many reasons as well. This was the place where you got your Ohio hunting and fishing licenses each year. It was the place where you waited in relative warmth in the winter, if you were going to New Concord High School, for Charlie Allen's caution-colored bus to pick you up. It was the place in the summer where the Muskingum County Library's boxy, bird-egg blue-and-white "bookmobile" parked every couple of weeks, under the shade of the huge old sugar-maple tree out front, to bring you opportunities for educational advancement, books of humor, a vast library of romance novels with lurid covers, scratchy phonograph records, and other items of education and entertainment that you didn't even have to pay for unless you brought them back late.

Whissel's Grocery was the place where most motorists living in or passing through Sonora stopped to get their gas or oil, and homeowners bought kerosene in both cans and bottles for their home heaters.

An undated Zanesville *Times Recorder* clipping showing the late Leland McClelland with the watercolor of our store that I watched him paint one summer afternoon. At left, behind the big maple tree, is the Methodist parsonage. I would love to locate this painting and convince the present owner that, to me, it is priceless, and I should own it. It is probably mildewing in somebody's garage around Zanesville. I would take real good care of it.

Eventually, it became the site of the first (and only) public pay phone booth in Sonora, a seven-foot-high, three-foot-square glass-and-aluminum box with clear windows and red-painted lower panels that was anchored by concrete-imbedded bolts next to our two Sohio gas pumps by the Ohio Bell Telephone Company. It had a white fluorescent light that we could turn off and on whenever we felt like it from a switch in the back of our store, a cardboard-covered telephone book that contained both white and yellow page listings, and blue government pages as well, and a squeaky bifolding door that you were able to close to make it harder for everyone standing around to hear you but mainly to keep out the June bugs and moths on summer nights which were attracted by the booth's bright lights and we didn't have any problem with being around the store until we got the telephone booth.

To enter Whissel's Grocery, the Sonora Post Office, or the Sohio gasoline service station, being all one and the same building, you had to rise six or eight feet above the Sonora Road level. This you could accomplish in at least three ways. The most dangerous way was to walk along the well-worn sandy path from the south that paralleled Sonora Road, passing through the shade of a dozen old maple trees that picket-lined the row of front yards that were all about four feet higher than the road. This was the most dangerous approach to our store because, as you passed by the final maple tree before reaching the set of concrete steps to the elevated porch, you entered a no-man's land, where at least two or three kids could be waging war with feathered wooden darts with sharp steel tips. The usual dart target consisted of the thin square cardboard insert from a Reese's Cup that was stuck in the bark of the maple, but accidents were known to happen. (Sorry about your left leg, Pamela Francis.) However, since this was the gentlest climb to the level of the porch, it was the preferred route of most of Sonora's elderly residents, who unfortunately also happened to be the slowest dart-dodgers.

Most store and post office patrons chose to use the broad concrete steps and sidewalk at the northeast corner of the store. This approach route was the slowest and steepest but safest, although winter snows tended to drift over the steps and sidewalk and kept us busy with shakers of rock salt and various snow shovels.

The third approach option was to get to the same porch steps by vehicle, driving up a short, limestoned grade and parking alongside our kerosene pump and padlocked "oil house," wherein we stored tin cans and cardboard cartons of 10W-30 and 10W-40 motor oil, transmission fluid, and windshield washer mixer. This approach route had the major disadvantage of causing your vehicle to be parked on a slope, in an era of simply not trusted or seldom-used parking brakes. At least one car or truck each year would slide backwards down this slope and into the path of some unsuspecting passing motorist on Sonora Road, causing a lot of both driver and pedestrian excitement. In winter, there was the additional hazard of packed snow and ice, which helped keep a backwards-sliding vehicle rolling into the path of oncoming traffic even if its driver applied the brakes.

The often-hazardous sidewalk approach was the one chosen by old Charlie Hanes early one summer morning. Charlie Hanes was a near look-alike for Charlie Chaplin, except for his thin gray hair, his battered straw hat, his oval eyeglasses, and the heavy rubber overshoes that he wore on most days, both winter and summer. Like Chaplin, Charlie Hanes had a cane, although he used it more for go than for show. Almost every morning, Charlie would walk slowly along Sonora Road from his home a block away to check his mail at the post office. Among the kids of Sonora, Charlie was rumored to be worth about a million dollars, although his actual assets, while still substantial, probably amounted to somewhat less. (It was also rumored that penurious Charlie wanted to be buried under a used tombstone when he died.) Charlie lived by himself, and

never bothered anybody, so far as we could tell. He more or less minded his own business, which was a very novel idea in a small midwestern town in the 1950s. We kids, on the other hand, pretty much minded *everybody's* business. We knew every house in Sonora inside out and upside down. We knew everyone's best traits and worst habits. Being kids, we knew it all. So we knew almost to the exact minute when old Charlie would be walking out Sonora Road to the post office to check his mail, when he would be starting up to climb up the first few concrete stoops by the Sohio gas pumps, and how he wouldn't much notice the small cardboard King Edward cigar box that was sitting on our first sidewalk stoop, stuffed to its green gills with smoking firecrackers, just waiting for old Charlie to pass by to explode.

The best-laid plans take a lot of planning. Here, around 1950, I think about where I am going to place the exploding cigar box that got Charlie Hanes so excited about 10 years later.

Charlie must have jumped high enough to see clean over the tallest catalpa trees next door in Phillips's front yard. It was the best fireworks display that Sonorans had seen in years, even if it had been seen by only a few kids. When the whole fused string of firecrackers exploded, at the very same time, the sturdy little cigar box was blown apart at its seams. All four sides and the lid simply shattered, in a puff of gray-white smoke and cardboard confetti that would have made even old King Edward proud to be an American. If Charlie had not been almost deaf at the time, the noise of the explosion alone would have killed him. Even so, the unanticipated onslaught of the blinding smoke, the shock-wave sound, and the billion flying bits of cardboard was enough to put an unusual spring in Charlie's step, and a heightened wariness in his morning post-office walk for days after the incident. A doctor might have told Charlie, over the phone, to take two aspirin and send in the five dollars, and his blood pressure would be back to normal in a couple of weeks. We improved Charlie's health immediately, for free, by stimulating his sagging pulse rate. Of course, Charlie probably ended up dying sooner than he otherwise might have, but we all have to make sacrifices.

## - OF FIRES AND FOGGY MORNINGS -

The front of our store, which faced east and looked almost directly across Sonora Road at Jack and Alma Greiner's house, was nearly all glass. To both the left and the right, there were four large rectangular panes. One set of four panes comprised the east wall of the post office cubicle, where the dust-smoted rays of early morning sunlight beamed down on a turn-of-the-century oak desk. The other quartet of panes bore an arch of blocked white letters that promoted Salada Tea.

The east wall of windows ended the aisle where we stood to obtain certain shelved items for customers, ring out their purchases, and record their charges on little notebooked tablets that made a carbon copy when you wrote down the items and their cost. In the middle of the store's street-side wall were two matching wooden doors, each with a single pane of glass. One door served as the main entrance to the store, the other was largely unused. It had an after-hours mail drop/slot box on the outside (with lockable interior access) and a fluorescent Meadow Gold Dairy sign on the inside that no one passing within two hundred yards of at night could miss. Over these doors was another, horizontal pane of glass, about six feet wide, in a bisected wood-framed window that could be cranked opened on hot summer days to create a cooling draft when a fat-bladed motorized metal fan was turned on at the rear of the large rectangular room.

The floor of the store consisted of one-by-four tongue-and-groove pine boards, butted end-to-end and laid diagonally. These dark-stained boards were protected periodically by a liberal application of linseed oil. The floor was swept regularly, using a big straw broom and a coarse green powder to hold down the dust. The walls and ceiling of this twenty-by-forty-foot room were white-painted plaster over lath, and may or may not have been insulated with finely shredded paper. At the rear of the store, Dad had installed a large fuel-oil furnace, the warm but never hot air from which was forced by its insultingly inefficient fan through sheet-metal ducting that ran almost all the way from the rear of the store to the front. Upward branches of this duct work also provided the only source of heat for the three bedrooms in our house, all of which happened to be located directly over the store. Alongside the three bedrooms was a dimly lit hallway that was terminated at its west end by a set of vinyl-carpeted stairs. At the foot of the stairs were three doors: a seldom-used one that allowed you to exit the house over a sheltered cellar door on which I usually parked my Whizzer motorbike, another one that opened to our kitchen (which was directly behind the store), and a third door that led to our dining room, which was next to our living room, from which you also

220

could enter the rear of the store when you heard someone come in and you were in the living room on family business.

From the store's ceiling hung three rows of chain-suspended fluorescent lights, with bare bulbs either four or eight feet long. Forming a

Here is a pre-appointment shot of Sonora's postmaster with a couple of his flapper friends who shall remain anonymous (only because I have absolutely no idea who they are). Until I found this photo recently, I would not have believed that Dad ever would have posed for it, particularly wearing that hat and that sweater. Also, I have absolutely no idea why these two women are holding hands, but they seem to be very...happy. Maybe Dad actually was a past *minister*, not a post *master*. Say good night, Gracie. ("Good night, Gracie.") In his spare time, Dad sold bridges in Brooklyn. ("Say the magic word....") Every Friday night, Dad taught Sunday School.

rough square, with the largest set of lights sort of centered in the room, these fixtures provided more than enough illumination to carry on grocery or post office business at any hour of the day or the night. Hanging from an eye-hook, screwed into the twelve-foot ceiling over the main check-out counter and always ready for use, was a gothic C-shaped metal string dispenser. This was a bare-bones invention that held a tightly wound cone of twisted cotton string. It had a threaded slide that rose and fell on the C-shaped frame as you jerked on the string below. The string remained taut as you bundled and tied paper packages. We had three or four sizes of brown Kraft paper bags to choose from, but many items—especially meats—were always wrapped first in a nearly translucent slick white paper, then re-wrapped in other white or pinkish Kraft paper that we ripped from rolls and secured with several windings of string from a second suspended dispenser at the rear of the store, alongside a thumb- threatening motorized meat-slicer.

In the spring of the year, on your left by the post office as you entered the store, would be a two-shelved Burpee's Seed rack. Almost every family in Sonora grew its own assorted vegetables in a backyard garden, and a large number of those plants got their start from packets and boxes of seed that had been purchased at our store. There would always be a chart, on both the rack itself and the packets and boxes, showing the several different growing zones

The turn-of-the-century oak roll-top desk that Dad bought in the 1940s for use in the post office, where it remained until he retired. Dad then put the valuable desk at the back wall of his garage, and bumped into it frequently with his pickup truck, until I finally rescued and refinished it. It's now safe in Jackson, Wyoming.

around the country. By noting which growing zone you were in, you would know when the respective seeds should be planted if you hoped to harvest a fully matured crop by first frost. Sonora's growing climate was such that, if you got your seeds in the ground some time after the last snow but any time before the Fourth of July, you would usually harvest a bumper crop before the first frost. At an early age I advanced from mere store sweeper to store stock boy, one of whose duties was to unpack the

Burpee's Seed box each spring, bolt its two slanted particle-board shelves to its four aluminum legs, and mix up the various seed boxes and packets so badly that nobody could find what they were looking for if they tried. This was a marketing scheme that I'm proud to say that I invented, and it still seems to be used with great commercial success today. By placing the seed packets and boxes in no organized order, I figured, a confused customer would have to look through a lot of things that he or she had not intended to buy, and might just find even more to purchase. This worked out so well with seeds that I tried the same mix-up scheme on our bushel baskets of potatoes and onions, crates of oranges, boxes of bananas, and bunches of grapes. But it never seemed to work nearly so well with any of those items as it did with the packets and boxes of Burpee seeds, so I never tried to patent the process. Somebody else probably figured out later what the problem was and made a fortune.

Uncle Dave pushes Mom on the tricycle that Dad bought her so she could go to her bingo games in Zanesville (seven miles away). Notice the row of huge catalpas along Sonora Road. At left is the Greiner home, at right the house that Dave and Eileen bought years later. Whissel's Grocery is just off Dave's left shoulder, next to the front porch post that my brother Jim accidentally destroyed. I have no idea who the dog is, but it sure is ugly enough to have belonged to Mom.

On your right, as you entered our store, you would walk by a set of certified weighing scales with a big stylishly filigreed arrow that swept clockwise around an outer circle of lines and numbers that neatly divided your bagged purchase of lima or pinto beans, brown or white sugar, or other loose products into ounced parts of a pound. This scale was used far less than another illuminated one with numbers that rolled like those of a slot machine. It sat squarely atop the middle of the double-glassed, refrigerated meat case, near the rear of the store where customers could—and usually did—check closely to see that their slices of meat weighed at *least* as much as you assured them they did. It was no problem at all if you were a bit over the weight that they had ordered (so long as you didn't try to charge them for that added weight). It was a major felony if your cuts fell a bit short of the requested weight, particularly if you presumed to charge them for a slice more than they actually received. And you weighed the meat *before* you placed it on the weightless wrapping paper, not after, thank you very much. Sonora was a tough town.

Next to the graduated scales, on your right as you came in the store, was an electric mechanical cash register and a non-electrified hand-cranked adding machine. These went through many spools of ribbon and rolls of paper, and were so important to the operation that you made sure that spare ribbons and rolls were always handy. As with the meats, close attention was paid by most customers to your register and adding machine punch-ins, and most customers wanted to take home the tape. It was not unusual to receive a telephone call hours after a customer had left the store, once she got her groceries and other goods home and unpacked, politely questioning the price of this item or that and why a particular amount was pennies different from what she had expected, and threatening to shoot you and burn your store down if you didn't take care of the mistake immediately. I don't know how Dad or Mom explained their occasional over-ring, but I always blamed mine on the federal government and gave them Richard Nixon's personal telephone number in Washington, D. C., to call, and his address to write to, although I don't think anybody ever actually did.

Under the main check-out counter were two big barrels, one aluminum and one wood-staved and metal-banded, both lidded and both for beans, one for dark red kidneys and white bush beans, and the other for greenish-white limas. Between this counter and the short section of wall under the big storefront windows was a wooden bench, on which there were usually four or five boxes of cigars, including King Edward Imperials ("America's Mildest Cigar"), which sold for six cents each, Dutch Masters Panatelas, and Tampa Nuggets, which for a dime promised "A Good Smoke" that was "Good as Gold." Also sitting on this bench were a portable General Electric radio, the ugliest artificial Christmas tree in the world in season, small packets of cigarette paper, a little red manual

224

cigarette-rolling machine, and an assortment of tinned tobaccos. Upon request, we would actually roll individual cigarettes for customers. Some of these hand-made cigarettes somehow went up in smoke in the tall weeds north of the Keystone Feed Mill.

Those who preferred ready-made cigarettes could find fifteen or more brands sold by the box or the carton, along with three or four kinds of tin-canned pipe tobacco, next to the window bench, on a shelf under several rows of assorted tin cans, paper bags and glass jars of coffees. This bay of shelves was next to another that contained bags and boxes of sugar, cans of Carnation and Pet Milk condensed milk, canned creamed and whole-kernel corn, and a selection of canned fruits like peaches, pears, plums, chunky and sauced apples, and apricots. Canned apricots was our worst-selling fruit.

The next bay of shelves housed at waist level a pigeon-holed cabinet in which rested dozens of small tablets, each with the name of a customer who had a charge account with us. In these pages were found both the dietary preferences of certain Sonora families as well as a good indication of their financial condition. It was common for many customers to be months or even years in arrears on these booked IOUs. But Dad and Mom denied additional credit to only a few fall-behinds whenever they simply asked for it. Some of these customers owed the store hundreds of dollars (when twenty cents would buy a loaf of bread, and a gallon of gasoline was only a few pennies more), and the store was always carrying thousands of dollars in uncollected and mainly uncollectible consumer debt.

Mustards, pickles, ketchups (or catsups), mayonnaise, Aunt Jemima and Log Cabin syrups, and several kinds of Heinz and Campbell's canned soups were next down the wall, followed by Arm & Hammer's multi-purposed baking powder, baking soda, Pillsbury and Betty Crocker cake mixes, and twenty or more flavors of Jell-O brand gellatins (black raspberry was my personal favorite).

All along the north wall on the highest shelf—and thus at the very top of the food pyramid—stacked clear to the ceiling, were a dozen different cereals. Our best sellers seemed to be Wheaties, Cheerio's, Kellogg's Sugar Frosted Flakes (my personal favorite—they were GRR-EA-TT), Rice Krispies, and the round cardboard boxes of oatmeal that showed some smiling pilgrim or puritan guy on the box wearing a big hat that curved up on each side. I don't know why he was always smiling, because he never outsold the constantly changing athletes on Wheaties boxes.

## - OF FIRES AND FOGGY MORNINGS -

To reach the cereal boxes, and to lower them without bringing down a dozen boxes on your head, you had to use a stepladder or an arm-extending grabber that I eventually became an expert with. Using this clever, claw-like invention, I tried to show off whenever I could, particularly in front of comely young female customers. The grabber was a wooden pole about five feet long, with a steel rod that ran up its side. There were two hinged handles that you squeezed, one to close the semi-circular pincers at the upper end of the pole around your intended abductee, the other in the middle of the pole to keep the pincers tightly closed. My best trick with this grabber was to remove the lowest of three stacked boxes of cereal and let the top two slide down without losing them all and others to gravity and making myself look like an idiot.

Directly in front of nearly this whole wall of shelves was the most popular section of our store, if you asked any kid in town. End-to-end there were two long candy cases with glass tops, glass fronts, glass sides, and pressed-board doors in the rear that you slid sideways to gain access. These three-tiered cases were packed with as many kinds of candy as a drooling tot could dream about having all in one place at the same time, probably close to a hundred sugar variations on any given day. On the lower of the two shelves was box after box of candies like bubble gum, twists, mints, gummy characters, caramel things that had great white stuff in their center, and hollow chocolate balls, all of which sold for a penny per piece, two-for-a-penny or even three. On the top shelf were things like Clark bars, Reese's Cups (my personal favorite), mint patties, several brands of chewing gum, and, in boxes featuring the head-to-head profiles of two bearded brothers who apparently knew a lot about sore throats, absolutely terrible-tasting cough drops. These lozenges tasted so bad that the two men had to register at hotels using the name "Smith." Our top-shelf items normally cost a nickel. Under the bottom shelf, on the base level of the case, we displayed round and long balloons of various colors, boxed rolls of exploding paper caps for toy cap pistols, and spare boxes of the quicker-selling items that were displayed above.

Several times a year the glass candy cases would be topped with a cardboard tray or two of caramel-covered green-skinned granny apples, which were plastered with ground nuts and packaged upside-down individually in a paper wrapper with a wooden stick stuck in them. Each of these carameled apples cost a whole ten cents. Only in the winter would we also have similar apples for sale that were coated by a hard red glossy glaze of shiny sugar that you couldn't bite off if you tried but always stuck like cement to your teeth if you did.

## - THE GENERAL STORE-

Our worst storekeeping fears would be realized when some six-year-old candy buyer would come in to buy candy with no more than a penny or two in his tightly closed palm—probably a bribe from some parent who would have paid a lot more to get him out of the house. Grabbing one of the smallest of our five sizes of Kraft brown bags, we would follow the kid to the candy case with both fear and trepidation.

"Gimme one of dose," he would open his purchase negotiations, fighting the sniffles of a summer cold. "How mush are dose tings beside 'em?"

"You mean these?" we would ask, in all innocence, pointing to the nearest adjacent box.

"No. Not dose. Da udder way."

We would hold a hand over the box of candy on the other side of his original purchase, praying for an earthquake, a flash flood, or a tornado to strike, hoping against hope.

"Yeah. Dose. How mush are dose?"

"Two for a penny."

"How many can I get for two pennies?"

"Four."

"How mush would tree cost?" (Trick question?)

"You can't buy tree...three. You have to buy either two or four."

"Let me tink about it."

He would pause in place for a moment, to tink about it, then slowly work his way down to the other end of the candy case, leaving several of his oily fingerprints all the way on the glass front, and dripping drool on the woven wood baskets of onions and potatoes below.

"Are dose good?"

"They're very good. Do you want one?"

"What doody taste like?"

"Well, they're kind of chocolatey. You would really like them."

"I don't want any. Are dose tings in front of 'em still tree for a penny?"

"Yes. They're always tree for a penny."

"Can I get two of 'em?" (Trick question?)

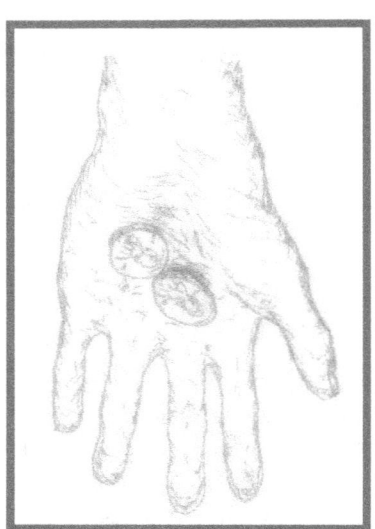

"No. You have to buy dose tree at a time."

"Okay. Gimme a penny's worth. How mush do I got left?"

"Well, how mush did you have to start with?"

"Dis mush."

He would hold out his hand.

There would be, maybe, two cents in it.

"You have two cents. With the first candy you bought, you don't have any more pennies."

"But I gotta have some bubble gum. Ain't da bubble gum tree for a penny?"

"Yes. The bubble gum is tree for a penny. But you don't got no more pennies. You only had two pennies to start with, and you done bought one of dese for a penny and tree of dose for another penny. You're plum out of pennies, pal."

"Well, can I put back da ting dat was one for a penny and get some bubble gum?"

"Yes. You can put dat back and get some bubble gum."

"Okay. Give me tree pieces of bubble gum. But I changed my mind on dose udder tings. Put dem back, and let me have two of dose white tings. Are dey still two for a penny?"

## - THE GENERAL STORE-

"Well, the price is supposed to be ten for a nickel, but since you're such a good customer, I'll make you a special deal today and sell them to you two for a penny. So, now you want tree pieces of bubble gum and two of dese...these white things, right?"

"I'm not sure. I tink I just want a balloon."

This could go on for fifteen minutes or more, testing especially the patience of Dad. In the end, we sometimes gave a kid a whole bag of assorted candy just to get him out of the store. You had to wonder if that had been his strategy all along.

Each winter some new oil-painting of a Christmas character, such as Santa Claus or a warm- and- fuzzy feeling, snow-covered rural landscape, would appear on the front glass of the candy case. If you timed it just right, you could stand and watch me paint it.

In 1979, to recognize his gardening skills and his hard-won expertise (particularly in pole beans and yellow tomatoes), I gave Dad the small trophy at right, which I had modified from something I had won. It used to have small, beanlike vines, but they all disappeared over the decades.

On the pine-board floor, directly in front of the candy case, were three or four bushel baskets that contained red potatoes, white potatoes, and big and small round onions. Our customers would usually ask for these items two or five pounds at a time, and we would duly bag and weigh them. Closer to the front door was a shelved metal wire rack with Cheetos, pretzels, and three sizes of potato chips in bags that sold for a nickel, a dime, and twenty-five cents for the jumbo-giant family size.

Across the aisle from the candy case was our bread and pastry racks. White and brown breads, rolls, cakes, cookies, donuts, and several other pastry products from the Baker Bread Company on Eighth Street in Zanesville and Cannon's Bakery in Dresden were kept fresh by drivers who delivered every other day or so. *(See Chapter Twenty: "The Dough Boy")*

On the floor, in front of the bread and pastry racks, were baskets or boxes of bunched bananas, peaches, apples, pears, grapes, oranges, or tangerines, depending on the season and what Mom was hungry for when Dad drove in to Miller's Produce in Zanesville to place and pick up an order. I occasionally went with him, and was always overwhelmed by the blast of pleasantly pungent natural scents when we walked back through the long dark building to pick up our produce. It was always much better than going with Dad to one of the "meat houses," either David Davies or Rittberger Brothers in Zanesville, to obtain bloody pieces of dead cows,

**Dad could grow anything in his huge garden behind the store, including red and hangover yellow tomatoes, pole beans, strawberries, corn, and potatoes.**

pigs, lambs, turkeys, chickens, or whatever. Behind the bread and pastry racks was an ice-cream cabinet, with three double sets of top-opening insulated doors and a frost build-up problem that just wouldn't quit. From this cabinet customers served themselves pint, quart, and gallon containers of ice cream, popsicles on dual wooden sticks, various-flavored bars, and ice-cream sandwiches (my personal favorite).

Our store's whole south wall, from Charlie Oliver's rural-patron postal pigeon holes in the front to our thumb-threatening meat cutter counter at the rear, was shelved with hand and laundry soaps, blueings, dyes, canned dog and cat foods, and several sizes of men and women's work and cotton gloves. At the very end of the white wooden shelves we stocked first-aid products—suspiciously near, I always thought, our motorized meat slicer. On similar shelves beyond the meat counter, by the door that led down the rickety wooden stairs to our cool, carved-stone cellar, were rolls of paper towels, two different sizes of boxed Kleenex, certain bathroom products that had universal application, and a couple of products from Modess and Kotex that, at your age, you weren't supposed to know what they were used for and had to hide in a brown paper bag as soon as possible to avoid embarrassing any female customers.

Across most of the rear of the store was our refrigerated meat case containing both pre-packaged sliced meats of several varieties and whole hunks of balogna, spiced loaf, minced loaf, Dutch loaf (my personal favorite), ham, and other meats that we would slice thick or thin to order, steak, beef, bacon, chicken, pork, and other meats that Dad would pick up at "the meat house" or Shirer's would deliver from up near Otsego. Other perishables, such as celery, carrots, cabbages, and similar vegetables, were obtained mainly from Miller's in Zanesville, and were also kept in this refrigerated cabinet.

On no particular schedule, but always during the winter, a staved barrel full of smelly dead fish stored in brine would sometimes appear directly in front of the meat case. I never knew where it came from, but I was always glad to see it go. Five decades later, I can still smell those fish, and that is probably why I never developed much of a taste for seafood.

For a few precious summer days, our meat case cooler would be filled—for about a half-hour only each day—with two or three dozen heaping quart baskets full of huge Pocahontas and Ever-Bearer strawberries that Dad and I grew in our whole-acre garden behind the store. Having made discrete inquiries during their morning mail run as to the possible availability of our beautiful berries, several housewives would flood the store around noon to scarf them up before they disappeared. Once I had picked, sorted, cleaned, and basketed berries for an entire morning, I could expect to receive the handsome price of fifty cents a heaped, full-sized quart for all of my efforts. Well, to be fair, Dad had a little bit to do with growing them.

Our garden, which was always Dad's pride and joy, also produced a quantity of potatoes for sale in the store, along with plenty more for our own table. Dad's overgrown garden was also responsible for many other vegetables on our table, including green (bush) beans, lima (pole) beans, onions, lettuce, radishes, pickles, beets, carrots, and about every other vegetable that you could grow in Southeastern Ohio. He especially loved to grow red and yellow tomatoes. He referred to his yellow tomatoes as "hangovers," because they were so big that the slices hung over the edges of any sandwich bread that you put them on. We also grew raspberries and blackberries. Dad's super-sized garden was growing from the last frost of spring to the first frost of fall, and was always far more productive than we could handle, forcing Dad to give his excess items to relatives, neighbors, friends, foes, and anyone else he could think of or could con or connive off the street.

Until Dad bought a motorized meat slicer, we made all of those cuts by hand on a large wooden tree-stump sort of block that stood near the meat case on four stubby legs, using two large knives that Dad kept super sharp. Two meat cleavers also were kept on this cutting table, for tackling big-boned items like beef and porkchops. The table was kept clean with a scrub-brush kind of tool that had stiff steel tines that cut away not only grease and grime but also the wood top of the table, causing it to shrink smaller each year. I don't know what happened to the missing wood.

All the way to the rear of the store were two other refrigerated cases. One held pint, quart, half-gallon, and gallon glass bottles and waxed cardboard containers of pasteurized, homogenized, and chocolate milk, orange juice, and buttermilk (Mom's personal favorite). The other cooler contained bottles of soda pop that sold for five or ten cents. Thirty-two liter bottles of some popular flavors like Coca-Cola, Pepsi-Cola, 7-Up, orange, and grape were amassed like Caesar's infantry divisions on the floor in front of the meat case. (And the late Mrs. Margaret Barnett thought I never learned anything in her Latin I and II classes; all I would say to her now, after 45 years, is *"Omnia Gallia in tres partes divisa est!"*) Those biggest bottles each sold for a quarter.

A return deposit of two cents on the smaller bottles, five cents on the larger, and ten cents on the jumbos was added upon purchase, but the bottles were nearly always returned for a refund, either by those who originally had purchased the pop or by one of the younger Sonora boys who went around town in search of the precious items to redeem for candy money. I stacked the empty bottles in wood, 24-count cases on the open porch that Dad built right under my bedroom window, and the empties were picked up periodically by the drivers of soda-pop delivery trucks with "No Riders" signs slapped on their windshields.

Dad and Mom ran Whissel's Grocery from the early 1940s to well into the Sixties. They sold the store to Donna Steinman, sister of my former brother-in-law, Dunkin' Dave, although Dad stayed on as postmaster until he died, when Mom became Sonora's first, and last, postmistress. She continued working at the store until December of 1977, when a failed chimney flue allowed flames from the old open fireplace in our former living room (which was now rented out) to set the building

After the fire. The big glass windows in front had been boarded over, the gas pumps and oil shed removed. At left is the parsonage. Between the brick chimneys on the second floor was my bedroom window, from which my brother Jim ran the radio aerial wire that sparked the Phillips porch post fire.

ablaze. Before the volunteer fire department could bring the fire under control, the one-time community center was gutted. It was such an historic moment, for not just Sonora but a sizeable region, that a news team from *WHIZ-TV* in Zanesville was sent out to Sonora to document it. (They somehow never interviewed my brother, Jim.)

To the accomplished firewatchers of Sonora, the fiery end to Whissel's Grocery and the town's fourth-class post office was a pretty good show that would have been even better if it could have happened at night. To more thoughtful observers, however, the historic fire seemed somehow to signify the end of an era. It was the loss not only of a local landmark, but of a way of life that entailed illusions, daydreams, the under-appreciated innocence of almost everything, and a roseate future that had appeared preordained for self, family, friends, town, county, state,

At left, our front porch (swing missing). Behind it were our living room, dining room, and the indoor bathroom that Dad built to replace the outhouse that my brother Jim burned down. The tri-masted TV antenna, erected in the 1950s, was still standing. *(Both fire photos from the* WHIZ-TV *television news broadcast.)*

country, and world. It was the crowning, going-out blaze of glory for, perhaps, Sonora's most-memorable era. A half-century later, from the grim perspective of a war-divided, terrorist-infested world that seems to be politically corrupt, economically insatiable, environmentally unrepentant, and historically unschooled, it is both comforting and somehow saddening to remember those halcyon days gone by. Ahead may be fallen arches and failing memories, but still fresh are the foggy mornings and seldom-told stories from a small town in the 1950s that are absolutely, positively true. Sort of.

Sonora, Ohio, circa 1955, looking east. At bottom right, the back nine of the Jaycees Public Golf Course. Follow the B&O Railroad tracks to Sonora Road, hang a left, and go north through the town of Sonora. At the C.R. 64 (Norfield Road) intersection, swing right and re-cross the tracks, go by St. Paul's Cemetery, take a sharp right at Dick Gibbon's, then a left to go down to old Route 40 near the Little Salt Creek bridge. Go south on the East Pike until the Sonora Road intersection (out of drawing at right), take that up and over George Hill, crossing Pleasant Grove Road, back to Sonora. At top left in this drawing is Bill Burwell's pig farm, just east of Leonard Orndorff's farm. Near the National Road at top right is the farm and slaughterhouse of Harmon Brock. At left center are the coal strip mines where Bobby Shirer and I played cowboy. Every effort has been made to include all homes, most outbuildings, and several trees where they actually were (notice the catalpas). Other details include Sonora's ballpark, the Keystone feed mill and weed patch, Sonora School's playground (and outhouses), all alleys, and creeks.

# EPILOGUE

## Another Beginning

*I*t was hot. Even for the middle of July it was hot. Even with a humidity level that was a bit lower than normal it was hot. It was one of those mid-Ohio summer scorchers that made him want to do nothing but find an easy book to read and a cool place to read it, grab a water-cooled bottle of Pepsi from the store's pop case to sip on, and filch a frozen cherry popsicle from the frosty ice-cream freezer for immediate relief.

He could imagine just how miserable this humid heat would be in a cramped seacoast city like New York, Baltimore, San Francisco, Seattle, or Los Angeles, where the humidity was always high because of the nearby water. On the other hand, since he had never actually been to New York, Baltimore, San Francisco, Seattle, or Los Angeles, he really had no idea how bad a hot day like this would be in those cities. All he knew for certain was that here in Sonora, even with no big bodies of water close by to influence the weather, it was hot. Too hot.

Of course, he could have taken his mind off the heat by going fishing, but that would have meant digging for bait, and that would have made him even hotter. He also could have gone swimming in Stage's algae-covered duck pond, but on a day like this that would have been like jumping into a saucepan of warm noodle soup. He could have coaxed some of the guys into a couple of innings of baseball, but in this heat that, too, would have taken extra effort. But all of those heat-escaping possibilities, and others, had gone by the wayside that morning with the word from his father that a trip into Zanesville was on tap. Since his thirteenth birthday was only two days away, he thought it prudent to spend the morning just marking time around the house, waiting for the trip to begin. It was shortly after his usual summer lunch of artificially sweetened orange juice and two Dutch loaf sandwiches slabbed with sliced raw onion and smothered in French's yellow mustard that the start flag was waved.

"Ready?" his dad asked, seeing him at the squeaking, spring-closed screen door to their plastic screen-protected back porch.

"I'm ready," he replied. "I just don't know where we're going."

"Maybe that's why they call it a surprise."

"It would really surprise me if it didn't have something to do with my birthday."

"Hm. I forgot all about your birthday. When is it? The nineteenth? I think it is. Are you going to be eleven or twelve this year?"

"Thirteen," he smiled.

"Oh?" said his dad, faking ignorance. Carl Whissel knew very well how old his youngest son would be on this birthday. He always knew such things. "Well, let's go. Where's the dog?"

At the first sound of their voices across the back yard, their dog Pepi had risen from his half-nap in the cool, locust-shaded grass by the barn, stretched his aging muscles slowly, and hurried to join them. It sounded like they were headed off somewhere, and wherever they went, he went. Whenever they went, he went. Whatever that meant, in terms of Pepi being his own dog, he had no idea. But for years Pepi had always accompanied them in their vehicles, and he had always been anxious to go. He trotted a little faster, not about to risk being left behind.

"Here he comes."

All three of them, the boy, his dad and their dog, piled in to the battered red short-bed Chevy pickup truck. As always, the truck had been parked near the white picket fence that separated their back yard from the narrower strip of grass on the outer, north side. In some earlier age, the faded board fence, with its one-by-four boards trimmed by inverted "v"s, may have been effective in keeping dogs and babies on one side or the other. But now, in the late 1950s, the fence served the purpose of neither protection nor containment. It was not even aesthetically attractive, being always in a terminal phase of peeling paint. It no longer had even a swinging gate to latch or unlatch as you left or entered the property from the cindered alleyway parking area.

Each of them tried to avoid the sudden draft of hot air that poured out when the pickup's doors were cracked, but failed to dodge it; knowing that they would be going to town, one of them should have thought about rolling down the truck's windows that foggy morning, before the air inside could heat up. Now it was too late; they would just have to make the best of it. In keeping with his self-assumed right of first entry, Pepi hopped in, quickly found his place in the middle of the scorching vinyl seat, sat up ramrod straight, and began scouting around for cats to curse and other dogs that he could warn out of their way with a menacing bark or two.

Fred had to slam the passenger side door three times to make it stay shut. His dad needed only two tries on the driver's side to achieve the same result. As soon as they were settled, both of them rolled down the side windows, and pivoted the wing ones open. Maybe the afternoon's slight breeze would be a bit of help in cooling down the cook-stove interior of the cab. In mid-July, the red-painted steel pickup, sitting with closed windows in the southeastern Ohio sun, was about as perfect a magnet for attracting heat as Detroit could have devised. They wouldn't get much real relief from the heat until the truck started rolling. With a single wrist wrenching of the silver-plated ignition key, the engine turned over. In less than a minute, they were on Sonora Road, trucking towards town.

"Reach down below there and make sure your vent is open," his father ordered.

The unseen vent was open—as it had been since about April—but the air being sucked through it from the engine compartment was still warm. Already Pepi was beginning to pant. As they neared the First Street intersection George Smith saw and saluted them with a quick wave from his one-kneed kneel in the freshly roto-tilled dirt of his vegetable garden. A few rows over, an undercover army of long green worms already had lunched an assault on the underside of the leaves of his yellow-tomato plants. George had discovered the worm eaters only that morning, and planned to take the battle to them later on when the day cooled off. But for now, he was intent on merely inspecting his bush beans for bugs. It seemed like there was always something to do in a garden. George Smith spent almost as much summer time in his garden as Carl Whissel did in his, on the hillside one-acre plat behind the general store.

## - EPILOGUE – ANOTHER BEGINNING -

As they next rolled down the slight slope by her small squarish house on the right, his Grandma Minnie Jones was trying to beat the heat by gliding back and forth in the metal swing on her newly repainted front porch. Like a metronome, her wrinkled hand waved a splayed paper fan back and forth before her face with a steady beat. She was often seen gliding on her elevated porch perch, where besides keeping cool she could keep up with Sonora's comings and goings. Instantly aware of the truck coming down the hill, and who was in it, Minnie made a cursive movement that involved more motion with her hand than it did with her arm, and greeted them as they went by. Fred wondered if she would have been so quick to wave if his dad had been in the truck alone. But in small-town Sonora, in the 1950s, everyone always waved at everyone else, even if they didn't really like them.

Shortly after they crossed the B&O railroad tracks, they saw several young and older Sonorans wading in the tepid, algae-ringed waters of Stage's duck pond, seeking what coolness the warm wetness afforded, feathers and all. Just beyond, at the foot of George Hill, he saw two of his buddies easing down the bridge bank carrying freshly cut sassafras poles and tin cans containing earthworms to fish in Little Salt Creek. They soon saw him too, and waved, and he waved back, thinking that if they were going to fish under the bridge itself they probably weren't going to catch anything. He and his friend David Francis had cleaned out that pool a couple of days ago.

With help from two gear-crunching downshifts, the old red pickup climbed the north side of George Hill, slowed for the "S" curves near the top, crested the hill at Sonora Road's intersection with Pleasant Grove Road, and coasted down the straighter south side, shooting towards the two round oil tanks and adjacent pump at the bottom and the right-winged on-ramp to the East Pike. The downhill roll, with its increased speed, sent an appreciated cooling breeze into the truck. As they reached the top of the short ramp to the highway, he saw several cars and trucks parked in front of his uncle Pee Wee's Crossroads Cafe, their drivers apparently taking refuge from the heat under the beer joint's big ceiling fans or behind frosted foamy mugs of Blatz or Budweiser. There was very little traffic on the National Road; it was not until they neared the first panels of the boarded white fence that surrounded escavator C. M. Luburgh's escavated pond that they even saw a single vehicle headed east—another pickup truck. It was just too hot today to drive if you did not absolutely have to. Riding over the heat-reflecting highway on a motorcycle today would have been uncomfortable. On down the highway they saw few vehicles surrounding Mickey's Drive-In, even fewer around the Greenlawn Restaurant, but then neither of those eateries normally had any real business before six o'clock or seven. And unlike uncle Pee Wee's Crossroads Café, neither of those popular pull-ups had any help from draft beer or 80-proof alcohol to cool their mid-day customers.

"So," his dad questioned, at long last crossing the heated stream of steady silence. "Did you ever ask Wendell Derry if he could use your help this year in his hay fields?"

Fred was glad to open a conversation, regardless of the topic. Maybe the simple task of talking would help him forget the heat for awhile. By now, Pepi had lost all interest in the trip, and was slobbering a constant stream while he tried to figure out how he could curl up most comfortably on the hot seat and catch some sleep.

"Wendell said we would just have to wait to see what kind of a crop he has," Fred reported. "But if there's a lot of hay, he'll for sure need someone to help him, and the job's mine if I want it. I told him to call me."

"A man can always use more money," his father philosophized. "Working in the hay fields isn't too bad a way to get it."

"Well, it's a lot better than putting up straw, I'll say that. I'm not sure I'll ever do that again. Last year I almost died. That black junk gets in your nose and mouth and you just can't breathe. It isn't so bad with hay, but it's still not as good as anything else I can imagine. Selling Grit sure is a lot easier than any farm job I've found. And if Bobby Shirer would give up his Times Recorder route, I could get that, too. At least he lets me substitute for him every once in a while. But I think I make more money from finding golf balls at the golf course than anything else. Yesterday I came home with almost five dollars."

"A man can always use more money," his dad assured him.

For as long as he could remember, there always seemed to be plenty of money in the Whissel family. For years, since before he could even remember, his dad had been Sonora's postmaster. Being a government job, that must have paid pretty well, although he never had the slightest idea how much his dad actually earned, from that or any of his other full- and part-time occupations. In addition to being Sonora's postmaster, for several years Carl Whissel had quality-checked newly blown bottles at the Hazel-Atlas Glass Company in Zanesville, working eight-hour shifts with start times that rotated backwards from morning to midnight to afternoon. A steady stream of money also flowed in from the family's grocery/service station operation, although the three-a-week raids that his wife Edith made on its cash drawer for her bingo stake must have slowed the flow a little. But whenever Carl pulled out his venerable leather wallet, and shooed all of the moths away, the big bill pocket always seemed to be stuffed with big bills.

The long-renown Y-Bridge in Zanesville, Ohio. Just out of frame at the left is a roller dam on the Muskingum River (which continues southward at top). A (since-removed) vertical lift over the canal at top left halted lower Main Street vehicles for canal traffic flow. At lower right is the Licking River, with its own dam. At mid-bridge, a city bus leaves West Main Street. Opting for the third, Linden Avenue leg of the bridge, at lower left, would take you past the Lind Arena (a bingo parlor/roller skating rink), through commercial, industrial, and residential areas, and eventually to Ellis Dam, where Dad and I spent many a night daydreaming.

The Whissel family's general store/service station was also their home. The many rooms of the residence wrapped around the south side and the westward back of the big store showroom, and the home's three-in-line bedrooms were situated directly over it. Not only did "the store" account for a fairly continuous flow of cash, but it also provided all of the Whissel family's groceries, gasoline, and general household supplies as well—things that *most other families had to pay retail to buy. When the Whissels needed more meat, more milk, a can of Campbell's soup, a loaf of bread, or whatever, all they had to do was walk from their kitchen into the store and get it, at any hour of the day or night. Best of all, there was never any need to ring-in these "purchases," no charge slips or vouchers to fill out. They simply took what they wanted from the store when they needed it and let the IRS worry about the missing items each April. The non-cash benefits of the store, of course, should have been considered other household income. But the way Carl Whissel figured it, he was handing enough of his hard-earned income over to the government already. If they wanted any more of it they would just have to work for it, like he did. The store also was the source of a fair share of their home heat, since its old oil furnace was ducted along the big showroom's flaking plaster ceiling, and sent some of its lukewarm air up through cast-iron registers into the second floor's three boxy bedrooms, each with a single center light and a thin crappy clothes closet.*

*Slowing to look both ways at the railroad tracks at the foot of Greenwood hill on the outskirts of Zanesville, it was necessary for his dad to floor-shift the transmission down into second gear to make the grade. Seeing the grove of tall old trees, and the graves of hundreds of tombstoned former residents in Greenwood Cemetery, off to the right, seemed to have a welcomed chilling effect on Fred as they climbed the hill. At the very top of the steep grade, they passed by the misty glassed greenhouse of Hilltop Florists on the left. At the intersection itself, the traffic light was turning red, and they were forced to stop.*

*"Didn't think it would be this hot today," his dad observed. "It'll probably rain later on—those clouds up there look pretty dark. I'd say we'd better get a move on."*

*The thought struck him that they were moving just about as fast as they could while sitting still at a red light. As they waited, two men in their wasted fifties or sixties came weaving out of Phil Joseph's red-bricked Bar and Grill on the left, staggered straight as a sidewinder rattlesnake across the street without looking either way, let alone both, and pretty much fell into either side of a badly beat-up car that was parked in front of Hilltop Grocery. Lucky for them that no traffic was coming. They must not have been able to find their ignition keys, since the car was still parked and the engine was still silent as his dad drove by them. Looking over, he saw them arguing loudly and belligerently—apparently over who was to blame for misplacing the car keys. They soon began throwing what had to be powerless punches, each at least as likely to injure himself as the other.*

## - EPILOGUE – ANOTHER BEGINNING -

*"Damned drunks" was all his father had to say, glancing over and shaking his head in disgust as they drove by.*

*They continued down Market Street past the tiny White Castle with its great little 12-cent pickled-and-onioned hamburgers, past the old brick Market House, all the way to Second Street. This was one of his dad's favored routes to bypass the downtown Zanesville traffic, and it was nearly always faster than going down the multi-lighted Main Street. They turned left from Market and went south a block, where they turned right onto the lower end of Main Street, bounced over the several sets of used and unused railroad tracks, rolled across the rusting canal lift bridge, and began crossing Zanesville's world-famous Y-Bridge. (You could cross the bridge here and still be on the same side of the Muskingum River.) Looking down he could see that the level of the brown waters boiling white foamy bubbles over the rocks in both the Muskingum and the Licking Rivers was low. On the Muskingum, the sun-silvered waters had to make an extra effort just to tumble over the roller-dam obstruction. Atop the dam, a few men and boys had walked almost half way across the Muskingum on the exposed rollers and were now fishing for carp, probably, or catfish, hopefully, in the shallow pools just below the dam. A sudden storm, a flash flood, he thought, and they would all be whisked clear down to McConnelsville before anyone even found their bodies. On the other hand, he had to admit that the fishing might be better out there, where a cast from shore couldn't land a lure. So maybe it was worth the risk.*

*"Any idea yet where we're going?" his dad asked.*

*"I still don't have a clue," he conceded. "The last time we did this, I ended up with a bowling ball. We turned right up here and went up to that little hole-in-the-wall on Linden Avenue."*

*"Not this time," his dad assured him, with a grin. "But I don't think you'll have much trouble liking what I've got picked out for you this year— unless you want another bowling ball."*

*He had no idea. This trip was a complete puzzle. When his dad was buying him a new baseball glove, or similar sporting gear, they went in to Clossman's Hardware at the head of Main Street or—much less often—to Bonifield's Hardware on Sixth. For shop tools and such, it was always Sears. For most clothes they went to J. C. Penney's on Fifth Street, next door to Sears. His bicycles they had always bought at that shop on Sixth Street— what was its name? He couldn't remember. In any event, since they were* headed this time in a whole different direction, his dad must have something entirely new in mind. Exactly what that might be he had no idea. Anyway, it was almost too hot to even think about it; he would find out soon enough. As they came to the middle of the river, they turned left, stopping briefly in response to the traffic sign, and rolled on to West Main. It was only a few blocks farther on that they saw the huge billows of black smoke rising up ahead of them. At the next intersection, all four feeds of traffic had been halted by police squad-car barricades. A number of ruby-red fire engines, with the unrestricted right of way that their use, speed, size, and water-barreled weight afforded them, were bouncing into the intersection from the left, and were being hurried through it by the waving arms of a blue-shirted cop who was standing in the center of the intersection. On the right, a few doors down West Main, a small business of some sort apparently was being written into Zanesville's history books in inky smoke and flames.

"Well, this has turned out to be a dig for no potatoes," his father lamented, repeating one of his stock sayings for about the ten-thousandth time. "Looks like we can either sit here and wait it out or we can try to go around. It's probably going to take a while to clean up this mess."

"I sure hope they weren't selling my birthday present," he moaned in mock dismay.

"I don't know what they were selling," his dad pointed out, "but they won't be selling any more for awhile. See how the fire is shooting through the roof? When that happens, you can almost bet that the building will be a total loss. I think I'm going to turn down this alley, and see if we can't work our way around it. The place we need to get to is only a couple of more blocks on the other side of the fire. I'll be damned if I'm going to drive all the way to town in this heat and then be turned back by a fire."

"Okay by me. I have no idea where we're going anyway, so when we get there I probably won't even know it." He reached over and flapped Pepi's ears. The dog looked at him like he was hot, which he had to be, and drooled still more sticky saliva onto the truck's vinyl seat. But he seemed to appreciate the coolness of the air stirring on his ears, and showed it with a smile.

Making the detour around the fire was not quite as easy as it could have been. Other drivers on West Main had decided to find a way around the fire as well, and some side street traffic was still approaching the main thoroughfare, getting more and more jammed up the closer it came. There were no lights, only stop signs on the secondary streets, so the overload of automobiles, commercial trucks, and a few other pickups was causing mass transit confusion. Added to the heat of the afternoon, this was all they needed.

It must have taken them a good half-hour to drive no more than three blocks beyond the burning building, but the extra effort had turned out to be worth it. As they entered the parking area of a business that he had only half-noticed in earlier drive-bys, there seemed to be two dozen shiny new motorcycles sitting around. After parking the truck and entering the shop, they must have seen half again as many bikes on display in the showroom. Over by a big plate-glass window, a salesman was telling a man who was seated on one of the motorcycles how well it seemed to fit him. "This bike was just made for you," the salesman said. From the look on the man's face, he seemed to actually believe it.

"Be with you in a minute," the salesman said to them, raising an arm and snapping off a salute with his extended index finger. He followed his dad towards an opening at the rear of the main showroom. It was obvious that his old man had been here before, and knew exactly where he was going. In the dim light that seeped through a dirty window and dripped from a fluorescent fixture in the center of the room, he could see that most of the filthy floor of this smaller showroom was filled with motorbikes, both new and used, and that the walls were lined with hooks and shelves holding assorted biking accessories. As his dad pulled out his venerable wallet, shooed away the moths, and began counting out several big bills on a glass showcase, he saw a sign on one wall that said "Whizzer."

You could have stretched his smile clear across the wide Muskingum. No, this was not going to be another bowling ball birthday. This boy was about to become a biker.

# Another Ending

*I*t had been a successful hunt. The two boys, Jhon and Carl, had each shot a squirrel. He himself had taken two, both nice fox squirrels that had been sitting on branches high up in a hickory, cutting their nuts. The boys, as he had hoped, had been excited about going squirrel hunting for the first time. He was glad that they not only had each gotten a squirrel, but had seemed to enjoy the woodland experience as well.

"Mine was higher up than yours," Carl argued. "I could just barely see it."

"Yeah, right," replied his older brother. "I had to shoot through three branches and a bunch of leaves to get mine. What about it, Grandpa? Who made a better shot? Me or him?"

"Well," he mused, "they both were good shots, for your first time hunting. I'm really surprised that you both got a squirrel. I don't think I shot one the first time I went hunting." He paused to think. "That was more than fifty years ago."

"You must be having fun then, Grandpa," Carl calculated. "They say that's what happens when time flies. Are we going to go hunting again tomorrow?"

"I'm game," Jhon added, with a smile on his face as he slowly came to appreciate his unintentional humor. "Get it?"

"Jhon, you are so dumb," Carl said, sighing his disgust. "You didn't even realize that you were making a joke. That was purely accidental."

"Boys, boys," their grandfather interrupted. "Enough bickering. Is that all you fellows do all day long? It must drive your mother nuts. But to answer your question, if you want to go again tomorrow we will—if it's okay with your dad and mom. Do you want to go in the morning again? Or do you want to wait until late afternoon?"

"I about got my fill of getting up before daylight in this one trip," Jhon replied. "If it's all the same to you, I'd rather go in the afternoon."

"Okay with me, Grandpa," Carl agreed. "I didn't really want to get up either while it was still dark and go squirrel hunting. Once was about enough—and your burnt bacon-and-eggs breakfast was really bad."

"You're both pansies," their grandfather chided. "Here I am over sixty years old and there you are at—what? eleven and thirteen?—and I can get out and about better than either of you with two hands tied behind my back."

They both had to think about that one for a minute.

"What's having your hands tied behind your back got to do with walking in the woods?" Carl asked, confused.

"That was just an expression, dummy," Jhon explained. "It didn't mean beans about applesauce."

Now Carl was really confused. He had no idea what beans had to do with applesauce, let alone walking in the woods with your hands tied behind your back. He decided just to stay silent and give it some more thought.

"If we go tomorrow afternoon, you'll have to be a lot quieter in the woods than you were this morning," their grandfather cautioned. "Making all of that noise with your feet was bad enough on leaves and branches made soft by the foggy morning. It just won't do if you go tromping around like that in the afternoon, when everything's dry. The squirrels'll hear you for sure. Plus, they won't still be half-asleep like they were this morning when we got to that first tree before daybreak."

"My head still hurts from when you cuffed me," Carl stewed. "I didn't mean to break that branch with my foot."

"Oh, come on," his grandfather replied. "I didn't knock you any ways near as hard as my Dad used to hit me when I did the same thing. I know you didn't mean to break the branch. Jhon knows you didn't mean to break the branch. Probably even your dead squirrel knows you didn't mean to break the branch. That's not the point. The point is, I told you several times

247

*that you had to walk softly, and there you went swishing through the leaves like you had no idea what I was talking about. You were bound to step on a branch sooner or later. Your head doesn't really hurt, does it?"*

*"No," Carl admitted. "But it could have if I didn't duck."*

*"Okay, then. Let's forget about it, and I won't smack you any more—unless you deserve it."*

*"Are we going to go to the same place, Grandpa?" Jhon asked.*

*"No. First off, we shot the only squirrels that were in those trees," he answered. "But the difference between a woods in the morning and afternoon is like night and day. We'll have to find somewhere else tomorrow, where we can creep up on the squirrels while they are cutting their nuts without scaring them. I know another place where we should be able to do that—if you fellows keep quiet."*

*The old Pontiac Star Chief was coming into town. As they rounded a bend, they saw a broadening column of black smoke and orange flames rising from a house. The flames flared wildly through the asphalt-shingled roof of the one-story dwelling, curled around its eaves, shot through the smashed front door, and exploded the windows into shards. The water being sprayed by a dozen volunteer firemen onto the house from several serpentined canvas hoses was, at most, a mere technicality. While the water turned some of the fire's tremendous heat into steam, it was apparent to all who watched that the dwelling was going to be a total loss. This family's entire history, all of its possessions, every tangible item that was inside the house, would soon be nothing more than a pile of smoldering ashes, melted metal, glazed glass, and charcoaled wood. Nothing but memories would remain.*

*"Wow!" shouted Carl. "Looks like that is one house that they aren't going to save. Wonder if anybody was in it."*

*"Probably not," his grandfather replied. "I've been to a lot of home and building fires in my time, and what they try to do first thing is get anybody out that may be in there. Doesn't look to me like those firemen are showing any great concern about somebody being trapped inside. All they are trying to do now is keep the fire from spreading to the other houses."*

*Traffic on the street, in both directions, was stopped. The block was filled with lime-green and fire-engine-red firefighting vehicles, black-lettered* white police cars, flashing multi-colored emergency lights, heavy-coated firemen, and light-helmeted police officers. There was no way to drive through this organized confusion, and now no way to back out, since two more cars had followed the Pontiac into the street and were also stopped. It was going to be a while before this mess was cleaned up.

"Well, this is a dig for no potatoes," he said. "I guess we'll just have to sit here and watch the show, since we can't go forward, can't back up, and there are no side streets to turn down."

Heavy smoke was rolling in puffy black balloons above the house. A light wind carried the incandescent smoke eastward for a block or two where, like the family's furniture, clothing, photographs, and dreams, it just drifted away, disappearing almost indiscernibly slowly in the hot haze of the summer afternoon.

"This reminds me of a fire I once saw, when I was a boy about your age," the grandfather told them.

"Oh, no. Here we go again," moaned Jhon. "Is this going to be another story about So-nora, O-hio?"

"Go ahead and tell us, Grandpa," Carl consented  "Don't mind him. He's just an idiot. Tell us about the fire you saw. Looks like it's going to be a while before this mess is cleaned up."

"Okay," Jhon agreed. "We've probably heard it before, and we'll probably hear it again, but you might as well tell us. It will help put this little baby to sleep."

"Who you calling a baby?" Carl shot back. "You're the one who had to sleep with the light on until he was seven!"

"Okay, boys!  Enough! Listen up."

# Home Again

*H*ow long they had sat there waiting for the fire to be extinguished was anybody's guess. All of the rest of the traffic had moved on, escorted through the final fire department and police vehicles by the white-helmeted cops who, apparently, had left with them. Only a few weary firemen and a single pumper truck remained behind to put the last of the ashes to bed. The house had simply disappeared. The only thing left standing where it had been was a burnt brick chimney. It was now late afternoon.

In the right front seat Carl, his youngest grandson, was slumped over against the door, probably reliving his first squirrel hunt. Behind them, Carl's older brother, Jhon, was stretched out across the rear seat, sawing logs. He had no idea how many of his stories they had heard before conking out. Most likely his ramblings would have put anyone to sleep. An old man telling old stories to a new generation. The boys also had to be a bit tired, since they had walked a good ways in the woods, both going in and coming out.

It was almost dark as he pulled the old Pontiac in to his daughter's driveway. Obviously concerned, she was waiting at the front door, still wiping dry the pan that she had been rinsing in the kitchen sink when she heard his approach. As he turned off the engine she placed the pan down on a hall table, strolled along the concrete walk until she reached the passenger side of the car, and carefully opened the rear door.

"Well, this certainly is a pretty picture," she smiled. "Sound asleep. Have you been telling them your old war stories again?"

"Now, Poo. No need to get nasty. We simply got stuck in traffic at a house fire over on Ash and had to wait it out; there were cars behind us. I guess the boys just got tired, with all of the excitement."

"Okay. I'll buy that. Better wake them up."

## - EPILOGUE - HOME AGAIN -

*The boys were foggy as they returned to the real world. Both gave a quick shake, to help them see again, but soon fought off the haze and were almost embarrassed that their mother had seen them asleep from exhaustion.*

*"We all got a squirrel, Mom," Carl hastened. "Grandpa got two. And we saw a house burn down."*

*"I had the longest shot," Jhon added. "I knocked that sucker clear out of the top of the tree. Carl could have killed his with a rock."*

*"I'll bet," she said. "Did you have fun?"*

*"Can we go again tomorrow?" Carl asked. "Grandpa said we can go someplace else if we go in the afternoon. Mom, Grandpa bopped me on the head."*

*"What?"*

*"It wasn't anything," he assured her. "Carl just stepped on a branch and broke it, giving us away. So I sort of gave him a love pat."*

*She looked at him suspiciously. "Did he really hurt you?" she asked Carl.*

*"Well, not really. But it could have really hurt if it had been harder."*

*"I see. And you still want to go again?"*

*"Yeah! It was awesome!"*

*"It was so cool," Jhon added. "You hear this squirrel way up in the top of the tree cutting his nuts, and you have to be really quiet as you walk around trying to get a clear shot. All of a sudden you see the squirrel. It sees you, and it's all about who shoots first and asks questions later. BLAM! Right between the eyes. And the squirrel comes crashing down through the branches, landing deader than a door nail. Grandpa said he'll take them home and clean them. Then he'll bring them over for us to eat."*

*"I'll have to see that to believe it," she said. "Grandpa is probably going to end up with four squirrels for dinner.*

*Well, are you coming in, Dad?"*

"Actually, I had better get on home. Your mom is probably wondering what became of us. I told her we would be back hours ago."

"She's already called me three times."

"Grandpa was telling us war stories again," Carl ratted. "While we were sitting at the fire he was telling us about So-nora."

"I thought so," she said. "Neil said he also drove by the fire and it was almost out two hours ago. He said those poor people lost everything they had."

"It was a sight to see," her father admitted. "I'll have to say that."

"Funny Neil didn't see your car at the fire," she puzzled. "It's hard to miss it. At least he didn't say anything about seeing it. You must have come in from a different direction."

"Well, come over here and get your coats out of the trunk, boys. I'll take your guns home and clean them tonight." He unlocked the trunk lid. "I'll call you tomorrow about the time we need to leave. Is it going to be okay with you if they go again, Poo?"

"Sure. Why not? Get them out of the house again. You probably have a million more stories to tell them. And all of them are absolutely, positively true. Sort of."

They exchanged smiles and good-byes, and he backed down the driveway while his daughter walked towards the house with a son on either arm. They all turned and waved good-bye.

It was several blocks farther to his own house, and he tripped the automatic garage door opener with the radio-frequency remote as he pulled in the driveway, easing the old Pontiac to a stop just short of his workbench. Checking to make certain that he wasn't leaving anything in the car that needed to go inside on the first trip, he got out, closed the car door, and began walking towards the entrance to the hallway between their kitchen and dining room. He would come back out for the squirrels and his shotgun, after saying hello to his wife, Barbara.

He paused in mid-stride, spun on his heels with the relief of a man much younger, who had arrived at some clear conclusion after a soul-searching debate with himself, and walked over to the corner of his garage, where a dusty brown canvas tarpaulin served the same purpose as the late great Leonard Wisecarver's. Carefully, ceremoniously, he removed the tarp from the ancient Whizzer motorbike. Freed of its dark cape, the bike gleamed like new. Its chrome reflected bright proof that the Whizzer had been polished recently. Both belts were like new—not yet wrapped with even the first round of friction tape. Not a speck of dust spoiled the bike's maroon and white paint. Not a gob of excess grease clung to its chain and chromed axles. And there were no tell-tale pools of oil on the concrete floor to indicate a leaking gasket anywhere on the engine. The Whizzer was in prime operating condition, almost as good as new more than a half-century after it was manufactured.

He stood there admiring the bike only a few seconds before walking to the end of the workbench to get a red plastic two-gallon container of gasoline. And a large white plastic funnel. Removing the tank's chromed gas cap, he poured a gallon or so of the malodorous gasoline into the metal tank, wiped up what he had spilled with a soft rag, and replaced the cap.

Moving a couple of cardboard boxes out of the way, he rolled the bike backwards alongside the car, until it was well outside the garage, then reversed direction and turned a half-circle to head the old Whizzer down the slight grade of the driveway. For a moment he considered straddling the bike and simply coasting it into the street. But he decided instead to walk along beside the old Whizzer and let it roll smoothly down the driveway, squeezing the right caliper front-wheel brake handle to slow and then stop its progress.

My, God, he thought, I haven't done this in years.

He wasn't even sure he could do it any more.

But he certainly was going to give it a try. He reached down under the gas tank, felt for the choke lever, and flipped it forward to its fully closed position. The time had come. It was now or never.

Taking a deep breath, he began running alongside the Whizzer down the street, towards the west, into the setting sun. Faster, faster—he knew he wouldn't be able to keep this up for long—the shining bike sped. When he thought the right moment had arrived, when just enough speed and momentum had been generated by his churning old legs, he turned the left handgrip to engage the spark and build compression. A finely tuned mixture of gas and air flowed into the engine's single cylinder. With a puffing, *coughing, booming wheeze, the ancient engine turned over. And began to run on its own.*

*"Waa-hoo!" he celebrated, flipping his right leg over the big leather seat and placing both feet on the pedals. "Leonard, you greasy old son-of-a-gun, you're still the best mechanic who ever lived!" He reached down and opened the choke, then gave the engine more throttle. The Whizzer responded by smoothing out its running and picking up speed.*

*And with one of the broadest smiles that his face had held in nearly fifty years, he was once again a young boy in the small-town of Sonora, riding off into the sunset to find still another fire, to remember still another foggy morning.*

## Illustrations:

**Drawings by the author:** vi, 12, 15, 23, 28, 33, 34, 35, 40, 42, 50, 51, 53, 57, 63, 70, 71, 81, 83, 84, 87, 89, 102. 104, 105, 107, 108, 111, 119, 121, 124, 126, 131, 132, 135, 137, 158, 162, 166, 170, 192, 201, 203, 207, 218, 228, 230 235

**Photos by the author:** 9, 10, 24, 78, 93, 94, 96, 97, 138, 139, 140, 142, 144, 147, 149, 152, 155, 157, 159 (2), 164, 183, 186, 198, 210, 212, 214, 222, 229, 230

**Painting by the author:** 49

**Photos in author's collection:** 18, 19, 22, 25, 38, 44, 45, 47, 52, 54, 55, 58, 67 (2), 73, 85 (2), 113, 123, 127, 128, 129, 151, 154, 160m 200, 202, 204, 205, 208 (2), 209, 211, 213, 219, 221, 223
Internet search, source unknown: 22, 66, 69, 70, 75, 77, 133, 158

**The (Zanesville) Times Recorder (c):** 141, 142, 216

**TV Guide (c):** 168, 169

**WHIZ-TV (c):** 233, 234

## About the Author

Fred Whissel, a native of Sonora, Ohio, owned and operated a storefront business (Audio Video Country) in Jackson, Wyoming, with his wife for 20 years. He holds a B.S. in journalism (1968) from Ohio University, where he studied creative writing under Walter Tevis (The Hustler). He has won several state, national, and military awards as an editor, investigative reporter, editorial writer, and photographer for various U.S. Army Security Agency and civilian newspapers. Prior to moving his family to Jackson in 1984 he was public affairs manager at Ohio Power Company. His first **lulu.com** contribution, Save Yourself! How You CAN Troubleshoot Your Own Audio/Video Problems, was published in June, 2007, and is a self-illustrated book of how-to help and how-NOT-to humor relating some of his experiences with such personages as Harrison Ford, Gerry Spence, Bo Derek, and Robert Ballard. His first **lulu.com** novel, Bear Edges, was published in July, 2007. It is a slightly revised reprint of the novel that was first published in 2003 by Canada's Trafford Publications. His next **lulu.com** work is scheduled to be a book of drawings, Sports in Jackson Hole, lampooning assorted foibles of both tourists and residents in Wyoming's toniest town (according to Tom Brokaw). Also planned for publication in 2007 are a book of the favorite newspaper editorials that he has written (including "Best Editorial" winners in both 1972 and 1973 in Ohio Associated Press competition), a compilation of short stories, and a compilation of screenplays. He is married to Barbara A. Whissel. They are the proud parents of Jhon, Alicia, and Carl, who attended universities in Wyoming and Ohio. Whissel is presently listed as a work-disabled security screener at the Jackson Hole Airport.